The Gift

Cecelia Ahern

The Gift

WM
WILLIAM MORROW
An Imprint of HarperCollinsPublishers

Rocco and Jay—
The greatest gifts,
Both, at the same time

Contents

The Gift

CHAPTER I

An Army of Secrets

I F YOU WERE TO STROLL down the candy-cane fa-
cade of a surburban neighborhood early on Christmas morning, you couldn't help but observe how the
houses in all their decorated, tinseled glory are akin to
the presents that lie beneath the Christmas trees within.
For each holds its secrets inside. Peeping through a crack
in the curtains to get a glimpse of a family in Christmas-
morning action is to poke and prod at the present's
wrapping; it's a captured moment that's kept away from
all prying eyes. In the calming yet eerie silence that ex-
ists only on this morning every year, these homes stand
shoulder to shoulder like painted toy soldiers: chests
pushed out, stomachs tucked in, proud and protective
of all within, like an Army of Secrets.

And houses on Christmas morning are indeed trea-
sure chests of hidden truths. A wreath on a door like a
finger upon a lip; blinds down like closed eyelids. Then,
at some unspecified time, a warm glow will appear beyond the drawn curtains, the smallest hint of something

happening inside. Like stars in the night sky gradually appearing to the naked eye, lights go on behind the blinds and curtains in the half-light of dawn. One at a time, like tiny pieces of gold being revealed as they're sieved from a stream, room by room, house by house, the street begins to awaken.

The Christmas-morning calm makes it seem as though a strange happening in the world has caused everybody to scutter to their hiding places. The emptiness on the streets doesn't instill fear, though; in fact, it has the opposite effect. It presents a picture postcard of safety, and, despite the seasonal chill, there's warmth. And while outside is somber, inside each household is a world of bright frenzied color, a hysteria of ripping wrapping paper and flying colored ribbons. Christmas music and gastric delights fill the air with fragrances of cinnamon and spice and all things nice. Exclamations of glee, of hugs and thanks, explode like party streamers. These Christmas days are indoor days, not even a sinner lingering outside. Only those in transit from one home to another dot the streets. Cars pull up and presents are unloaded. Sounds of greetings and invitation from open doorways, which waft out to the cold air, are only teasers as to the festivities occurring inside. Then, just as you're soaking it up and sharing the invitation—ready to stroll over the threshold a common stranger but feeling a welcomed guest—the front door closes and traps everything back inside, as a reminder that it's not your moment to take.

In this particular neighborhood of toy houses, one soul wanders the streets. This soul doesn't quite see the beauty in the secretive calm. This soul is intent on a war, wants to unravel the bow and rip open the paper to reveal what's inside door number twenty-four.

It is not of any importance to us what the occupants of door number twenty-four are doing, though, if you must know, a ten-month-old, captivated by the large green flashing prickly object in the corner of the room, is beginning to reach for the shiny red bauble that reflects a pudgy hand and gummy mouth. This, while a two-year-old nearby rolls around in wrapping paper, bathing herself in glitter like a hippo in muck. Beside them, *He* wraps a new necklace of diamonds around *Her* neck as she gasps, hand flying to her chest, and shakes her head in disbelief, just as she's seen women in the black-and-white movies do.

None of this is important to *our* story, though it means a great deal to the soul who stands in the front garden of house number twenty-four, trying to look through the living room's drawn curtains. Fourteen years old and with a dagger through his heart, he can't see what's going on, but his imagination has been well nurtured by his mother's bedtime stories and now by her daytime weeping, and so he can guess.

Ready now, he raises his arms above his head, pulls back, and with all his strength pushes forward and releases the object in his hands. Then he stands back to watch with bitter joy as a fifteen-pound frozen turkey smashes through the window of the living room of number twenty-four. The drawn curtains act once again as a barrier between him and them, slowing the bird's flight through the air. And with no life left to stop itself now, it—and its giblets—descend rapidly to the timber floor inside, where it's sent spinning and skidding along to its final resting place beneath the Christmas tree. His gift to them.

People, like houses, hold their secrets. Sometimes the secrets inhabit them, and sometimes people inhabit their secrets. They wrap their arms tight to hug them close, twist their lying tongues around the truth. But, like gravy left overnight, the truth is a thin layer of film that forms and covers the surface. The truth prevails, rises above all else. It squirms and wriggles inside, grows until the swollen tongue can't wrap itself around the lie any longer, until the time comes when it needs to spit the words out and send truth flying through the air and crashing into the world like . . . well, like a frozen dead bird through a living room window. Truth and time always work alongside each other.

This story is about people, secrets, and time. About people who, not unlike wrapped parcels, cover themselves with layers and layers until they present themselves to the right ones who can unwrap them and see inside. Until that happens they lie under a tree, being poked and prodded by unwelcome hands. Sometimes you have to give yourself to somebody in order to see who you are.

Sometimes you have to let that person unravel things to get to the core.

This is a story about people who find out who they are. About people who are unraveled and whose cores are revealed to all who count. And those who count are finally revealed to them. Just in time.

CHAPTER 2

A Morning of Half Smiles

POLICE SERGEANT RAPHAEL O'REILLY MOVED slowly and methodically about the cramped staff kitchen of Howth Police Station, his mind going over and over the revelations of the morning. Known to others as Raphie, pronounced *Ray-fee*, he was fifty-nine years old and had one more year to go until his retirement. He'd never thought he'd be looking forward to that day until the events of this morning had grabbed him by the shoulders and turned him upside down like a snow globe, forcing him to watch all his preconceptions sprinkle away. With every step he took he heard the crackle of his once-airtight beliefs under his boots. Of all the events and moments he had experienced in his forty-year career, what a morning this one had been.

He spooned two heaps of instant coffee into his mug. The mug, shaped like an NYPD squad car, had been brought back from New York by one of the boys at the station as his Christmas gift this year. He pretended the sight of it offended him, but secretly he found it comforting. Gripping it in his hands during the morning's Kris Kringle reveal, he'd time-traveled back to a Christmas fifty years ago when he'd received a toy police car from his parents. It was a gift he'd cherished until he'd abandoned it outside overnight and the rain had done enough rust damage to force his toy men into early retirement. He held the mug in his hands now, almost tempted to run it along the countertop making siren noises before crashing it into the bag of sugar, which would, incidentally, cascade into his mug.

Instead, he checked around the kitchen to ensure he was alone and added half a teaspoon of sugar to his mug. Then, a little more confident, he coughed to disguise the crinkling sound of the sugar bag as he pushed his spoon down once again and quickly fired a heaping teaspoon into the mug. Having now gotten away with two spoons, he became cocky and reached into the bag one more time.

"Drop your weapon, sir," a female voice from the doorway called with authority.

Startled by the sudden presence, Raphie jumped, the sugar from his spoon spilling all over the counter. It was a mug-on-sugar-bag pileup. Time to call for backup.

"Caught in the act, Raphie." His colleague Jessica joined him at the counter and whipped the spoon from his hand.

She took a mug from the cupboard—a Jessica Rabbit novelty mug, another comical Christmas gift—and slid her namesake across the counter to him. Porcelain Jessica's voluptuous breasts brushed against his car, and the boy in Raphie thought about how happy his men inside would be.

"I'll have one, too."

"Please," Raphie corrected her.

"Please," she imitated him, rolling her eyes.

Jessica was a new recruit. She'd joined the station just six months ago, and already Raphie had grown more than fond of her. He had a soft spot for the twenty-six-year-old, five-foot-four athletic blonde who always seemed willing and able, no matter what her task was. He also felt she brought a much-needed feminine energy to the all-male team at the station. Many of the other men agreed, but not quite for the same reasons as Raphie. He saw her as the daughter he'd never had. Or the daughter he'd had, but lost. He shook that thought out of his head as he watched Jessica cleaning the spilled sugar from the counter.

Despite her strong energy, her almond-shaped eyes— such a dark brown they were almost black—buried something below. As though a top layer of soil had been freshly added, and pretty soon the weeds or whatever was decaying beneath would begin to show through. Her eyes held a mystery that he didn't much want to explore, but he knew that whatever it was, it drove her forward during those challenging times when most sensible people would go the opposite way.

"Half a spoon is hardly going to kill me," he added grumpily, after tasting his coffee, knowing that just one more spoonful would have made it perfect.

"Are you actually *trying* to give yourself another heart attack?"

Raphie reddened. "It was a heart *murmur*, Jessica, nothing more, and keep your voice down," he hissed.

"You should be resting," she said more quietly.

"The doctor said I was perfectly normal."

"Then the doctor needs his head checked. You've never been perfectly normal."

"You've only known me six months," he grumbled.

"Longest six months of my life," she scoffed. "Okay then, pass me your mug, you can have the brown," she said, feeling guilty. She shoveled a spoon into the brown sugar bag and emptied a heaped spoonful into his coffee.

"Brown bread, brown rice, brown this, brown that. I remember a time when my life was in Technicolor."

"I bet you can remember a time when you could see your feet when you looked down, too," she said without a second's thought.

In an effort to dissolve the sugar in his mug completely, she stirred the spoon so hard that a portal of spinning liquid appeared in the center. Raphie watched it and wondered: If he dived into that mug, where would it take him?

"If you die drinking this, don't blame me," she said, passing the coffee back to him.

"If I do, I'll haunt you until the day you die."

She smiled, but the light of it never reached her eyes, fading somewhere between her lips and the bridge of her nose.

He watched the portal in his mug begin to die down, his chance of leaping into another world disappearing fast along with the coffee's steam. Yes, it had been one hell of a morning. Not much of a morning for smiles. Or maybe it was. A morning for half smiles, perhaps. He couldn't decide.

Raphie handed Jessica her mug of steaming coffee—black with no sugar, just as she liked—and they both leaned against the countertop, facing each other, their lips blowing on their coffee, their feet touching the ground, their minds in the clouds.

He studied Jessica, her hands wrapped around the mug's cartoon figure as she stared intently into her coffee as though it were a crystal ball. How he wished it was; how he wished they had the gift of foresight to stop so many of the things they witnessed every day. Her cheeks were pale, a light red rim around her eyes the only giveaway to the morning they'd had.

"Some morning, eh, kiddo?"

Those almond-shaped eyes glistened, but she stopped herself and hardened. She nodded and swallowed the coffee in response. He could tell by her attempt to hide the grimace that it burned, but she took another sip as if in defiance. Standing up even against the coffee.

"My first Christmas Day on duty, I played chess with the sergeant for the entire shift," he said.

She finally spoke. "Lucky you."

"Yeah." He nodded, remembering. "Didn't see it that

way at the time, though. Was hoping for plenty of action."

Forty years later he'd gotten what he'd hoped for, and now he wanted to give it back. Return the gift. Get his time refunded.

"You win?"

He snapped out of his trance. "Win what?"

"The chess game."

"No," he chuckled. "Let the sergeant win."

She ruffled her nose. "You wouldn't see me letting you win."

"I wouldn't doubt it for a second."

Guessing his coffee had now cooled to the right temperature, Raphie finally took a sip. He immediately clutched at his throat, coughing and sputtering, feigning death and knowing immediately that despite his best efforts to lift the mood, it was in poor taste.

Jessica merely raised an eyebrow and continued sipping.

He chuckled softly before the silence continued.

Then, "You'll be okay," he assured her.

She nodded again and responded curtly, as though she already knew. "Yep. You call Mary?"

He nodded. "Straight away. She's with her sister." A seasonal lie, a white lie for a white Christmas. "You call anyone?"

She nodded but averted her gaze, not offering more, never offering more. "Did you, em . . . did you tell her?"

"No. No."

"Will you?"

He gazed into the distance. "I don't know. Will you tell anyone?"

She shrugged, her look as unreadable as always. Then she nodded down the hall at the holding room. "The Turkey Boy is still waiting in there."

Raphie sighed. "What a waste." Of a life or of his own time, he didn't make clear. "He's one that could do with knowing."

Jessica paused just before taking another sip, and fixed those near-black almond-shaped eyes on him from above the rim of the mug. Her voice was as solid as faith in a nunnery, so firm and devoid of all doubt that he didn't have to question her certainty.

"Tell him," she said firmly. "If we never tell anybody else in our lives, at least let's tell him."

CHAPTER 3

The Turkey Boy

RAPHIE ENTERED THE INTERROGATION ROOM as though he was entering his own living room and was about to settle himself on his couch with his feet up for the day. There was nothing threatening about his demeanor whatsoever. Despite his height of six feet two, he fell short of filling the space his physical body took up. He was bent over in contemplation, his eyebrows mirroring the angle by drooping over his pea-sized eyes. The top of his back was slightly hunched, as though he carried a small shell there as shelter. But on his front his belly provided an even bigger shell. In one hand he held a Styrofoam cup, in the other his half-drunk NYPD mug of coffee.

The Turkey Boy glanced at the mug in Raphie's hand. "Cool. Not."

"So is throwing a turkey through a window."

The boy smirked at that and started chewing on the end of the string on his hooded top.

"What made you do that anyway?"

"My dad's a prick."

"I gathered it wasn't a Christmas gift for being father of the year. What made you think of the turkey?"

The boy shrugged. "My mam told me to take it out of the freezer," he offered, as if by way of explanation.

"So how did it get from the freezer to the floor of your dad's house?"

"I carried it most of the way, then it flew the rest." He smirked again.

"When were you planning on having dinner?"

"At three."

"I meant what day. It takes a minimum of twenty-four hours of defrosting time for every five pounds of turkey. Your turkey was fifteen pounds. You should have taken the turkey out of the freezer three days ago if you intended on eating it today."

"Whatever, Ratatouille." He looked at Raphie as if the man was crazy. "If I'd stuffed it with bananas, too, would I be in less trouble?"

"The reason I mention it is because if you had taken it out when you should have, it wouldn't have been hard enough to go through a window. Otherwise this may sound like premeditation to a jury, and no, bananas and turkey isn't a clever recipe."

"I didn't plan it!" the boy squealed, showing his age.

Raphie drank his coffee and watched the young teenager.

The boy looked at the Styrofoam cup Raphie had

placed before him and wrinkled his nose. "I don't drink coffee."

"Okay." Raphie lifted the Styrofoam cup from the table and emptied the contents into his mug. "Still warm. Thanks. So, tell me about this morning. What were you thinking, son?"

"Unless you're the fat bastard whose window I threw a bird through, then I'm not your son. And what's this, a therapy session or an interrogation? Are you charging me with something or what?"

"We're waiting to hear whether your dad is going to press charges."

"He won't." The boy rolled his eyes. "He can't. I'm under sixteen. So if you just let me go now, you won't waste any of your time."

"You've already wasted a considerable amount of it."

"It's Christmas Day, I doubt there's much else for you to do around here." He eyed Raphie's stomach. "Other than eat doughnuts."

"You'd be surprised."

"Try me."

"Some idiot kid threw a turkey through a window this morning."

He rolled his eyes again and looked at the clock on the wall ticking away. "Where are my parents?"

"Wiping grease off their floor."

"Those people are not my parents," he spat. "At least *she's* not my mother. If she comes with him to collect me, I'm not going."

"Oh, I doubt very much that they'll come to take you home with them." Raphie reached into his pocket and took out a chocolate candy. He unwrapped it slowly, the wrapper rustling in the quiet room. "Did you ever notice the strawberry ones are always the last left over in the tin?" He smiled before popping the candy in his mouth.

"I bet nothing's ever left in the tin when you're around."

Raphie ignored the jab. "So I was saying, your father and his partner—"

"Who, for the record"—the boy interrupted Raphie and leaned close to the recording device on the table— "is a whore."

"They may pay us a visit to press charges."

"Dad wouldn't do that," the boy said with a swallow, his eyes tired and puffy with frustration.

"He's thinking about it."

"No, he's not," the boy whined. "If he is, it's probably because *she's* making him. Bitch."

"It's more probable that he'll do it because it's currently snowing in his living room."

"Is it snowing?" The boy looked like a child again, eyes now wide with hope.

Raphie sucked on his candy. "Some people just bite right into chocolate; I much prefer to suck it."

"Suck on this." The boy grabbed his crotch.

"You'll have to get your boyfriend to do that."

"I'm not gay," he huffed, then leaned forward, and

the child returned. "Ah, come on, is it snowing? Let me out to see it, will you? I'll just look out the window."

Raphie finished his candy and leaned his elbows on the table. He spoke firmly. "Glass from the window landed on the ten-month-old baby."

"So?" the boy snarled, bouncing back in his chair, but he looked concerned. He began pulling at a piece of skin around his nail.

"He was beside the Christmas tree, where the turkey landed. Luckily he wasn't cut. The baby, that is, not the turkey. The turkey sustained quite a few injuries. We don't think he'll make it."

The boy looked both relieved and confused at the same time.

"When's my mam coming to get me?"

"She's on her way."

"The girl with the"—he cupped his hands over his chest—"big jugs told me that two hours ago. What happened to her face, by the way? You two have a lover's tiff?"

Raphie bristled over how the boy spoke about Jessica, but kept his calm. The kid wasn't worth it. Was he even worth sharing the story with at all?

"Maybe your mother is driving very slowly. The roads are very slippery right now."

The Turkey Boy thought about that again and looked a little worried. He continued pulling at the skin around his nail.

"The turkey was too big," he said after a long pause. He

clenched and unclenched his fists on the table. "She bought the same-sized turkey she used to buy when he was home. I don't know why, but she thought he'd be coming back."

"Your mother thought this about your dad," Raphie confirmed, rather than asked.

The boy nodded. "When I took it out of the freezer, it just made me crazy. It was too big."

Silence again.

"I didn't think the turkey would break the glass," he continued, quieter now and looking away. "Who knew a *turkey* could break a window?"

Then he looked up at Raphie with such desperation that, despite the seriousness of the situation, Raphie had to fight a smile at the boy's misfortune.

"I just meant to give them a fright. I knew they'd all be in there playing happy family."

"Well, they're definitely not anymore."

The boy didn't say anything but seemed much less smug and angry than when Raphie had first entered.

"A fifteen-pound turkey seems very big for just three people," Raphie said, trying to keep the conversation going.

"Yeah, well, my dad's a fat bastard, what can I say."

Raphie decided he was wasting his time. Fed up, he stood to leave.

"Dad's family still used to come for Christmas dinner every year," the boy caved in, calling out to Raphie in an effort to keep him in the room. "But they decided not to come this year, either. The turkey was just too bloody big for the two of us," he repeated, shaking his head. Dropping the bravado act, his tone changed. "When will my mam be here?"

Raphie shrugged. "I don't know. Probably when you've learned your lesson."

"But it's Christmas Day."

"As good a day as any to learn a lesson."

"Lessons are for kids."

Raphie smiled at that.

"What?" the boy spat defensively.

"Well, I learned one today."

"Oh, I forgot to add *retards* to that, too."

Raphie made his way to the door.

"So what lesson did you learn then?" the boy asked quickly, and Raphie could sense in his voice that he didn't want to be left alone.

Raphie stopped and turned, feeling sad, looking sad.

"It must have been a pretty shit lesson," the boy said.

"You'll find that most lessons are."

The Turkey Boy sat slumped over the table, his un-zipped hoodie hanging off one shoulder, his small pink ears peeping out from his greasy shoulder-length hair, his cheeks covered in pimples, his eyes a crystal blue. He was only a child.

Raphie sighed. Surely he'd be forced into early retirement for telling this story. He walked back to the table, pulled out a chair, and sat down.

"Just for the record," Raphie said, "*you* asked *me* to tell you this."

CHAPTER 4

The Shoe Watcher

L OU SUFFERN ALWAYS HAD TWO places to be at one time. When asleep, he dreamed. In between dreams, he ran through the events of the previous day while making plans for the next, so when he was awakened by his alarm at six a.m. every day, he never felt very rested. When in the shower, he rehearsed presentations, often while responding, one hand outside the shower curtain, to e-mails on his BlackBerry. While eating breakfast he read the newspaper, and when being told rambling stories by his five-year-old daughter, he listened to the morning news. When his thirteen-month-old son demonstrated a new skill each day, Lou's face displayed interest, his mind feeling the exact opposite. When kissing his wife good-bye, he was usually thinking of someone else altogether.

Every action, movement, appointment, doing, or thought of any kind was layered by another. Driving to work was also a conference call by speakerphone. Breakfasts ran into lunches, lunches into pre-dinner drinks,

drinks into dinners, dinners into after-dinner drinks, after-dinner drinks into . . . well, that depended on how lucky he got. On those lucky nights when he felt himself appreciating his luck and the company of another, he, of course, would convince those who wouldn't share his appreciation—namely his wife—that he was in another place. To them, he was stuck in a meeting or at an airport, finishing up some important paperwork, or buried in the maddening traffic. Two places, quite magically, at once.

Everything overlapped, and he was always moving, always had someplace else to be, always wished that he was elsewhere, or that, thanks to some divine intervention, he could be in both places at the same time. He spent as little time as possible with each person during his day, but always left them feeling that it was enough. He wasn't a tardy man; he was precise, always on time. In his personal life he may have been a broken pocket watch, but in business he was a master timekeeper. He strove for perfection and possessed boundless energy in his quest for success. However, it was these bounds—so eager to attain his ever-growing list of desires, so full of ambition to reach new dizzying heights—that caused him to soar above the heads of the people who mattered most in life. Nothing, and no one, could lift him higher than a new deal at work.

On one particularly cold Tuesday morning, along the continuously developing dockland of Dublin city, Lou's black leather shoes, polished to perfection, strolled confidently across the sight line of one particular man. This man watched the shoes in movement that morning, as he had yesterday and as, he assumed, he would tomorrow. There was no best foot forward for this man; for both feet were equal in their abilities. Each stride was equal in length, the heel-to-toe combination so precise; his shoes always pointing forward, heels striking first and then pushing off from the big toe, flexing at the ankle. Perfect each time. The footsteps rhythmic, almost magical as they hit the pavement. There was no rushing or heavy pounding with this man, as was the case with the seemingly decapitated others who raced by at this hour, their heads still back at home on their pillows. No, his shoes made a tapping sound as intrusive and unwelcome as the patter of raindrops against a windowpane, the hem of his trousers flapping slightly like a flag in a light breeze on the eighteenth hole.

The watcher half expected the slabs of pavement to light up as the man stepped on each one, and for him to break out into a tap dance about how swell and dandy the day was turning out to be. And as the watcher was soon to find out, a swell and dandy day it was most certainly going to be.

Usually these shiny black shoes beneath the impeccable black suit would float stylishly by the watcher, through the revolving doors, and into the grand marble entrance of this latest modern glass building to be squeezed through the cracks of the quays and launched up into the Dublin sky. But this morning the shoes stopped directly before the watcher. And then they turned, making a gravelly noise as they pivoted on the cold concrete. The watcher had no choice but to lift his gaze from the shoes.

"Here you go," Lou said, handing him a coffee. "It's an Americano; hope you don't mind, they were having problems with the machine, so they couldn't make a latte."

"Take it back then," the watcher said, turning his nose up at the cup of steaming coffee being offered to him.

This was greeted by a stunned silence.

"Only joking." The watcher laughed at the man's startled look, and very quickly—in case the joke was unappreciated and the gesture was rethought and withdrawn—reached for the cup and cradled it with his numb fingers. "Do I look like I care about steamed milk?" The watcher grinned, before his expression changed to a look of pure ecstasy. "Mmmm." He pushed his nose up against the rim of the cup to smell the coffee. He closed his eyes and savored it, not wanting the sense of sight to take away from this divine smell. The cardboard cup was so hot, or his hands so cold, that the liquid burned right through to his fingers, sending torpedoes of heat and shivers through his body. He hadn't known how cold he was until he'd felt this heat.

"Thanks very much indeed," he said to the man.

"No problem. I heard on the radio that today's going to be the coldest day of the year." The shiny shoes stamped the concrete slabs, and the man's leather gloves rubbed together as proof of his word.

"Well, I'd believe them, all right. Never mind the brass monkeys, it's cold enough to freeze my own balls off. But this will help." The watcher blew on the drink slightly, preparing to take his first sip.

"There's no sugar in it," Lou apologized.

"Ah, well then." The watcher rolled his eyes and quickly pulled the cup away from his lips. "I can let you off for the steamed milk, but forgetting to add sugar is a step too far." He offered it back to Lou.

Getting the joke this time, Lou laughed. "Okay, okay, I get the point."

"Beggars can't be choosers, isn't that what they say? Though is that to say choosers can be beggars?" The watcher raised an eyebrow and smiled and finally took his first sip. So engrossed in the sensation of heat and caffeine traveling through his cold body, he hadn't noticed that suddenly he, the watcher, became the watched.

"Oh. I'm Gabe." He stuck out his hand. "Gabriel, but everyone who knows me calls me Gabe."

Lou reached down and shook his hand. Warm leather to cold skin. "I'm Lou, but everyone who knows me calls me a prick."

Gabe laughed. "Well, that's honesty for you. How's about I call you Lou until I get to know you better."

They smiled at each other and then were quiet in the sudden awkwardness. Two little boys trying to make friends in a school yard. The shiny shoes began to fidget slightly, *tip-tap, tap-tip,* Lou's side-to-side steps a combination of trying to keep warm and trying to figure out whether to leave or stay.

"Busy this morning, isn't it?" Gabe said easily.

"Christmas is only a few weeks away, always a hectic time," Lou agreed.

"The more people around, the better it is for me," Gabe said as a twenty-cent went flying into his cup on the ground. "Thank you," he called to the lady who'd barely paused to drop the coin. From her body language one would almost think it had fallen through a hole in her pocket rather than being an intended gift. He looked up at Lou with big eyes and an even bigger grin. "See? Coffee's on me tomorrow." He chuckled.

Lou tried to lean over as inconspicuously as possible to steal a look at the contents of the cup. The twenty-cent piece sat alone at the bottom.

"Oh, don't worry. I empty it now and then. Don't want people thinking I'm doing too well for myself." He laughed. "You know how it is."

Lou agreed, but at the same time he didn't.

"Can't have people knowing I own the penthouse right across the water," Gabe added, nodding across the river.

Lou turned around and gazed across the river Liffey at Dublin quay's newest skyscraper. With its mirrored glass it was almost as if the building was the Looking Glass of Dublin city center. From the re-created Viking longship that was moored along the quays to the many cranes and new corporate and commercial buildings that framed the Liffey to the stormy, cloud-filled sky that surrounded the higher floors, the building captured it all and reflected it back to the city like a giant plasma screen. At night the building was illuminated in blue and was the talk of the town, or at least it had been in the months following its launch. The next best thing never lasted for too long, as he knew well.

"I was only joking about owning the penthouse, you know," Gabe said, seeming concerned that his humor was a little off today.

"You like that building?" Lou asked, still staring at it in a trance.

"That's one of the main reasons I sit here. That, and because it's busy right along here, of course. A view alone won't buy me my dinner."

"We built that," Lou said, finally turning back around to face his new acquaintance.

"Really?" Gabe took him in a bit more. Mid to late thirties, dapper suit, his face cleanly shaven, smooth as a baby's behind, his dark groomed hair with even speckles of gray throughout, as though someone had taken a saltshaker to it. Lou reminded Gabe of an old-style movie star, emanating suaveness and sophistication, all packaged in a full-length black cashmere coat.

"I bet it bought you dinner." Gabe laughed, feeling a slight twinge of jealousy at that moment, which bothered him, since he hadn't known any amount of jealousy until now. Since meeting Lou he'd learned two things that were of no help, and there he was, all of a sudden cold and envious, when previously he had been warm and content. Bearing that in mind, and despite always being happy with his own company, he foresaw that as soon as he and this gentleman were to part ways, he would experience a loneliness he had never been previously aware of. He would then be envious, cold, *and* lonely. The perfect ingredients for a nice homemade bitter pie.

In fact, the building had bought Lou more than dinner. It had gotten the company a few awards, and, for him personally, a house in Howth and an upgrade from his present Porsche to the new model—the latter arriving right after Christmas, to be precise, but Lou knew not to announce that to the man sitting on the freezing cold pavement, swaddled in a flea-infested blanket. Instead, Lou smiled politely and flashed his porcelain veneers, as usual doing two things at once. Thinking one thing and saying another.

"Well, I'd better get to work. I just work—"

"Next door, I know. I recognize the shoes." Gabe smiled. "Though you didn't wear those yesterday. Tan leather, if I'm correct."

Lou's neatly tweezed eyebrows went up a notch. Like a pebble dropped in a pool, they caused a series of ripples to rise on his as-yet-un-Botoxed forehead.

"Don't worry, I'm not a stalker." Gabe allowed one hand to unwrap itself from the hot cup so he could hold it up in defense. "If anything, you people keep turning up at my place."

"Incredible." Lou laughed, self-consciously looking down at his shoes. "I've never noticed you here before," he thought aloud.

"All day, every day," Gabe said, with false perkiness in his voice.

"Sorry . . ." Lou shook his head. "I'm always running around the place, on the phone with someone or late for someone else. Always two places to be at the same time, my wife says. Sometimes I wish I could be cloned, I get so busy." He laughed again.

Gabe gave him a curious smile, then nodded toward Lou's feet. "Almost don't recognize them standing still. No fire inside today?"

Lou laughed once more. "Always a fire inside there, believe you me." He made a swift movement with his arm, and, like the unveiling of a masterpiece, his coat sleeve slipped up just far enough to reveal his gold Rolex. "I'm always the first director into the office, so there's no great rush." He observed the time with great concentration, and in his head he was already leading his first meeting of the day.

"You're not the first in this morning," Gabe said.

"What?" The meeting in Lou's head was interrupted, and he was back on the street again, outside his office, the cold Atlantic wind whipping at their faces.

Gabe scrunched his eyes shut tight. "Brown loafers. I've seen you walk in with him a few times. He's in already."

"Brown loafers?" Lou laughed, first confused, next

impressed, and then quickly concerned as to who had made it to the office before him.

"You know him—a pretentious walk. The little suede tassels kick with every step, like a mini cancan. It's like he throws them up there purposely. They've got soft soles, but they're heavy on the ground. Small wide feet, and he walks on the outsides. Soles are always worn away on the outside."

Lou's brow furrowed in concentration.

"On Saturdays he wears shoes like he's just stepped off a yacht."

"Alfred!" Lou said, recognizing the description. "That's because he probably *has* just stepped off his ya—" But then he stopped himself. "He's in already?"

"About a half hour ago. In a kind of a rush, by the looks of it, accompanied by another pair of black slip-ons."

"Black slip-ons?"

"Black shoes. Male shoes. A little shine but no design. Simple and to the point. Can't say much else about them apart from the fact they move slower than the other shoes."

"You're very observant." Lou examined him, wondering who this man had been in his previous life, before landing here on the street. At the same time, his mind was on overdrive, trying to figure out who these people were. Alfred showing up to work so early had him nervous, an emotion that was rare for Lou.

Recently, a colleague of theirs—Cliff—had suffered

a nervous breakdown, and this had left them excited—yes, excited—about the opening up of a new position. Providing Cliff didn't get better, which Lou secretly hoped for, major shifts were about to take place in the company, and any unusual behavior by Alfred was questionable. In fact, for Lou, any of Alfred's behavior at any stage was questionable.

Gabe winked. "Don't happen to need an observant person in there for anything, do you?"

Lou parted his gloved hands. "Sorry."

"No problem, you know where I am if you need me. I'm the fella in the Doc Martens." He lifted his blanket to reveal his high black boots.

"I wonder why they're in so early." Lou looked at Gabe as though he could provide the answer.

"Can't help you out there, I'm afraid, but they had lunch last week. Or at least they left the building at what's considered the average joe's lunchtime, and then came back together when that time was over. What they did in between is just a matter of clever guesswork." He chuckled.

"What day was that lunch?"

Gabe closed his eyes again. "Friday, I'd say. He's your rival, is he, brown loafers?"

"No, he's my friend. Kind of. More of an acquaintance, really." On hearing the news of this lunch, Lou, for the first time, showed signs of being rattled. "He's my colleague, but with Cliff having a breakdown it's a great opportunity for either of us to, well, you know . . ."

"Steal your sick friend's job," Gabe finished for him with a smile. "Sweet. The slow-moving shoes? The black ones?" Gabe continued. "They left the office the other night with a pair of Louboutins."

"Lou . . . Loub—what are they?"

"Identifiable by their lacquered red sole. These particular ones had one-hundred-and-twenty-millimeter heels."

"Millimeters?" Lou questioned. Then, "Red sole, okay." He nodded, absorbing it all.

"You could always just *ask* your friend-slash-acquaintance-slash-colleague-slash-rival who he was meeting," Gabe suggested, with a glint in his eye.

Lou didn't respond directly to that. "Right, I'd better run. Things to see, people to do, and both at the same time, would you believe?" He winked. "Thanks for your help, Gabe." He slipped a ten-euro note into Gabe's cup.

"Cheers, man," Gabe beamed, immediately grabbing the bill from the cup and tucking it into his pocket. He tapped it with his finger. "Can't let everyone know, remember?"

"Right," Lou agreed.

But, at the exact same time, he didn't agree at all.

CHAPTER 5

The Thirteenth Floor

G OING UP?"
There was a universal grunt and nodding of heads from inside the crammed elevator as the door opened on the second floor to an inquiring gentleman who looked in at the sleepy faces with hope. All but Lou responded, since he was too preoccupied with studying the gentleman's shoes, which stepped over the narrow gap and into the confined space. Brown brogues shuffled in and then turned around 180 degrees, in order to face the front.

Lou was looking for red soles and black shoes. Alfred had arrived early and had lunch with black shoes. Black shoes left the office with red soles. If Lou could find out who owned the red soles, he'd know who she worked with, and then he'd know who Alfred was secretly meeting. This convoluted process made more sense to Lou than simply asking Alfred, which Lou thought said a lot about the nature of Alfred's honesty.

"What floor do you want?" A muffled voice came

from the corner of the elevator, where a man was well hidden—possibly squashed. As the only person with access to the buttons, he was forced to deal with the responsibility of comandeering the elevator stops.

"Thirteen, please," the new arrival said.

There were a few sighs and one person tutted.

"There is no thirteenth floor," the disembodied voice replied. "You either want the twelfth floor or the fourteenth floor. There's no thirteen."

"Surely he needs to get off on the fourteenth floor," somebody else offered. "The fourteenth floor *is* technically the thirteenth floor."

"So you want me to press fourteen?" the muffled voice asked impatiently.

"Em . . ." The man looked from one person to the other with confusion as the elevator ascended quickly. He watched the numbers go up on the monitor above and then dived into his briefcase to find his schedule.

Lou pondered the man's confusion with irritation. It had been his suggestion that there be no number thirteen on the elevator panel, but of course there was a thirteenth floor. There wasn't a gap with *nothing* before getting to the fourteenth floor; the fourteenth didn't hover on some invisible bricks. The fourteenth *was* the thirteenth, the very floor his office was on. Perfectly simple.

He himself exited on the fourteenth floor, his feet immediately sinking into the spongy plush carpet there. He strode through reception toward his office and his secretary, arms swinging, lips whistling, while the lost man in the brown brogues wandered aimlessly in the wrong direction, eventually knocking lightly on the door of the broom closet at the end of the corridor.

"Good morning, Mr. Suffern." His secretary, Alison, greeted him without looking up from her papers.

He stopped at her desk and looked at her with a puzzled expression. "Alison, call me Lou like you always do, please."

"Of course, Mr. Suffern," she responded, refusing to look him in the eye.

While he settled in and Alison moved about her desk, Lou tried to get a glimpse of the soles of her shoes. Once again avoiding his eye, she returned to her desk to type, and as inconspicuously as possible, Lou bent down to tie his shoelaces and peeked through the gap in her desk.

She frowned and crossed her long legs. "Is everything okay, Mr. Suffern?"

"Call me Lou," he repeated, still puzzled.

"No," she said rather moodily, and looked away. She grabbed the diary from her desk. "Shall we go through today's appointments?" Standing, she made her way around the desk.

Tight silk blouse, tight skirt. His eyes scanned her body before getting to her shoes.

"How high are your heels?"

"Why?"

"Are they one hundred and twenty millimeters?"

"I've no idea. Who measures heels in millimeters?"

"I don't know. Some people. *Gabe.*" He smiled, following her as they walked into his office and trying to get a glimpse of her soles.

"Who the hell is Gabe?" she muttered.

"Gabe is a homeless man." He laughed.

As she turned around to question him, she caught him with his head tilted, studying her.

"Do you have red soles?" he asked her, making his way to the gigantic leather chair behind his desk, in which a family of four could live.

"Why, did I step in something?" She stood on one foot and hopped around lightly, trying to keep her balance while checking her soles, appearing to Lou like a dog trying to chase its tail.

"It doesn't matter." He sat down at his desk wearily.

She viewed him with suspicion before returning her attention to the schedule. "At eight thirty you have a phone call with Aonghus O'Sullibháin about needing to become a fluent Irish speaker in order to buy that plot in Connemara. However, I have arranged, for your benefit, for the conversation to be in English . . ." She smirked and threw back her head like a horse, pushing her mane of highlighted hair off her face. "At eight forty-five you have a meeting with Barry Brennan about the slugs they found on the Cork site—"

"Cross your fingers they're not rare," he groaned.

"Well, you never know, sir; they could be relatives of yours. You have some family in Cork, don't you?" She still wouldn't look at him. "At ten—"

"Hold on a minute." Despite knowing he was alone with her in the room, Lou looked around, hoping for backup. "Why are you calling me *sir*? What's gotten into you today?"

She looked away, mumbling what sounded like "Not you, that's for sure."

"What did you say?" But he didn't wait for an answer. "I've a busy day. I could do without the sarcasm, thank you. What happened to my eight o'clock meeting? And why isn't there anything at nine thirty?"

"I thought that it would be a good idea to make fewer appointments in the future." She blushed slightly. "Instead of these manic days spent darting around, you could spend *more* time with *fewer* clients. Happier clients."

"Yes, then Jerry Maguire and I will live happily ever after. Alison, you're new to the company, so I'll let this go, but this is how I like to do business, okay? I like to be busy. I don't need two-hour lunch breaks and school-work at the kitchen table with the kids." He narrowed his eyes. "You mentioned happier clients; have you had any complaints?"

"Your mother. Your *wife*," she said through gritted teeth. "Your brother. Your sister. Your daughter."

"My daughter is five years old."

"Well, she called when you forgot to pick her up from Irish dancing lessons last Thursday."

"That doesn't count," he said, rolling his eyes, "because my five-year-old daughter isn't going to lose the company hundreds of millions of euro, is she?" Once again he didn't wait for a response. "Have you received any complaints from people who do *not* share my surname?"

Alison thought hard. "Did your sister change her name back after the separation?"

He glared at her.

"Well then, no, sir."

"Again, what's with the *sir* thing?"

"I just thought," she said, her faced flushed, "that if you're going to treat me like a stranger, then that's how I'll treat you, too."

"How am I treating you like a stranger?"

She looked away.

He lowered his voice. "Alison, we're at the office; what do you want me to do? Tell you how much I enjoyed screwing your brains out in the middle of discussing our appointments?"

"You didn't screw my brains out; we didn't quite get that far."

"Whatever." He waved his hand dismissively.

Alison's jaw tightened. "Oh yes, and Mr. Patterson's secretary called to ask me to remind you not to miss any more meetings today." She seemed to get satisfaction from relaying the message. "It seems Alfred mentioned to Mr. Patterson that you missed the meeting with Alan Fletcher yesterday."

"Alfred made that appointment *after* he learned I'd be out for an hour," Lou said, shooting up from his chair. "You know that."

"Yes, I do." She smiled sweetly.

"Did you tell Mr. Patterson that?"

"No, I—"

"Well, call him and tell him," he snapped. "Make sure he knows."

Lou's blood boiled. He spent his life running from one thing to another, missing half of the first in order to make it to the end of the other. He did this all day, every day, always feeling like he was catching up in order to get ahead. It was long and hard and tiring work. He had made huge sacrifices to get where he was. He loved his work, was totally and utterly professional, and was dedicated to every aspect of it. So to be called out on missing one meeting that had not yet been scheduled when he had taken an hour off angered him.

It also angered him that it was family, his mother, that had caused this. It was she on the morning of the meeting whom he had had to collect from the hospital after a hip replacement. He felt angry at his wife for talking him into doing it when his suggestion to arrange a car had sent her into a rage. He felt angry at his younger sister, Marcia, and his older brother, Quentin, for not doing it instead. He was a busy man, and the one time he was forced to choose family over work, he had to pay the price. He hated the excuses that other colleagues used—funerals, weddings, christenings, illnesses—and swore he'd never bring his personal life into the office. To him, it was a lack of professionalism. Either you did the job or you didn't.

He paced by his office window, biting down hard on his lip and feeling such anger he wanted to pick up the phone and call his entire family and tell them, "See? See, this is why I can't always be there. See? Now look what you've done!"

"Right." His heart began to slow down, now realizing what was going on. His dear friend Alfred was up to his tricks. Tricks that Lou had assumed, up until now, he was exempt from. Alfred never did things by the book. He looked at everything from an awkward angle, came at every conversation from an unusual perspective, always trying to figure out the best way he could come out of any situation at someone else's cost.

Lou's eyes searched his desk. "Where's my mail?"

"It's on the twelfth floor. The intern got confused by the missing thirteenth floor."

"The thirteenth floor isn't missing! *We are on it!* What is *with* everyone today? Tell the intern to take the stairs from now on and count his way up. That way he won't get confused. Why is an intern handling the mail anyway?"

"Harry says they're short-staffed."

"Short-staffed? It only takes one person to get in the elevator and bring my bloody mail up." His voice went up a few octaves. "A monkey could do that job. There are people out there on the streets who'd die to work in a place like . . ."

"What?" Alison asked, but she got only the back of Lou's head because he'd turned around and was looking out his floor-to-ceiling windows at the pavement below, a peculiar expression on his face reflected in the glass.

She got up and slowly began to walk away. For the first time in the past few weeks, she felt a light relief that their fling, albeit a fumble in the dark, was going no further, because perhaps she'd misjudged him, perhaps there was something wrong with him. She was new to the company and hadn't quite sussed him out yet. All she knew of him was that he reminded her of the White Rabbit in *Alice in Wonderland*, always seeming late, late, late for a very important date, but managing to get to every appointment just in the nick of time. He was cordial to everybody he met and was successful at his job. Plus, he was handsome and charming and drove a Porsche, and those things she valued more than anything else. Sure, she'd felt a slight twinge of guilt when she had spoken to his wife on the phone, but then it was quickly erased by his wife's absolute naïveté when it came to her husband's infidelities. Besides, everybody had a weak spot, and any man could be forgiven if his Achilles' heel just happened to be Alison.

"What shoes does Alfred wear?" Lou called out, just before she closed his office door.

She stepped back inside. "Alfred who?"

"Berkeley."

"I don't know." She frowned. "Why do you want to know?"

"For a Christmas present."

"Shoes? You want to get Alfred a pair of *shoes*? But

I've already ordered the Brown Thomas hampers for everyone, like you asked."

"Just find out for me. But don't make it obvious. Just casually inquire, I want to surprise him."

She narrowed her eyes with suspicion. "Sure."

"Oh, and that new girl in accounts. What's her name . . . Sandra, Sarah?"

"Deirdre."

"Check her shoes, too. Let me know if they've got red soles."

"They don't. They're from Top Shop. Black ankle boots, suede, with watermarks. I bought a pair of them last year. When they were in fashion." With that, she left.

Lou sighed, collapsed into his oversized chair, and held his fingers to the bridge of his nose, hoping to stop the migraine that loomed. Maybe he was coming down with something. He'd already wasted fifteen minutes of his morning talking to a homeless man, which was totally out of character for him, but he'd felt compelled to stop for some reason. Something about the young man demanded that Lou stop and offer him his coffee.

Unable to concentrate on his schedule, Lou once again turned to look out at the city below. Gigantic Christmas decorations adorned the quays and bridges— oversized mistletoe and bells that swayed from one side to the other, thanks to the festive magic of neon lights. The river Liffey was at full capacity and gushed by his window and out to Dublin Bay. The pavements were aflow with people charging to work, keeping in time with the currents, following the same direction as the tide. They power walked by the gaunt copper figures dressed in rags, statues that had been constructed to commemorate those during the famine who had been forced to walk these very quays to emigrate. Instead of carrying small parcels of belongings, Irish people of today's district now carried Starbucks coffee in one hand, briefcases in the other. Women walked to the office wearing power suits and sneakers, their high heels packed away in their bags. A whole different destiny and endless opportunities awaiting them.

The only thing that was static out there was Gabe, tucked away in a doorway near the building entrance, wrapped up on the ground and watching the shoes march by, the opportunities for him not quite as hopeful. Though only slightly bigger than a dot on the pavement thirteen floors down, Lou could see Gabe's arm rise and fall as he sipped from his cup, making every mouthful last, even if by now the coffee was surely cold.

Gabe intrigued Lou. Not least because of his talent for recanting every pair of shoes that belonged in the building, as if he had a photographic memory, but, more alarmingly, because the person behind those crystal-blue eyes was remarkably familiar. In fact, Gabe reminded Lou of himself. The two men were similar in age, and, given the right grooming, Gabe could very easily have been mistaken for Lou. He seemed a personable, friendly, capable man. Yet how different their lives were.

At that very instant, as though feeling Lou's eyes on him, Gabe looked up. Thirteen floors up and Lou felt like Gabe was staring straight at his soul, his eyes searing into him.

This confused Lou. He knew that the glass on the outside of the building was reflective, knew beyond any reasonable doubt Gabe couldn't possibly have been able to see Lou. But there he stood staring up, his chin to the air, with a hand across his forehead to block out the light, in almost a kind of salute. He was probably looking at a reflection of something, Lou reasoned; a bird perhaps had swooped by and caught his eye. That's right, a reflection was all it could be. But so intent was Gabe's gaze, which reached up the full thirteen floors to Lou's office window and all the way into Lou's eyes, that it made Lou wonder. Before he knew it he lifted up his hand, smiled tightly, and gave a small salute to the man below. But before he could wait for a reaction, he wheeled his chair away from the window and spun around, his pulse rate quickening as though he'd been caught doing something he shouldn't.

The phone rang. It was Alison, and she didn't sound happy.

"Before I tell you what I'm about to tell you, I just want to remind you that I qualified from UCD with a business degree."

"Congratulations," Lou said.

She cleared her throat. "Here you go. Alfred wears size eight brown loafers. Apparently he's got ten pairs of the same shoes and he wears them every day, so I don't think the idea of another pair as a Christmas gift would go down too well." She took a breath. "As for the shoes with the red soles, Melissa bought a new pair and wore them last week, but they cut into her ankle so she went to return them, but the shop wouldn't take them back because it was obvious she'd worn them because the red sole had begun to wear off."

"Who's Melissa?"

"Mr. Patterson's secretary."

"I'll need you to find out from her who she left work with every day last week."

"No way, that's not in my job description!"

"You can leave work early if you find out for me."

"Okay."

"Thank you for cracking under such pressure."

"No problem, it means I can get started on my Christmas shopping."

"Don't forget my list."

So Gabe had been right about the shoes and wasn't a lunatic, as Lou had secretly suspected. He remembered Gabe asking if Lou needed an observant eye around the building, and right then and there he rethought his earlier decision.

"And can you get me Harry from the mailroom on the phone. I'm going to cure his little short-staffing problem. Then take my spare shirt, tie, and trousers downstairs to the guy sitting at the entrance. Take him to the men's room first, make sure he's tidied up, and then show him down to the mailroom. Harry will be expecting him. His name is Gabe."

"What?"

"Gabe. It's short for Gabriel. But call him Gabe."

"No, I meant—"

"Just do it. Oh, and Alison?"

"What?"

"I really enjoyed our kiss last week, and I look forward to screwing your brains out in the future."

He heard a light laugh slip from her throat before the phone went dead.

He'd done it again. While in the process of telling the truth, he told a total and utter lie. Almost an admirable quality, really. And through helping Gabe, Lou was also helping himself; a good deed was indeed a triumph for the soul. But Lou also knew that somewhere beneath his plotting and soul saving there lay another plot, a saving of a very different kind. That of his own skin. And even deeper down in this onion man's complexities, he knew that this outreach was prompted by fear. Not just by the very fear that—had all reason and luck failed him—Lou could so easily be in Gabe's position at this very moment. In a layer so deeply buried from the surface, there lay the fear of a reported crack—a blip in the fine engineering of Lou's career. As much as he wanted to ignore it, it niggled. The fear was there; it was there all the time, but it was merely disguised as something else for others to see.

Just like the thirteenth floor.

CHAPTER 6

A Deal Sealed

WHEN LOU'S MEETING WITH MR. Brennan—
about the thankfully not rare but still problem-
atic slugs on the development site in County Cork—was
close to being wrapped up, Alison appeared at his office
door, looking anxious, and with the pile of clothes for
Gabe still draped in her outstretched arms.

"Sorry, Barry, we'll have to wrap it up now," Lou said
in a rush. "I have to run. I've two places to be right now,
both of them across town, and you know what traffic is
like." And just like that, with a porcelain smile and a firm
warm handshake, Mr. Brennan found himself suddenly
back in the elevator, descending to the ground floor, his
winter coat draped over one arm and his paperwork
stuffed into his briefcase and tucked under the other.
Yet, at the same time, it had been a pleasant meeting.

"Did Gabe say no?" Lou asked Alison.

"There was no one there." She looked confused. "I
stood at reception calling and calling his name—God, it
was so embarrassing—and nobody came. Was this part

of a joke, Lou? I can't believe, after you made me show the Romanian rose seller into Alfred's office, that I'd fall for this again."

"It's not a joke." He took her arm and dragged her over to his window.

"But there was no man there," she said with exasperation.

He looked out the window and saw Gabe still in the same place on the ground. A light rain was starting to fall, spitting against the window at first and then quickly making a tapping sound as it turned heavier. Gabe pushed himself back farther into the doorway, tucking his feet in closer to his chest and away from the wet ground. He lifted the hood from his sweater over his head and pulled the drawstrings tightly, which from all the way up on the thirteenth floor seemed to be attached to Lou's heartstrings.

"Is that not a man?" he asked, pointing out the window.

Alison squinted and moved her nose closer to the glass. "Yes, but—"

He grabbed the clothes from her arms. "I'll do it myself," he said.

As soon as Lou stepped through the lobby's revolving doors, the icy air whipped at his face. His breath was momentarily taken away by a great gush, and the rain alone felt like ice cubes hitting his skin. Gabe was concentrating intently on the shoes that passed him, no doubt trying to ignore the elements that were thrashing around him. In his mind he was elsewhere, anywhere but there. On a beach where it was warm, where the sand was like velvet and the Liffey before him was the endless sea. While in this other world he felt a kind of bliss that a man in his position shouldn't.

His face, however, didn't reflect all this. Gone was the look of warm contentment from that morning. His blue eyes were colder as they followed Lou's shoes from the revolving doors all the way to the edge of his blanket.

As Gabe watched the shoes, he was imagining them to be the feet of a local man working at the beach he was currently lounging on. The local was approaching him with a cocktail balanced dangerously in the center of a tray, the tray held out high and away from his body like the arms of a candelabra. Gabe had ordered this drink quite some time ago, but he'd allowed the man this small delay. It was a hotter day than usual. The sand was crammed with glistening, coconut-scented bodies, and the muggy air was slowing everybody down. The flip-flop-clad feet that approached him now sprayed him with grains of sand with each step. As they neared him, the grains became splashes of raindrops, and the flip-flops became a familiar pair of shiny shoes. Gabe looked up, hoping to see a multicolored cocktail filled with fruit and tiny paper umbrellas on a tray. Instead, he saw Lou, with a pile of clothes over his arm, and it took him a moment to adjust once again to the cold, the noise of the traffic, and the hustle and bustle that had replaced his tropical paradise.

Lou also didn't look like he had this morning. His hair had lost its Cary Grant–like sheen and neatly combed forelock, and his shoulders appeared to be covered in dandruff as the drops falling from the sky nested in his expensive suit, leaving dark patches on the fabric. He was uncharacteristically windswept, and his usually relaxed shoulders were instead hunched high in an effort to shield his ears from the cold. His body trembled, missing his cashmere coat like a sheep who'd just been sheared and now stood knobbly-kneed and naked.

"You want a job?" Lou asked confidently, but it came out quiet and meek, as half his volume was taken away by the wind.

Gabe simply smiled. "You're sure?"

Confused by his reaction, Lou nodded. He wasn't expecting a hug and a kiss, but his offer seemed almost *expected*. This he didn't like. He was more atuned to a song and a dance, an ooh and an aah, a thank-you and a declaration of indebtedness. But he didn't get this from Gabe. What he did get was a quiet smile, and, after Gabe had thrown off the blanket from his body and raised himself to his full height, a firm, thankful—and, in spite of the temperature, surprisingly warm—handshake. It was as though they were already sealing a deal Lou couldn't recall negotiating.

Standing at exactly the same height, they gazed directly into each other's blue eyes, Gabe's from under the hood that was pulled down low over his eyes, monk-like, boring into Lou's with such intensity that Lou had to blink and look away. At the same time, a doubt entered Lou's mind, now that the mere thought of a good deed was becoming a reality. The doubt came breezing through like a stubborn guest through a hotel lobby with no reservation, and Lou stood there, confused at what to do next. Where to put this doubt. Keep it or turn it away. He had many questions to ask Gabe, many questions he probably should have asked before offering the job, but there was only one that he needed to ask right then.

"Can I trust you?" Lou asked.

He had wanted to be convinced, for his mind to be put at ease, but he did not count on receiving the kind of response he was about to hear.

Gabe barely blinked. "With your life."

The Presidential Suite for the gentleman and his word.

CHAPTER 7

On Reflection

GABE AND LOU LEFT THE icy air outside and entered the warmth of the marble lobby. Suddenly surrounded by walls, floors, and pillars of granite covered by swirls of creams, caramels, and Cadbury-chocolate colors, Gabe was tempted to lick the surfaces. He had known he was cold, but until he felt this warmth he'd had no idea just how cold.

Lou felt all eyes on him as he led the rugged-looking man through reception and into the men's room on the ground floor. Not quite sure why, Lou took it upon himself to check each toilet cubicle before talking.

"Here, I brought you these." Lou handed Gabe the pile of clothes, which were slightly damp now. "You can keep them."

He turned to face the mirror to comb his hair back into its perfect position, wiped away the raindrops from his shoulders, and tried his best to return to normality—physically and mentally—as Gabe slowly sifted through the pile. Gray Gucci trousers, a white shirt, a gray-and-white-striped tie. He fingered them all delicately, as though a single touch would reduce them to shreds.

After Gabe discarded his blanket in the sink and went into one of the stalls to dress, Lou paced up and down past the urinals, responding to phone calls and e-mails on his BlackBerry. He was so busy with his work that when he looked up at one point, he didn't recognize the man standing before him and returned his attention to his device. But then he slowly reared his head again, realizing with a start that it was Gabe.

The only thing that showed this was the same man was the dirty pair of Doc Martens beneath the Gucci trousers. Everything else fitted perfectly, and Gabe stood before the mirror, looking himself up and down as though in a trance. The woolen hat that had covered Gabe's head had been discarded, revealing a thick head of black hair similar to Lou's, though far more tousled. The warmth had replaced the coldness in his body, making his lips full and red and his cheeks nicely rosy instead of the frozen, pallid color of before.

Lou didn't quite know what to say, so, sensing a moment that was far deeper than he was comfortable with, he splashed around in the shallow end instead.

"That stuff you told me about the shoes, earlier?"

Gabe nodded.

"That was good. I wouldn't mind if you kept your eyes open for more of that kind of thing. Let me know now and then about what you see."

Gabe nodded.

"Have you somewhere to stay?"

"Yes." Gabe looked back at his reflection in the mirror. His voice was quiet.

"So you've an address to give Harry? He'll be your boss."

"You won't be my boss?"

"No." Lou took his BlackBerry again and began scrolling for nothing in particular. "No, you'll be in another . . . department."

"Oh, of course." Gabe straightened up, seeming a little embarrassed for thinking otherwise. "Right. Great. Thanks so much, Lou, really."

Lou nodded it off, feeling embarrassed, too. "Here." He handed Gabe his comb from his pocket while looking the other way.

"Thanks." Gabe took it, held the comb under the tap, and began to shape his messy hair. Then Lou hurried him on and led him back out of the men's room and through the marble lobby to the elevators.

Gabe offered the comb back to Lou as they walked.

Lou shook his head and waved his hand dismissively, looking around to make sure nobody waiting by the elevators had seen the gesture. "Keep it. You have an employer number, social security number, things like that?" he rattled off at Gabe.

Gabe shook his head, looking concerned. His fingers ran up and down the silk tie, as though he was afraid it would run off.

"Don't worry, we'll sort that out. Okay," Lou started

to move away as his phone began ringing, "I'd better run."

"Of course. Thanks again. Where do I go?"

"Down a floor. The mailroom," he said quickly, before answering his phone.

Gabe looked surprised at first, and then his pleasant face returned, and he smiled at Lou.

Lou knew that offering Gabe a job was a great gesture and that there was nothing wrong with the mailroom, but somehow he felt that it wasn't enough, that the young man standing before him was not only capable but expectant of much more. There was no reasonable explanation for why on Earth he felt this—Gabe was as warm, friendly, and appreciative as he had been the very first moment Lou had met him—but there was something about the way he looked, standing there. There was just . . . something.

"Do you want to meet for lunch or anything?" Gabe asked hopefully as soon as Lou snapped his phone shut.

"No can do," Lou replied, his phone starting to ring again. "I've such a busy day ahead, you know . . ." He trailed off as the elevator doors opened and people began filing in. Gabe moved to step in with Lou.

"This one's going up," Lou said quietly, his words a barrier to Gabe's entrance.

"Oh, okay." Gabe took a few steps back. Before the doors closed and a few last people scurried in, Gabe asked, "Why are you doing this for me?"

Lou swallowed hard and shoved his hands deep into

his pockets. "Consider it a gift." And the doors closed.

When Lou reached the fourteenth floor a minute later, he was more than surprised as he headed to his office to see Gabe pushing a mail cart around the floor, depositing packages and envelopes on people's desks. At the same time as his mouth tried to formulate words, his mind ran through how long it must have taken Gabe to get from the basement to this floor. It was simply impossible. He stared at Gabe, openmouthed.

Gabe looked around and back at Lou with uncertainty, smoothing down the new tie he'd been given and checking to make sure he hadn't dirtied it. "This is the thirteenth floor, isn't it?" he asked.

"It's the fourteenth," Lou replied breathlessly, speaking the words more out of habit and barely noticing what he was saying. He held his hand to his forehead, which was hot. "You got here so quickly . . . How did you, I mean . . ."

Gabe looked at him and waited for the rest of the sentence, his face perfectly expressionless, giving away nothing.

"Lou," Alison hissed. "Your sister's on the phone. Again."

Lou didn't respond, unable to tear his eyes away from Gabe's.

"Lou?" Alison said a little more urgently. "It's Marcia. About your dad's seventieth party."

Finally Lou managed to speak but still stood cemented to the floor. "Tell her I'm out."

"But what about the party?"

"Tell her I'll organize it. Or at least you will," he said distractedly, finally able to move his eyes away. He reached for his coat. "Make sure you find out the date."

"It's the twenty-first. Same date as the office holiday party," she whispered loudly, covering the handset.

"Change it then," he said as he went into his office to pick up his briefcase, then walked back out while wrapping his scarf tightly around his neck.

"The office party?"

"No," he said, wrinkling his nose up in disgust. "My father's party."

He caught Gabe's eye and saw a judging, accusing look. Once again it stopped him in his tracks. "No, actually, don't," he backtracked quickly to Alison. "I'll figure it out."

Gabe gave him a curious smile at that.

"Okay, I'm off." He finally broke his gaze with Gabe and power walked to the elevator, phone to his ear. Lou held Gabe's cool stare as the doors closed and the elevator slowly descended. A few seconds later it reached the ground level, and as the doors opened Lou caused a jam as he froze at the sight before him. While irritated people trying to get off snapped at him to move, eventually pushing passed him, Lou didn't even notice. He just stood there, staring at Gabe, who was a few feet in front of him.

Even as the elevator crowd cleared and headed out into the cold of the city, Lou remained alone in the elevator, his heart skipping a few beats as he watched Gabe standing by the security desk, the mail cart beside him.

Before the elevator doors closed again, trapping Lou inside, he slowly disembarked and made his way toward Gabe.

"I forgot to give this to you upstairs," Gabe said, handing Lou a thin envelope. "It was hidden beneath someone else's stack."

Lou took the envelope and didn't even look at it before crushing it into his coat pocket.

"Is something wrong?" Gabe asked.

"No. Nothing's wrong." Lou didn't move his eyes away from Gabe's face. "How did you get down here so quickly?"

"Here?" Gabe pointed at the floor.

"Yeah, here," Lou said sarcastically. "The ground level. You were just on the thirteenth floor. Just less than thirty seconds ago."

"I thought there was no thirteenth floor," Gabe responded coolly.

"Fourteenth, I meant," Lou corrected himself, frustrated by his gaffe.

"You were there, too, Lou." Gabe frowned.

"And?"

"And . . ." Gabe stalled. "I guess I just got here quicker than you." He shrugged, then unlatched the brake at the wheel of the cart with his foot and prepared to move. "You'd better run," Gabe said, moving away, echoing Lou's words from the morning. "Things to see, people to do." Then he flashed his porcelain smile, but this time it didn't give Lou the warm fuzzy feeling it had earlier. Instead, it sent torpedoes of fear and worry right to his heart and straight into his gut. Those two places. Right at the same time.

CHAPTER 8

The Quiet Life

I T WAS TEN THIRTY AT night by the time the city spat Lou out and waved him off to the coast road that led him home to his house in Howth, County Dublin. Bordering the sea, a row of houses lined the coast there, like an ornate frame to the perfect watercolor, windswept and eroded from a lifetime of salty air. In each house, at least one window with open curtains twinkled with the lights of a Christmas tree. As Lou drove, to his right he could see across the bay to Dalkey and Killiney. The lights of Dublin city twinkled beyond the oily black of the sea, like electric eels flashing beneath the darkness of a well.

Howth had been the dream destination for as long as Lou could remember. Quite literally, his first memory began there, his first feeling of desire, of wanting to belong and then of belonging. The fishing and yachting port in north County Dublin was a popular suburban resort on the north side of Howth Head, fifteen kilometers from Dublin city. A bustling village filled with pubs and fine fish restaurants, it was also a place with history: cliff paths that led past its ruined abbey, an inland fifteenth-century castle with rhododendron gardens, and lighthouses that dotted the coastline. It had breathtaking views of Dublin Bay and the Wicklow Mountains, or Boyne Valley beyond; only a sliver of land attached the peninsular island to the rest of the country . . . only a sliver of land connected Lou's daily life to that of his family. A mere thread, so that when the stormy days attacked, Lou would watch the raging Liffey from the window of his office and imagine the gray, ferocious waves crashing over that sliver, threatening to cut his family off from the rest of the country. Sometimes in those daydreams he was away from his family, cut off from them forever. In nicer moments he was with them, wrapping himself around them like a shield.

Behind the landscaped garden of their home was land—wild and rugged, covered by purple heather and waist-high uncultivated grasses and hay—that looked out over Dublin Bay. To the front they could see Ireland's Eye, and on a clear day the view was so stunning, it was almost as though a green screen had been hung from the clouds and rolled down to the ocean floor. Stretching out from the harbor was a pier that Lou loved to take walks along, usually alone. He hadn't always; his love for the pier had begun when he was a child, his parents bringing him, Marcia, and Quentin to Howth every Sunday, come rain or shine, for a walk along the pier. On those family days, Lou would disappear into his own world.

He was a pirate on the high seas. He was a lifeguard. He was a soldier. He was a whale. He was anything he wanted to be. He was everything he wasn't.

Yes, Lou still loved walking that pier, his runway to tranquillity. He loved watching the cars and the houses perched along the cliff edges fade away as he moved farther and farther from land. He would stand shoulder to shoulder with the lighthouse, both of them looking out to sea. After a long week at work, he could throw all of his worries out there, where they'd float away on the waves.

But the night Lou drove home after first meeting Gabe, it was too late to walk the pier. Driving past it, all he could see was blackness and the occasional light flashing on the lighthouse. And besides, the village itself wasn't its usual quiet hideaway. So close to Christmas, every restaurant was throbbing with diners, Christmas parties, and annual meetings and celebrations. All the boats would be in for the night; the seals would be gone from the pier, their bellies full with the mackerel thrown to them by visitors. Lou continued on the black and quiet winding road that led uphill to the summit and, knowing that home was near and that nobody else was around, put his foot down on the accelerator of his Porsche 911. He lowered his window and felt the ice-cold air blow through his hair, and he listened to the sound of the engine reverberating through the trees as he made his way. Below him, the city twinkled with a million lights, spying him winding his way up the wooded mountain like a spider among the grass.

Suddenly he heard a whoop, and then, looking in his rearview mirror, cursed loudly at the police car that came up behind him, lights ablazing. He eased his foot off the accelerator, hoping he'd be overtaken, but to no avail; the emergency was indeed him. He turned on his signal and pulled over, sat with his hands on the steering wheel, and watched the familiar figure climbing out of the police car behind him. The man slowly made his way to Lou's side of the vehicle, looking around as he did, as though taking a leisurely stroll.

The man parked himself outside Lou's door and leaned down to look into the open window.

"Mr. Suffern," he said without a note of sarcasm, much to Lou's relief.

"Sergeant O'Reilly." He remembered the name right on cue and threw him a smile, showing so many teeth he felt like a tense chimpanzee. "We meet again."

"Indeed. We find ourselves in a familiar situation," Raphie said with a grimace. "But I do enjoy our little chats. How is your new secretary coming along? Last month you were racing to the office because she had made a mistake with your schedule."

"Alison. Yes, she's doing just fine." Lou smiled.

"And Cliff, how is he? You were racing to the hospital the time before that."

"Still not good," Lou said somberly.

"You have his job yet?" Raphie asked softly.

"Not yet." Lou smiled again.

"So what's the emergency tonight?"

"My apologies. The roads were quiet, so I thought it would be okay. There's not a sinner around."

"Just a few innocents. That's always the problem."

"And I'm one of them, Your Honor." Lou laughed, holding his hands up in defense. "It's the last stretch of road before getting home, and trust me, I only put the foot down seconds before you pulled me over. Dying to get home to the family. No pun intended."

"I could hear your engine from Sutton Cross, way down the road."

"It's a quiet night."

"And it's a noisy engine, but you just never know, Mr. Suffern. You just never know."

"Don't suppose you'd let me off with a warning," Lou said, trying to work sincerity and apology into his best winning smile. Both at the same time.

"You know the speed limit, I assume?"

"Sixty kilometers."

"Correct. You were fifty above that."

Lou bit down on his lip and tried his best to look appalled.

Without another word the sergeant bolted upright, causing Lou to lose eye contact and suddenly be staring at the man's belt buckle. Unsure of what the sergeant was up to, he stayed seated and looked out the window to the stretch of road before him, hoping he wasn't about to gain more points on his license. With twelve as the maximum before losing his license altogether, he was perched dangerously close with eight. He turned and peeked at the sergeant and saw him grasping at his left pocket.

"You looking for a pen?" Lou called, reaching his hand into his inside pocket.

The sergeant winced and turned his back on Lou.

"Hey, are you okay?" Lou asked with concern. He reached for the door handle and then thought better of it.

The sergeant grunted something inaudible, the tone suggesting a warning of some sort. Through the side-view mirror, Lou watched him walk slowly back to his car. He had an unusual gait. He seemed to be dragging his left leg slightly as he walked. Was he drunk? Then the sergeant opened his car door, got inside, started up the engine, did a U-turn, and was gone. Lou frowned. His day—even in its twilight hours—was becoming increasingly more bizarre by the moment.

LOU PULLED UP TO THE driveway feeling the same sense of pride and satisfaction he felt every night when he arrived home. To most average people, size didn't matter. To Lou, size most certainly *did* matter. He didn't want to be average, and he saw the things that he owned as being a measure of the man that he was. He wanted the best of everything. Despite being on a safe cul-de-sac, one of only a few houses on Howth summit, he'd arranged for the existing boundary walls to be built up higher, and for oversized electronic gates with cameras to be placed at the entrance. The lights were out in the children's bedrooms at the front of the house, and Lou felt an inexplicable relief.

"I'm home," he called as he walked into the quiet house.

There was a faint sound of a breathless and rather hysterical woman calling out from the television room down the hallway. Ruth's exercise DVD.

He loosened his tie and opened the top button of his shirt and kicked off his shoes, feeling the warmth of the underfloor heating soothe his feet through the marble as he walked to the hall table to sort through the mail. His mind slowly began to unwind, the conversations of various meetings and telephone calls from the day all beginning to slow. Though they were still there in his head, the voices seemed a little quieter now. Each time he took off a layer of his clothes—his overcoat flung over the chair, his suit jacket on the table, his tie onto the table but slithering to the floor—or emptied his pockets—his loose change here, his keys there—he felt the events of the day fall away.

"Hello," he called again, louder this time, realizing that nobody—his wife—had come to greet him. Perhaps she was busy breathing to the count of four, as he could hear the exercise-DVD woman in the television room doing.

"Sssh!" he heard coming from the second level of the house, followed by the creak of floorboards as his wife made her way across the landing.

Being silenced bothered him. Throughout a day of nonstop talking, of clever words, of jargon, of persuasive and intelligent conversation—deal opening, deal development, deal closing—not one person at any point had told him to *Sssh*. That was the language of teachers and librarians. Not of adults in their own homes. He felt like he'd left the real world and entered a church. Only one minute after stepping through his front door, he felt irritated. That had been happening a lot lately.

"I've just put Bud down again. He's not having a good night," Ruth explained from the top of the stairs in a loud whisper. Lou also didn't like this kind of speech. This whispering was for children in class or teenagers sneaking out of their homes.

The "Bud" she referred to was their one-year-old son Ross. This nickname came about after their five-year-old daughter Lucy overheard Lou affectionately call her new baby brother *buddy* or *bud*, and understood it to be his name. Despite their initial corrections, Lucy's conviction remained and so, unfortunately for Ross, his nickname of Bud seemed to be sticking around.

"What's new?" he mumbled while searching through the mail for something that didn't resemble a bill. He opened a few and discarded them on the hall table. Pieces of ripped paper drifted onto the floor.

Ruth made her way downstairs, dressed in a velour tracksuit-cum-pajamas outfit—he couldn't quite tell the difference between what she wore these days. Her long, chocolate-brown hair was tied back in a high ponytail, and she shuffled toward him in a pair of slippers—the noise grating on his ears.

"Hi." She smiled, and for a moment the tired face dissolved, and there was a glimpse, a tiny flicker, of the woman he had married. Then, just as quickly, it disappeared again, leaving him to wonder if that part of her was there at all. Then she stepped up to kiss him on the lips.

"Good day?" she asked.

"Busy."

"But good?"

The contents of a particular envelope took his interest. After a long moment he felt the intensity of her stare.

"Hmm?" He looked up.

"I just asked if you had a good day."

"Yeah, and I said, 'Busy.'"

"Yes, and I said, 'But good?' All your days are busy, but all your days aren't good. I hope it was good," she said in a strained voice.

"You don't sound like you hope it was good," he replied, eyes down, reading the rest of the letter.

"Well, I did the first time I asked," she said evenly.

"Ruth, I'm reading my mail!"

"I can see that," she mumbled, bending over to pick up the empty, torn envelopes that lay on the floor.

"So what happened around here today?" he asked, opening another envelope. Another piece of paper fluttered to the floor.

"The usual madness. Marcia called a few times today, looking for you. When I could finally find the phone. Bud hid the handset again, the battery went dead, and it took me ages to find it. Anyway, she needs help with deciding on a venue for your dad's party. What did you tell her?"

Silence. She patiently watched him reading the last page of a document and waited for an answer. When he had folded the papers and dropped them on the table, he reached for another envelope.

"Honey?"

"Hmm?"

"I asked you about Marcia," she said, trying to keep her patience, then proceeded to pick up the new pieces of paper that had fallen to the floor.

"Oh yeah." He unfolded another document and became once again distracted by the contents.

"Yes?" she said loudly.

He looked up and gazed at her, as though noticing for the first time that she was standing there. "What were we saying?"

"Marcia," she said, rubbing her tired eyes. "We're talking about Marcia, but you're busy, so . . ." She began making her way to the kitchen.

"Oh, that. I'm taking the party off her hands. Alison's going to organize it."

Ruth stopped. "Alison?"

"Yes, my secretary. She's new. Have you met her?"

"Not yet." She slowly made her way back toward

him. "Honey, Marcia was really excited about organizing the party."

"And now Alison is." He smiled. "Not." Then he laughed.

She smiled patiently at the inside joke that she didn't understand.

Lou looked away. He knew that Marcia had loved organizing the party, that she'd been planning it for months. But in taking it out of her hands he was, in fact, making it easier on himself. He couldn't stand the twenty calls a day about cake tasting and whether or not he'd allow three of their decrepit aunts to stay overnight in his house or if he'd lend a few of his serving spoons for the buffet. Ever since her marriage had ended, Marcia had focused on this party. Maybe if she'd have given her marriage as much attention as she did the bloody party . . . Taking this off her hands was a favor to her and a favor to himself. Two things accomplished at once. Just what he liked.

Ruth took a deep breath, her shoulders relaxing as she exhaled. "Your dinner's ready." She began to move toward the kitchen again. "It'll just take a minute to heat up. And I bought that apple pie you like."

"I've eaten," he said, folding the letter he'd just finished and ripping it into pieces that fluttered to the floor. It was either the sound of yet more paper hitting the floor or his words that stopped her, but either way she froze.

"I'll pick the bloody things up," he said with irritation.

She slowly turned around and asked in a quiet voice, "Where did you eat?"

"Shanahan's. Rib-eye steak. I'm stuffed." He absent-mindedly rubbed his stomach.

"With who?"

"Work people."

"Who?"

"What's this, the Spanish Inquisition?"

"No, just a wife asking a husband who he had dinner with."

"A few guys from the office. You don't know them."

"I wish you would have told me."

"It wasn't a social thing. Nobody else's wives were there."

"I didn't mean—I'd like to have known so I wouldn't have bothered cooking for you."

"Christ, Ruth, I'm sorry you cooked and bought a bloody pie," he exploded.

"Sssh," she said, closing her eyes and hoping his raised voice wouldn't wake the baby.

"No! I won't sssh!" he boomed. "Okay?" He made his way into the parlor, leaving his shoes in the middle of the hallway and his papers and envelopes strewn across the hall table.

Ruth took another deep breath, turned away from his mess, and made her way to the opposite side of the house.

WHEN LOU REJOINED HIS WIFE a little while later, she was sitting at the kitchen table eating lasagna and a salad, the pie next in line, watching women in spandex jump around on the large plasma TV in the adjoining family room.

"I thought you'd eaten with the kids," he remarked after watching her for a while.

"I did," she said, through a full mouth.

"So why are you eating again?" He looked at his watch. "It's almost eleven. A bit late to eat, don't you think?"

"You eat at this hour." She frowned.

"Yes, but I'm not the one who complains that I'm fat and then eats two dinners and a pie." He laughed.

She swallowed the food, feeling like a rock was going down her throat. He hadn't noticed his words, hadn't intended to hurt her. He never intended to hurt her; he just did. After a long silence, during which Ruth lost her energy for anger and built up the appetite to eat again, Lou poured himself a glass of wine and joined her at the kitchen table. On the other side of the kitchen window the blackness clung to the cold pane, eager to get inside. Beyond it were the millions of lights of the city across the bay, like Christmas lights dangling from the blackness.

"It's been a weird day today," Lou finally said.

"How?"

"I don't know." He sighed. "It just felt funny. I felt funny."

"I feel like that most days," Ruth said.

"I must be coming down with something. I just feel . . . out of sorts."

She felt his forehead. "You're not hot."

"I'm not?" He looked at her in surprise and then felt his forehead. "It's this guy at work." He shook his head. "So odd."

Ruth frowned and studied him, not used to seeing him so inarticulate.

"It started out well." He swirled his wine around his glass. "I met a man called Gabe outside the office. A homeless guy—well, I don't know if he's homeless. He says he has a place to stay, but he was begging on the streets anyway."

At that the baby monitor began crackling as Bud started to cry softly. Just a gentle sleepy moaning at first. Knife and fork down, and with the unfinished plate pushed away, Ruth prayed for him to stop.

"Anyway," Lou continued, not even noticing, "I bought him a coffee and we got to talking."

"That was nice of you," Ruth said. Her maternal instincts were kicking in, and the only voice she could hear now was that of her child, his sleepy moans turning into full-blown cries.

"He reminded me of me," Lou said. "He was exactly like me, and we had the funniest conversation about shoes." He laughed, thinking back over it. "He could remember every single pair of shoes that walked into the building, so I hired him. Well, *I* didn't, I called Harry—"

"Lou, honey," she cut in, "do you not hear that?"

He looked at her blankly, irritated at first that she'd

interrupted his story, and then cocked his head to listen. Finally the cries penetrated his thoughts.

"Fine, go on," he sighed, massaging the bridge of his nose. "But as long as you remember that I was telling you about my day, because you're always telling me that I don't," he mumbled.

"What is that supposed to mean?" She raised her voice. "Your son is crying. Do I have to sit here all night while he wails for help until you've finished your story about a homeless man who likes shoes, or would you ever go and check on him of your own accord?"

"I'll do it," he said angrily, though not making a move from his chair.

"Fine, I'll do it." She stood up from the table. "I want you to do it without being reminded. You don't do it for brownie points, Lou, you're supposed to *want* to do it."

"You don't seem too eager to do it yourself now," he grumbled.

Halfway from the table to the kitchen door, she stopped. "You know you haven't ever taken Ross for one single day by yourself?"

"Whoa. You must be serious if you're actually using his real name. Where is all this coming from?"

It all came out at once now that she was frustrated. "You haven't changed his diaper; you haven't fed him."

"I've fed him," he protested.

The wails got louder.

"You haven't prepared one bottle, made him one meal, dressed him, played with him. You haven't spent any time with him alone, without me running in every five minutes to take him from you while you send an e-mail or answer a phone call. The child has been living in the world for over a year now, Lou. It's been over a *year*."

"Hold on." He ran his hand through his hair and held it there, clenching a handful of hair with a tight fist, a sign of his anger. "How have we gotten from talking about my day, which you always want to know so much about, to this attack?"

"You were so busy talking about *you* that you didn't hear your own child," she said tiredly, knowing this conversation was going the same place as every other argument they'd had recently. Nowhere.

Lou looked around the room and held out his hands dramatically, emphasizing the walls around them. "Do you think I sit at my desk all day twiddling my thumbs? No, I work my hardest trying to juggle everything so that you and the kids can have all this. So excuse me if I don't fill his mouth every morning with mashed banana."

"You don't juggle anything, Lou. You choose one thing over another. There's a difference."

"I can't be in two places at once, Ruth! If you need help around here, I've already told you: just say the word, and we can have a nanny here any day you want."

He knew he'd just walked himself into a bigger argument, and as Bud's wails grew louder on the baby monitor, he prepared for the inevitable onslaught. He almost added, "And I promise not to sleep with this one."

But that argument never came. Instead, Ruth's shoulders shrank as she gave up the fight and instead went to tend to her son.

Lou reached for the remote control and held it toward the TV like a gun. He pressed the trigger angrily and powered it off. The sweating spandexed women disappeared into a small circle of light in the center of the screen before diminishing completely.

He reached for the plate of apple pie on the table and began picking at it, wondering how this had all started, practically from the second he had walked in the door. It would end as it did so many other nights: he would go to bed and she would be asleep, or at least pretend to be. A few hours later he would wake up, work out, get showered, and go to work.

He sighed, and then on hearing the baby monitor crackle, he realized it had grown silent. As he headed toward it to turn it off, he heard a faint noise that made him reach for the volume dial. His heart sank as the sounds of Ruth's quiet sobs filled the kitchen.

CHAPTER 9

The Turkey Boy 2

"SO YOU LET HIM GET away?" A young voice broke into Raphie's thoughts.

"What's that?" Raphie snapped out of his trance and turned his attention back to the young teen who was sitting across the table from him.

"I said, you let him get away."

"Who?"

"The rich guy, Lou, in the flashy Porsche. He was speeding, and you let him get away."

"No, I didn't let him get away."

"Yeah, you did. You didn't give him any points or a ticket or anything. You just let him off. That's the problem with you lot, you're always on the rich people's side. If that was me, I'd be locked up for life. I only threw a bloody turkey, and I'm stuck here all day. And it's Christmas Day and everything."

"Shut your whining; we're waiting for your mother, you know that, and I wouldn't blame her if she does decide to leave you here all day."

The Turkey Boy sat back in his chair, sulking.

"So you're new to the area. You and your mother moved here recently?" Raphie asked.

The boy nodded.

"Where from?"

"The Republic of Your Ass."

"Very clever," Raphie said sarcastically.

They sat in silence. "So why did you leave the Porsche guy so quickly?" the boy finally asked, curiosity getting the better of him. "Did you chicken out or something?"

"Don't be daft, son; I gave him a warning," Raphie said, straightening up defensively in his chair, hoping his heart wouldn't give him another scare again. At least not now, not until after he'd finished the story.

"But that's illegal; you should have given him a ticket. He could kill someone speeding around like that."

Raphie's eyes darkened, and the Turkey Boy knew to stop his goading.

"Are you going to listen to the rest of the story or what?"

"How do you know all this, by the way?"

"I'm the police. It's my job."

"But the stuff with his wife and all, how do you know?"

"It's my job to find the story. To talk to everybody and piece it all together." And what a task that had been. "Now, are you ready to hear more?"

"Yeah, I am. Go on." The boy leaned forward on the table and rested his hand under his chin. "I've got all day." He smiled cheekily.

CHAPTER 10

The Morning After

A T 5:59 A.M., LOU AWOKE. The previous evening had gone exactly as predicted: by the time he had made it to bed, Ruth's back had been firmly turned, with the blankets tightly tucked around her, leaving her as accessible as a fig in a roll. The message was loud and clear.

Lou couldn't find it within himself to comfort her, to cross over the line that separated them in bed, in life, to make things okay. They had definitely reached a low point. Even as students, completely broke and staying in subpar accommodations, with temperamental heating and bathrooms they'd had to share with dozens of others, things had never been like this. Now they had a giant bed, so big that even when they both lay on their backs their fingers barely brushed when they stretched out. A monstrosity of space and cold spots in the sheets that couldn't be warmed.

Lou lay in bed and thought back to the beginning, when he and Ruth had first met at university—two nineteen-

year-olds, celebrating the winter finals. With a few
weeks' break ahead of them and test results far from
their minds, they had met at open-mike night in the International Bar on Wicklow Street. After that night, Lou
had thought about her every day while back home with
his parents for the holidays. With every slice of turkey,
every present he unwrapped, every family fight over
Monopoly, she was on his mind. Because of her he'd
even lost his title as the Count the Stuffing Champion
with Marcia and Quentin. Lou stared up at the bedroom
ceiling and smiled, remembering how each year he and
his siblings—paper crowns on their heads and tongues
dangling from their mouths—would get down to counting every crumb of stuffing on their plate, long after his
parents had left the table. Every year, Marcia and Quentin would join together to beat him, but his dedication—
some would say obsession—could never be matched.
But that year he had been beaten by Quentin, because
the phone had rung and it had been her, and the call had
been it for Lou.

The nineteen-year-old of that Christmas would
have longed for this moment right now. He would have
grabbed the opportunity with both hands, to be trans-
ported to the future just to have Ruth right beside him in
bed, in a fine house, with two beautiful children sleeping
in the next rooms. He looked over at Ruth now. She had
rolled onto her back, her mouth slightly parted, her hair
like a haystack on top of her head. He smiled.

She'd done better than him in those winter exams,

which was no hard task, but she did so the following three years, too. Studying had always come so easily to her, while he seemed to have to burn the candle at both ends in order just to scrape by. He didn't know where she ever found the time to think, let alone study, she was so busy leading the way through their adventurous nights on the town. They'd crashed parties on a weekly basis, stayed out all night, but Ruth still made it to the first lecture, with her assignments completed. She could do it all.

Any time he'd failed an exam and had been forced to repeat it, she'd been there, writing out facts and figures for him to learn. She'd turn study sessions into quiz-show games, introducing prizes and buzzers, quick-fire rounds and punishments. She'd dress up in her finery, acting as quiz-show host, assistant, and model, display-ing all the fine things he could win if he answered all the questions correctly. Even food shopping at the market was a game. "For this box of popcorn, answer me this," she'd say.

"Pass," he'd say, frustrated, trying to grab the box anyway.

"No passing, Lou, you know this one," she'd say firmly, blocking the shelves.

He often wouldn't know the answer at first, but she'd make him know it. Somehow she'd push him until he reached deep into a part of his brain that he didn't know existed and found the answer that he never realized he knew.

They'd planned to go to Australia together after university. A year's adventure away from Ireland before life started. They spent a year saving for the flights; Lou working as a bartender in Temple Bar while she tended tables. But then he failed his final exams, while Ruth passed with flying colors. He would have packed it in there and then, but she wouldn't let him, convincing him he could do it, as she always did.

In the year waiting for him to retake his classes, Ruth completed a business master's degree. Just for something to do. She never once rubbed it in his face or made him feel like a failure. She was always the friend, the girlfriend, the life and soul of every party, the A student and achiever.

So was that when he started resenting her? All the way back then? Was it because he never felt good enough, and this was his way of punishing her? Or maybe there was no psychology behind this; maybe he was just too weak and selfish to say no when an attractive woman so much as looked his way. Because when that happened, he forgot all sense of himself. He knew right from wrong, of course he did, but on those occasions he didn't particularly care. He was invincible, always thinking there would be no consquences and no repercussions.

Ruth had caught him with the nanny six months ago. There had been only a few times, but Lou knew that if there were levels of wrongness for having affairs, which in his opinion there were, sex with the nanny was pretty high. There had been nobody since then, apart from a fumble with Alison, which had been a mistake. That was one that scored low on the wrongness scale. He'd been drunk, she was attractive, but he regretted it deeply. It didn't count.

"Lou," Ruth snapped, breaking into his thoughts and giving him a fright.

He looked over at her. "Morning." He smiled. "You'll never guess what I was just thinking ab—"

"Do you not hear that?" she interrupted him.

"Huh?" He turned to his left and noticed the clock had struck six. "Oh, sorry." He leaned across and switched off the beeping alarm.

He'd clearly done something wrong because her face went a deep red and she fired herself out of bed and charged out of the room. It was only then that he heard Bud's cries.

"Shit." He rubbed his eyes tiredly.

"You said a bad wud," said a little voice from behind the door.

"Morning, Lucy," he said.

Her figure appeared then, a pink-pajamaed five-year-old, dragging her blanket along the floor behind her, her chocolate-brown hair tousled from her sleep. Her big brown eyes were the picture of concern. She stood at the end of the bed, and Lou waited for her to say something.

"You're coming tonight, aren't you, Daddy?"

"What's tonight?"

"My school play."

"Oh yeah, that, sweetie; you don't really want me to go to that, do you?"

She nodded.

"But why?" He rubbed his eyes again. "You know how busy Daddy is; it's very hard for me to get there."

"But I've been practicing."

"Why don't you show me now, and then I won't have to see you later."

"But I'm not wearing my costume."

"That's okay. I'll use my imagination. Mum always says it's good to do that, doesn't she?" He kept an eye on the door to make sure Ruth wasn't listening. "And you can do it for me while I get dressed, okay?"

He threw the covers off and, as Lucy started prancing around, he rushed around the room, throwing on sweats and a T-shirt in which to work out.

"Daddy, you're not looking!"

"I am, sweetheart. Come downstairs to the gym with me. There are lots of mirrors there for you to practice in front of. That'll be fun, won't it?"

A few minutes later he was on the treadmill. He turned on the TV and started watching Sky News, hardly noticing his daughter performing for him.

"Daddy, you're not looking."

"I am, sweetie." He glanced at her once. "What are you playing?"

"A leaf. It's a windy day and I fall off the tree and I have to go like this." She twirled around the gym and Lou looked back at the TV.

"What's a leaf got to do with Jesus?"

She shrugged, and he had to laugh.

"Will you come to see me tonight, pleeeease?"

"Yep," he said, wiping his face on a towel.

"Promise?"

"Absolutely," he said dismissively. "Okay, you go back up to your mum now. I've to take a shower."

TWENTY MINUTES LATER AND ALREADY in work mode, Lou went into the kitchen to say a quick good-bye to everyone. Bud was in his high chair, rubbing banana into his hair; Lucy was sucking on a spoon and watching cartoons at top volume; and Ruth was in her nightgown making Lucy's school lunch. She looked exhausted.

"Bye." He kissed Lucy on the head; she didn't budge, completely engrossed in her cartoon. He hovered above Bud, trying to find a place on his face that wasn't covered in food. "Eh, bye." He pecked him awkwardly on the top of his head. Then he made his way around to Ruth.

"Do you want to meet me there at six or go together from here?"

"Where?"

"The school."

"Oh. About that." He lowered his voice.

"You have to go; you promised." She stopped buttering the bread to look at him in anger.

"Lucy showed me the dance downstairs and we had a

talk, so she's fine about me not being there." He picked at a slice of ham on the cutting board. "Do you know why the hell she's a leaf in a nativity play?"

Ruth laughed. "Lou, I know you're playing with me. I told you to put this in your diary last month. And then I reminded you last week, and I called that woman Tracey at the office—"

"Ah, that's what happened." He clicked his fingers in a gosh-darn-it kind of way. "Wires crossed. Tracey's gone. Alison replaced her. So maybe there was a problem when they switched over." He tried to say it playfully, but Ruth's face of disappointment, hatred, and disgust, all rolled into one, stopped him.

"I mentioned it twice last week. I mentioned it yesterday morning. I'm like a frigging parrot with you, and you still don't remember. The school play tonight and then dinner with your mum, dad, Alexandra, and Quentin. And Marcia might be coming, if she can move around her therapy session."

"No, she really shouldn't miss that." Lou rolled his eyes. "Ruthy, please, I would rather stick pins in my eyes than have dinner with them."

"They're your family, Lou."

"All Quentin talks about are boats. Boats, boats, and more bloody boats. It is totally beyond him to think of any other conversation that doesn't involve the words *boom* and *cleat*."

"You used to love sailing with Quentin."

"I used to love sailing. Not necessarily with Quentin,

and that was years ago." He groaned. "And Marcia . . . it's not therapy she needs, it's a good kick in the ass."

"Tough," Ruth said, continuing with her lunch making. "Lucy is expecting you at the play, your parents are excited, and I need you here. I can't do the dinner and play host all on my own."

"Mum will help you."

"Your mother just had a hip replacement." Ruth was straining to keep her voice down.

"Don't I know it. I collected her from hospital and got into trouble for it, like I said I would," he grumbled. "While Quentin was off on his boat."

"He was racing, Lou!" She dropped the knife and turned to him, then seemed to switch gears. "Please." She kissed him softly on the lips, and he closed his eyes, lingering in the rare moment.

"But I've so much to do at work," he said quietly amid their kiss. "It's important to me."

Ruth pulled away. "Well, I'm glad something is, Lou, because for a moment there I almost thought you weren't human." She was silent as she finished buttering the bread fiercely, the knife hitting so roughly that it made holes. She slapped down slices of ham, tossed in a slice of cheese, then pushed down on the bread and sliced it diagonally with a sharp knife. She moved about the kitchen, slamming drawers and violently ripping tinfoil from the teeth of the packaging.

"We're not in this life just to work, Lou, we're in it to *live*. We have to start doing things together, and that means your doing things for me even when you don't want to, and vice versa. Otherwise, what's the point?"

"What do you mean 'vice versa'? When do I ever make you do anything you don't want to?"

"Lou," she gritted her teeth, "they're *your* bloody family, not mine."

"So cancel it! I don't care."

"You have family responsibilities."

"But I have more work responsibilities. Family can't fire me if I don't turn up to a bloody dinner, can they?"

"Yes, they can, Lou," she said quietly.

"Is that a threat?" He lowered his voice. "You can't throw comments like that at me, Ruth; it's not fair."

Ruth just looked at him and said nothing, allowing her stare to speak for her.

"Okay, fine, I'll do my best to be there," Lou said, both to please her and to get out of the house, yet not meaning a word of it. On her look, he rephrased it with more meaning. "I'll be there."

LOU ARRIVED AT HIS OFFICE at eight a.m. A full hour before another soul would arrive, even Alison. It was important for him to be the first in; it made him feel efficient, ahead of the pack. As he stepped out of the empty elevator into the quiet corridor, he could smell the products used by the cleaning staff last night. The scents of carpet shampoo, furniture polish, and air fresheners still lingered, as yet untainted by morning coffee and other human smells. It was still pitch-black outside at this early winter hour, and the office windows seemed cold and hard. Lou looked forward to leaving the empty corridors and getting to his office for his morning routine.

En route to his office he stopped suddenly in his tracks. Though Alison's desk was empty, as expected, Lou could see that his office door was ajar and the lights were on. He walked briskly toward it. Seeing Gabe moving around inside his office, he felt his heart begin pounding as the anger surged through him.

"Hey!" he yelled, and fired his fist at the door, punching it open and watching it swing violently. He opened his mouth to yell again, but before he could get his words out, he heard another voice coming from behind the door.

"My goodness, who's that?" came the startled voice of his boss.

"Oh, Mr. Patterson. I'm sorry," Lou said breathlessly, quickly stopping the door from slamming against the man's face. "I didn't realize you were in here." He rubbed his hand, his fist stinging and beginning to throb from punching the door. He looked from Mr. Patterson to Gabe uncertainly. "I'm sorry to have frightened you. I just thought that there was somebody in here who shouldn't be." His eyes landed on Gabe.

"Good morning, Lou," Gabe said politely.

Lou slowly nodded at him in acknowledgment, wanting nothing more right then than an explanation as to why Gabe and his boss were standing in his office at eight a.m.

He looked down at Gabe's empty mail cart and then at the files splayed out on his desk. He or Alison always tidied the papers on his desk at the end of every evening. He narrowed his eyes suspiciously at Gabe.

Gabe stared back unblinkingly.

"I was just chatting with young Gabe here," Mr. Patterson explained. "He told me that he started his job yesterday, and isn't he just wonderful for being the first into the office? That shows such dedication to the job."

"First in? Really?" Lou faked a smile. "Wow. Looks like you beat me to it this morning, because I'm usually the first one in." Lou turned to Mr. Patterson and offered an even bigger smile. "But you already knew that, didn't you, Gabe?"

Gabe returned the smile with equal sincerity. "You know what they say: the early bird catches the worm."

"Yes, it does. It catches it indeed." Lou glared at him through his grin. A glare and a grin. Both at the same time.

Mr. Patterson watched the exchange with growing discomfort. "Well, it's just after eight. I should leave."

"Just after eight, you say. That's funny." Lou perked up. "The mail hasn't even arrived yet. What, em, what exactly are you doing in my office then, Gabe?" His voice had an edge to it that was clearly recognizable.

"Well, I came in early to familiarize myself with the building," Gabe responded angelically.

"Isn't that wonderful?" Mr. Patterson asked, trying to break the tension.

"Yes, it is, but, Gabe, you already familiarized your-self with my office yesterday," Lou said tightly. "So I'm asking again, what are you doing here?"

"Now, now, Lou, I fear I must jump in here," Mr. Pat-terson said awkwardly. "I met young Gabe in the hall-way and we got talking. As a favor for me, I'd asked him to take some files to your office. He was delivering them to your desk when I realized I'd left one in my briefcase. But when I turned around to tell him, he was already gone. Poof! Just like that!" Mr. Patterson chuckled.

"Poof!" Gabe grinned at Lou. "That's me, all right."

"I like fast workers, but I must say I prefer fast *and* ef-ficient, and my goodness you certainly are that."

Gabe jumped in before Lou could say anything.

"Thank you, Mr, Patterson, and if there's anything else you'd like me to do for you, please let me know. I finish my shift at lunchtime and would be only too happy to help out for the rest of the afternoon. I'm keen to work."

Lou's stomach tightened.

"That's wonderful, Gabe, thank you, I'll keep that in mind. So, Lou," Mr. Patterson turned to face him, and Lou waited for Gabe, no longer a part of this conversa-tion, to leave. But he didn't. "I wonder if you'd be able to meet with Bruce Archer this evening. You remember him."

Lou nodded, his heart lifting as though he was a schoolboy again, wanting to please the teacher.

"I was supposed to meet with him, but I was reminded this morning of something else I have to attend."

"This evening?" Lou asked, happily kissing good-bye Lucy's play and dinner with his family. He'd been saved. "That's no problem. It would be a pleasure."

He felt Gabe's eyes sear into him.

In his mind, Lucy, dizzy from her twirling for him, dropped to the ground, and Ruth opened her eyes and pulled away from their morning kiss, his promise of less than an hour ago having already been broken. He felt a split second of guilt, which at least told him he was human, making him feel that he might actually be a good family man. Some of his colleagues felt no guilt at all.

"Great. Great. Well, Melissa can fill you in on the details. I have a big night tonight." Mr. Patterson winked at Gabe. "It's my little one's Christmas play. I'd forgotten all about it until he came running in this morning dressed as a star. I wouldn't miss it for the world."

"Oh, that's wonderful," Gabe said, his face lighting up. "He'd probably never forgive you if you weren't there. It's such an important night for him. You're a good father to go, as busy as you are."

Lou glared at Gabe.

"Well, thank you, Gabe," Mr. Patterson beamed, happy with the praise. "Right so, enjoy tonight, Lou, and well done for finding this lad." Mr. Patterson patted Gabe on the back.

"Morning, Laurence," Lou heard the familiar cheery call behind him and turned around to see Alfred join them in his office. "Is this a secret little meeting I didn't know about?" Alfred smiled, looking from Lou to Mr. Patterson.

Alfred was a tall man, six feet, with white-blond hair, kind of like an oversized Milky Bar kid who had melted and been molded back together by the hands of a child. He always spoke with a smirk on his face and in the kind of accent that came from being privately schooled in England. His nose was disjointed from his rugby days, and he swanned around the office, as Gabe had observed the previous day, kicking up the tassels of his loafers with the air of a naughty schoolboy who was up to tricks.

Alfred's eyes fell upon Gabe, then quite obviously looked him up and down in silence and waited to be introduced. Gabe imitated him, confidently giving Alfred the once-over right back.

"Nice shoes," Gabe finally said, and Lou looked down at the brown loafers Gabe had described yesterday.

"Thank you." Alfred looked a little put out.

"I also like your shoes, Mr. Patterson," Gabe commented, looking over at them.

In a slightly awkward moment, all eyes looked down at the men's feet. Lou's heart started pumping at a ridiculous rate at the sight of the black slip-ons and the brown loafers, the exact shoes Gabe had described the previous morning. So Alfred was meeting with Mr. Patterson. Lou looked from Alfred to Mr. Patterson, feeling a sense of betrayal. It wasn't official that Cliff's job was up for grabs, but if it was, Lou was hell-bent on making sure it would be his, not Alfred's. It now looked like he had a fight on his hands.

"Who are you?" Alfred finally asked Gabe after Mr. Patterson had bid them farewell.

"I'm Gabriel." Gabe held out his hand. "Friends call me Gabe, but you can call me Gabriel." He smiled.

"Charming. Alfred." Alfred reached out his hand.

Their shake was cold and limp, and their hands fell quickly by their sides.

"Do I know you?" Alfred narrowed his eyes.

"No, we've never actually met, but you may recognize me."

"Why's that, were you in a reality show or something?" Alfred studied him again, with a less confident smirk.

"You used to pass by me every day, just outside this building."

Alfred looked back at Lou with a slightly nervous smile. "Help me out here, pal."

"I used to sit at the doorway next door," Gabe continued. "Lou gave me a job."

Alfred's face eventually broke into a smile, the relief more than obvious on his arrogant face. His demeanor shifted and he became the big man on campus again, knowing that his position wasn't being threatened by a homeless man.

He laughed as he turned to Lou, making a face and using a tone that he didn't even attempt to disguise in Gabe's company. "You gave him a job, Lou?" he said.

"Well, isn't it the season to be jolly, indeed. What the hell is going on with you?"

"Alfred, just leave it," Lou replied, embarrassed.

"Okay." Alfred held his hands up and chuckled to himself. "You thought Patterson would like that one, didn't you? Clever thinking, Lou. You're really reaching high up into your sleeve for Cliff's job, aren't you?"

"I thought Cliff's job was still Cliff's?" Gabe said.

Alfred looked at him dismissively. "Only if he gets better."

"And Cliff isn't going to get better," Lou added, before he and Alfred both laughed, Lou looking slightly guilty for doing so, Alfred unashamedly throwing his head back and guffawing.

Gabe looked from one to the other, bemused.

"Hey, can I use your bathroom?" Alfred suddenly stopped laughing.

"What? No, not here, Alfred, just use the rest-rooms."

"Come on, don't be a jerk." His tongue sounded too big for his mouth as it rolled around his words. "I'll just be a second. See you around, Gabe; I'll try to aim my coins at your cart when you pass by," Alfred joked, giving Gabe the once-over again. He smirked and winked at Lou before making his way to Lou's private bathroom.

From the office, Lou and Gabe could hear loud sniffing behind the bathroom door.

"There seems to be a nasty cold going around this district," Gabe said.

Lou turned to him. "Look, I'm sorry, Gabe—he's, you know, don't take him seriously."

"Oh, nobody should ever take anybody seriously really; you can't control anything but what's inside this circle." Gabe's arms made a movement around his body. "Until we all do that, *nobody* can be taken seriously. Here, I got you this." He leaned down to the bottom tray of his cart and lifted up a Styrofoam cup of coffee. "I owe you from yesterday. It's a latte; the machine was back working again."

"Oh, thanks." Lou felt even worse now, totally conflicted as to how he felt about this man.

"So, you're going to dinner tonight?" Gabe undid the brake on the cart and started to move away, one of the wheels squeaking as he pushed it.

"No, just a coffee. Not dinner." Lou was unsure if Gabe wanted to be invited. "It's no big deal really. I'll be in and out in an hour at the most."

"Oh, come on, Lou," Gabe said with a smile, and he sounded alarmingly like Ruth. *Oh, come on, Lou, you know this one.* But he didn't finish the sentence in quite the same way. "You know these things always turn into dinner," Gabe continued. "Then drinks and then *whatever.*" He winked. "You must really want poor Cliff's job."

Lou bit the inside of his lip and nodded. With every fiber of his being he wanted that job.

"But is any of it worth it for the amount of trouble you'll be in at home, Aloysius?" he said in a singsong voice that chilled Lou to the bone.

Gabe made his way toward the elevator, the squeaking of the wheel loud in the empty hallway.

"Hey!" Lou called after him, but he didn't turn around. "Hey!" he repeated. "How did you know that? Nobody knows that!"

Even though he was alone in the office, Lou quickly looked around to make sure no one else had heard.

"Relax! I won't tell anyone," Gabe called back to him in a voice that made Lou feel far from reassured. Lou watched as Gabe pressed the call button for the elevator and lingered by the doors.

The bathroom door opened and Alfred exited, rubbing at his nose and sniffing. "What's all the shouting about? Hey, where did you get the coffee?"

"Gabe," Lou replied, distracted.

"Who? Oh, the homeless guy," Alfred said uninterested. "Really, Lou, what the hell were you thinking? He could wipe you out."

"What do you mean?"

"Come on, were you born yesterday? You've taken a man who has nothing and put him in a place where there is everything. Ever heard of a thing called temptation? Actually, forget I asked. It's *you* I'm talking to," he said. "You give in to that every time. Perhaps you and the homeless man aren't so different," he added. He chuckled and his chest wheezed, the result of his forty-a-day smoking habit.

"We're nothing alike," Lou spat, looking back down at the elevators to Gabe.

But Gabe was gone.

The elevator pinged and the doors opened, like welcoming arms ready to embrace the next guest. But there was nobody there. It waited, but nobody entered, and so it crossed its arms in a huff, and descended again.

CHAPTER 11

The Juggler

At five p.m., exactly the same time that Lou should have been leaving work in order to get home for Lucy's school play, he instead paced the floor of his office. Something Gabe had said had made him rethink his decision to miss the play; he couldn't think what exactly, and all he could feel was a ball of guilt nestled somewhere near his heart and his gut. It was an unfamiliar feeling. His office door was wide open, prepared for his eventual catapult launch down the corridor into Mr. Patterson's office, where he would announce he was unable to meet Bruce Archer for coffee. Not unlike Mr. Patterson, he too had family commitments. Tonight his daughter was going to be a leaf. But the thought of doing so made him weaken at the knees. Each time he reached the doorway he stopped short, and instead turned around and continued his pacing around his desk.

Gabe. Bloody Gabe. How on Earth had he allowed that man to get inside his head? He didn't care what Gabe thought about him. Gabe didn't know how Lou was with his family. Gabe didn't know how his family felt about him. He didn't know all the good things he did for them. The expensive holidays, the lavish gifts at Christmas.

Lou would do his job tonight without guilt. Just like he did every day.

He calmed himself and sat at his desk. Just as he prepared to call Alison to instruct her to pass on the message of his important meeting to his wife, he heard Alison call out cheerily, "Hi, Gabe."

Lou froze, and then for reasons unknown, found himself rushing behind the door, where he stood with his back to the wall and listened to their conversation through the open door.

"Hi, Alison."

"You look smart today, Gabe."

"Thanks. Mr. Patterson has asked me to do a few jobs for him around here, so I thought it would be a good idea to look a bit more respectable."

Lou peeked through the gap in the hinges of the door and spied Gabe, his new haircut combed neatly like Lou's. A new dark suit was draped over his shoulder and covered in plastic.

"You're working for Mr. Patterson? Wow, congratulations. So is the new suit part of the job?" Alison asked.

"Oh, this? This is just for me to have. You never know when a suit will come in handy." He smiled. "Anyway, I'm here to give you these for Lou. I think they're plans."

"But Lou just asked Mr. Patterson for these five minutes ago. How did you get them from the architect so quickly?" Alison checked the plans, confusion written across her face.

"Oh, I don't know, I just, you know . . ." Lou could see Gabe's shoulders shrugging.

"No, I don't know," Alison laughed. "But I wish I did. Keep working like this, and I wouldn't be surprised if Mr. Patterson gives you Lou's job."

They laughed and Lou bristled, making a note to make Alison's life hell right after this conversation.

"Is Lou in right now?"

"Yes, he is. Why?"

"Is he going to meet with Bruce Archer today?"

"Yes. At least I think so. Why?"

"Oh, no reason. Just wondering."

"Why, what's going on?" She lowered her voice. "What's the big deal about this evening? Lou's been acting funny about it. It's almost like he has a conscience about not going to his daughter's play." She giggled.

That was it. Lou couldn't take it anymore. He slammed his office door, no doubt startling them both. Then he sat down at his desk and picked up the phone.

"Yes?" Alison answered.

"Get me Harry from the mailroom on the phone, and after that call Ronan Pearson and check with him to see if Gabe collected the plans from him personally. Do this without Gabe's knowing. And then we'll have a talk about that conscience of mine," he snapped.

"Oh." She paused, embarrassed, then composed herself. "Yes, of course, just one moment, please," she said in her best telephone voice. "I'll connect you."

Lou adjusted his tie, cleared his throat, and spun around in his oversized leather chair to face the window. The day was cold but crisp, and there wasn't a breeze as holiday shoppers rushed to and fro, their arms laden with bags amid the flashing colors of numerous neon signs.

"Yello," Harry barked.

"Harry, it's Lou."

"What?" Harry shouted, machines and voices so loud behind him, Lou had no choice but to speak up. He looked around to make sure he was still alone before speaking. "It's Lou, Harry."

"Lou who?"

"Suffern."

"Oh, Lou, hi, how can I help you? Your mail end up on twelve again?"

"No, no, I got it, thanks."

"Good. That new boy you sent my way is a genius, isn't he?"

"He is?"

"Gabe? Absolutely. Everyone's calling me with nothing but good reviews. It's like he fell from the stars, I'm telling you. And he couldn't have come at a better time, that's no word of a lie. We were struggling, you know that. In all of my years in this job, this Christmas season is the wildest. Everything's getting faster and faster.

Well, it must be, because it's not me that's getting slower, that's for sure. You picked a good one, Lou. I owe you. So how can I help you today?"

"Well, about Gabe," Lou said slowly, his heart pounding in his chest. "You know he's taken on some other commitments in the building. Other work outside of the mailroom."

"I heard that all right, and I'm happy for him. He was as excited as anything this morning. Got a new suit and all on his break. I don't know where he found the time to get it; some of them in here can't even light their cigarette in that time. He's quick, that boy. Mr. Patterson seems to have taken a shine to him. I'd say it won't be long before he's out of here and up there with you."

"Yeah . . . anyway, I was just calling to let you know. I didn't want it to conflict with his work with you." Lou tried one more time. "You wouldn't want him to be *distracted*, with his mind on the other things he's doing for us. You know? It gets so manic up here, and we certainly don't want any problems."

"I appreciate that, Lou, but what he does after one p.m. is his own business. To be honest with you, I'm glad he's found something else. He gets his job done so quickly, it's a struggle to keep him busy."

"Right. Okay. So, if he acts up in any way, you just go ahead and do what you have to do, Harry. I don't want you to feel in any way obligated to keep him on for me. You know?"

"I know that, Lou, I do. He's a good lad; you've nothing to worry about."

"Okay. Thanks. Take care, Harry."

The phone went dead. Lou sighed and slowly spun around in his chair to replace the receiver. As he turned, he came face-to-face with Gabe, who was standing behind his desk and watching him intently.

Lou jumped, dropped the receiver, and let out a yelp. "Jesus Christ." He held his hand over his pounding heart.

"No. It's just me," Gabe said, blue eyes searing into Lou's.

"Have you ever heard of knocking? Where's Alison?" Lou leaned sideways to check her desk and saw that it was empty. "How long have you been there?"

"Long enough." Gabe's voice was soft, and it was that which unnerved Lou most. "Trying to get me in trouble, Lou?"

"What?" Lou's heart pounded wildly, still unrecovered from the surprise, and also alarmingly discomfited by Alison's absence and Gabe's proximity. The man's very presence disconcerted him.

"No." He swallowed, and he hated himself for his sudden weakness. "I just called Harry to see if he was happy with you. That's all." He was aware of the fact that he sounded like a schoolboy defending himself.

"And is he?"

"As it turns out, yes. But you must understand how I feel a responsibility to him for finding you."

"Finding me," Gabe said with a curious smile.

"What's so funny about that?"

"Nothing." Gabe continued to smile and began looking around Lou's office, hands in his pockets, with that same patronizing look that was neither jealousy nor admiration.

"It's five twenty-two p.m. and thirty-three seconds now," Gabe said, not even looking at his watch. "Thirty-four, thirty-five, thirty-six . . ." He turned to Lou. "You get the idea."

"So?" Lou stood up and put on his suit jacket and caught a glimpse at his watch to make sure. It was five twenty-two, on the nose.

"You have to leave now, don't you?"

"What does it look like I'm doing?"

Gabe wandered over to Lou's side and picked up three pieces of fruit from the bowl there—two oranges and an apple—which he inspected closely, one by one. "Decisions, decisions," he said. He held the three pieces of fruit in his hands.

"Hungry?" Lou asked, agitated.

"No," Gabe laughed. "You any good at juggling?"

That same feeling struck Lou's heart, and he realized exactly what it was that he didn't like about Gabe. It was questions like that, statements and comments that pierced Lou somewhere other than where they should.

"You'd better get that," Gabe added.

"Get what?"

Before Gabe could respond, the phone rang, and,

despite his preferring Alison to screen his calls, he dove for it.

It was Ruth.

"Hi, honey." He motioned to Gabe for privacy, but Gabe didn't leave and began juggling the fruit instead. Lou turned his back, and then, feeling uncomfortable with Gabe behind him, he faced forward again to keep an eye on his visitor. He lowered his voice. "Em, yeah, about tonight, something's come up and—"

"Lou, don't do this to me," Ruth said.

"It's just the play I won't make, sweetheart."

Gabe dropped the apple, which rolled across the carpet toward Lou's desk, and continued juggling with the oranges. Lou felt a childish sense of satisfaction that Gabe had failed.

"Lucy's heart will be broken," Ruth said sadly.

"Lucy won't even notice I'm not there, the place will be so dark. You can tell her I was there. Mr. Patterson asked me to meet with a client of ours. It's a big deal, and it could help with my getting Cliff's job, you know?"

"I know, I know. And then if you do get a promotion, you'll be away from us even more. Anyway, I don't want to get into this conversation now. So you'll make it home for dinner? Your mum just rang on the phone saying how much she's looking forward to it. You know, it's already been a month since you've seen them."

"It's not been a month. I saw Dad just"—he went quiet while calculating the time in his head—"well, maybe it's *almost* been a month."

A month? How the time had flown. For Lou, visiting his parents was a chore, like making the bed. After he had not done it for some time, the sight of the untidy blankets would play on his mind until he went to get it over and done with. He'd feel an instant sense of satisfaction it had been completed. But then he'd wake up the next day and know he had to go and do it all over again. The thought of his father complaining about how long it'd been since Lou's last visit made Lou want to run in the other direction. It made him feel guilty, but it also made him want to stay away longer.

"I might not make dinner, but I'll be there for dessert. You have my word on that."

Gabe dropped an orange, and Lou felt like punching his fist in the air in celebration. Instead, he pursed his lips and continued to make excuses to Ruth for everything, refusing to apologize for something that was totally out of his control. Lou finally hung up the phone and folded his arms across his chest.

"What's so funny?" Gabe asked, throwing the one remaining orange up and down in his hand.

"Not such a good juggler, are you?" Lou smirked.

"Touché." Gabe smiled. "You're very observant. Indeed, I'm not a good juggler, but it's not really juggling if I'd already chosen to drop those others and keep this one in my hand, is it?"

Lou frowned at the peculiar response and busied himself at his desk, putting on his overcoat and preparing to leave.

"No, Gabe, it's certainly not juggling if you *choose* . . ."
He stopped suddenly, realizing what he was saying and
hearing Ruth's voice in his head. His head snapped up,
feeling that cold chill again, but Gabe was gone and the
orange was left on his desk.

"Alison." Lou marched out of his office with the orange in his hand. "Did Gabe just walk out of here?"

"Em . . ." she said slowly. "He came up to my desk
about twenty minutes ago and—"

"Yeah, yeah, I know all that. He was in my office a
second ago and then he was gone. Just now. Did he walk
by?"

"Well, he must have, but—"

"Did you see him?"

"No, I was on the phone and—"

"Jesus." He punched the desk, startling Alison. "By
the way"—he dropped his voice and leaned in closer—
"does any of my mail ever come to me under a different
name?"

"What do you mean?" She frowned.

"You know—" He looked left and right and barely
moved his lips as he spoke. "Aloysius," he mumbled.

"Aloysius?" she said loudly.

He threw his eyes up. "Keep it down," he hissed.

"No." She lowered her voice. "I've never seen the
name Aloysius on any of the mail." Then she smiled,
snorted, and started laughing. "Why the hell would
there be Aloy—"

At his look, her words disappeared and her smile

faded. "Oh. Oh dear. That's a"—her voice went an oc-
tave higher—"*lovely* name."

LOU WALKED ACROSS THE NEWLY constructed Seán
O'Casey pedestrian bridge that linked the two rejuve-
nated north and south quays—the North Wall Quay
and Sir John Rogerson's Quay. One hundred meters
across the bridge brought him to his destination, the
Ferryman, the only authentic pub left on this stretch. It
wasn't a place for cappuccinos or ciabattas, and because
of that the clientele was specific. The bar contained a
handful of Christmas shoppers who'd wandered off the
beaten track to take a break and to wrap their purple-
fingered hands around heated glasses. The rest of the
place was filled with workers, young and old, winding
down after their day's work. Suits filled the seats, pints
and shorts filled the surfaces. It was just after six p.m.,
and people had already escaped the business district for
their nearest place of solace, to worship at the altar of
beers on tap.

Bruce Archer was one such person, propped at the
bar with Guinness in hand, roaring with laughter over
something somebody beside him had said. All around
him were suits. Shoulder pads to shoulder pads. Pin-
stripes and polished shoes and briefcases containing
spreadsheets, pie charts, and forward-looking market
predictions. None of them were drinking coffee. Lou
should have known. But as he watched them backslap-

ping and laughing loudly, he wasn't in the least bit surprised. So, really, he had known all along.

Bruce turned around and spotted him. "Lou!" he
shouted across the room in his heavy Boston accent.
"Lou Suffern! Good to see ya!" He stood from the stool,
walked toward Lou with his hand extended, and then,
gripping Lou's hand firmly, pumped it up and down
while thumping him enthusiastically on the back. "Let
me introduce you to the guys. Guys, this is Lou, Lou Suffern, works at Patterson Developments . . ." And so Lou
was lost in a sea of introductions, forgetting each name
the second he heard it and pushing the image of his wife
and daughter out of his head each time he shook a firm,
clammy, or limp hand. He tried to forget that he had for-
saken his family for this. He tried to forget as they pooh-
poohed his order of coffee and instead filled him with
beer, as they ignored his attempt to leave after one pint.
Then after the second. And again after the third. Tired
of a fight each time a round arrived, he let them change
his order to a Jack Daniel's, and as his cell phone rang he
also let their adolescent jeers keep him from answering.
And then, after all that, they needed to convince him no
more. He was there with them for the long haul, with
his phone on silent and vibrating every ten minutes with
a call from Ruth. He knew at this point that Ruth would
understand; if she didn't, then she was an extremely un-
reasonable person.

Then there was a girl catching his eye across the bar;
then there was another whiskey and Coke on the coun-

ter. All sense and reason had gone outside with the bar patrons having a smoke, and it was shivering out there, half thinking of hailing a taxi, half looking around for someone to take it home and love it. And then, too cold and frustrated, sense turned on reason and resorted to fisticuffs outside the bar, while Lou turned his back and took sole care of his ambition.

CHAPTER 12

Home Sweet Home

L OU REALIZED HE WAS FAR too drunk to chat up the attractive woman in the bar who had been eyeing him all night, when, in the process of joining her table, he stumbled over his own feet and managed to knock her friend's drink into her lap. Not the pretty one's lap, just her friend's. And while he mumbled something he thought was highly smooth and clever, it was obvious she thought it was sleazy and offensive. For there was a fine line between sleazy and sexy when you'd had as much to drink as Lou Suffern. He appeared to have lost the swagger of charm and sophistication that he'd possessed in heaps when he had first walked in this evening. His crisp white shirt and tie were now stained with whiskey and Coke, and his blue eyes, which usually had hypnotic effects, were now bloodshot and glassy. And so, too drunk to get anywhere with her—or her friend—the more sensible option seemed to be to walk back to his car. And drive home.

When he reached the cold and dark basement parking lot underneath his office building—a walk that took twenty minutes longer than it should have—he realized he had forgotten where he'd parked. He circled the center of the lot, pressing the button on his key and hoping the sound of the alarm or the flashing lights would give it away. Finally seeing the car lights, he closed one eye and focused on making his way to his Porsche.

"Hello, baby," he purred, rubbing up alongside of it—though less out of love but more because he'd lost his footing. He kissed the hood and climbed inside. Then, finding himself in the passenger's seat, where there was no steering wheel, he got back out and made his way around to the driver's side.

After a few moments of trying to get the key into the ignition, he cheered at the sound of the engine, then with his foot pushed the accelerator to the floor. Finally remembering to look up at where he was going, he screamed with fright. At the hood of the car stood a motionless Gabe.

"Jesus Christ!" Lou shouted, taking his foot off the accelerator and banging on the windshield with his hand. "Are you crazy? You're going to get yourself killed!"

Gabe's face was blurry through the windshield, but Lou would have bet his life that he was smiling. Then he heard a knock and he jumped, and when he looked over he saw Gabe peering in the driver's window at him. Lou lowered the window a slit.

"Hi."

"Hi, Gabe."

"You want to turn the engine off, Lou?"

"No. No, I'm driving home."

"Well, you won't get very far if you don't take it out of neutral." His tone was patient. "I don't think it's such a good idea for you to drive home. Why don't you get out and we'll get you a taxi home?"

"No, can't leave the Porsche here. Some crazy will steal it. Some looney tune. Some homeless vagabond." Then he started laughing hysterically. "Oh, I know. Why don't you drive me home?"

"No, no, I don't think that's a good idea, Lou. Come on out and we'll get you a taxi," Gabe said, opening the door.

"Nope. No taxi," Lou slurred, moving the clutch from neutral to drive. He pushed his foot down on the accelerator, and the car jumped forward with the door wide open; then it stopped, lurched forward, and stopped again. Gabe rolled his eyes and hung on to the door as the car jumped forward like a cricket.

"Okay, fine," Gabe said as Lou lurched the car forward again. "I'll drive you home."

Lou climbed over the gearshift into the passenger seat, and Gabe sat in the driver's seat. He didn't need to adjust the seat or mirrors as he and Lou, it seemed, were exactly the same height.

"You know how to drive?" Lou asked.

"Yes."

"Have you driven one of these before?" Lou asked, and then began laughing hysterically again. "Maybe there's one parked beneath your penthouse."

"Buckle up, Lou." Gabe ignored his comments and concentrated on getting Lou home alive. That task was very important at this point, very important indeed.

Gabe handled the car well. He brought them from the city to Howth smoothly, without once having to fidget for an indicator or search for the window wipers. He seemed at home in the sports car.

Lou noticed this and began to get irrationally jealous. "Actually, let me drive," he said grumpily, squirming in his seat to get out. "I don't like people thinking this is your car."

"It's dangerous to drink and drive, Lou. You could crash."

"So," he huffed childishly. "That's my problem, isn't it?"

"A friend of mine died not so long ago," Gabe said, his eyes on the road. "And believe me, when you die, it's anything *but* your problem. He left behind a right mess. So I'd buckle up if I were you, Lou."

"Who died?" Lou closed his eyes, ignoring Gabe's advice but giving up on his idea to drive. He leaned his head back on the rest. "How'd he die?"

"Car crash," Gabe said, pushing his foot down on the accelerator. The car jerked forward quickly, the engine loud and powerful in the quiet night.

Lou's eyes opened slightly, and he looked over at Gabe warily. "Yeah?"

"Yep. Sad, really. He was a young guy. Successful.

Young family. Lovely wife." He pressed his foot down harder on the accelerator.

Lou's eyes were fully open now.

"It just shows you never know when your time is up."

The speedometer neared one hundred kilometers in the fifty-kilometer zone, and Lou grabbed the door handle and held on tightly. He moved from his slouched position and was sitting up poker straight now, watching the speedometer and the blurred lights of the city across the bay whizzing by.

Lou began to reach for his seat belt then, but all of a sudden, as quickly as he had sped up, Gabe took his foot off the accelerator, checked his side mirror, turned on the signal, and moved the wheel steadily to the left. He looked at Lou's face, which had turned an interesting shade of green, and smiled as he stopped the car.

"Home sweet home, Lou."

It was only over the next few days, as the hangover haze had begun to lift, that Lou realized he didn't recall giving Gabe any directions to his home that night.

"MUM, DAD, MARCIA, QUENTIN, ALEXANDRA!" Lou announced at full boom. As he entered the house, he found Ruth sitting at the dining table filled with dirty plates and glasses. She was alone.

"I'm ho-ome," he sang. "Where is everybody?" He looked around. "Oh. I'm so sorry I missed dinner; it was such a busy evening at the office. Busy, busy, busy."

Even Lou couldn't keep a straight face with that excuse, and so he stood in the dining room, his shoulders moving up and down, his chest wheezing in a near-silent laugh.

Ruth froze, watching her husband with mixed feelings of anger, hurt, and embarrassment. Somewhere inside her there was jealousy, too. After returning from the school play, she'd put the kids to bed and run around the house all evening in order to get dinner ready and the house presentable. She was physically flushed and tired, but also mentally drained from trying to stimulate her children in all the ways a parent should—from being on her knees on the floor with Bud, to wiping tears off the face of a disappointed Lucy, who'd failed to find her father in the audience despite Ruth's attempts to convince her otherwise.

Ruth looked at Lou swaying in the doorway, his eyes bloodshot, his cheeks rosy, and she wished that she could be the one who threw caution to the wind and acted the idiot. But Lou would never stand for it—and she would never do it—and that was the difference between them. But there he was, swaying and happy, and there she was, static and deeply dissatisfied, wondering why on Earth she had chosen to be the glue holding it all together.

Gabe joined Lou awkwardly by the dining room door in the long heavy silence that followed. Ruth smiled at the stranger.

"Lou," Ruth said quietly, "perhaps you should have some water or coffee. I'll make some coffee."

Lou sighed loudly. "Am I an embarrassment, Ruth? Am I?" he snapped. "You told me to come home. I'm home!" He made his way to the living room across the hall, like a sailor aboard a rocky ship.

Gabe walked over to the table to Ruth. "Hello, Ruth, I'm very pleased to finally meet you."

She barely looked him in the eye as she limply took his hand.

"Hello," she said quietly. "Please excuse me while I take all this away." She stood up from the table and began carrying the leftover cheese plates and coffee cups into the kitchen.

"I'll help you," Gabe offered.

"No, no, please, sit down." She rushed into the kitchen with a load in her arms.

Gabe followed her anyway and found her leaning against the kitchen counter where she had placed the dirty plates, her back to him. Her head was down and her shoulders were hunched, all life and soul of the woman gone at that very moment. He placed the plates he had carried in beside the sink so that she knew he was there.

She jumped, alert to his presence, and composed herself, then turned around to face him.

"Gabe." She smiled tightly. "I told you not to bother."

"I wanted to help," he said softly then. "I'm sorry about Lou. I wasn't out with him tonight."

"No?" She folded her arms and looked embarrassed for not knowing.

"No. But I do work with him at the office. I was there late when he got back from the . . . well, from his coffee meeting."

"When he got back to the office? Why would he . . ." She looked at him with confusion before a shadow fell across her face as realization dawned. "Oh, I see. He was trying to drive home."

It wasn't a question, more a thought aloud, and so Gabe didn't respond, but she softened toward him.

"Right. Well, thank you for bringing him home safely, Gabe. I'm sorry I was rude to you, but I'm just, you know . . ." Emotion entered her voice and she stopped talking, and instead busied herself scraping food from the plates into the trash.

"I know. You don't have to explain."

From the living room they heard Lou let out a "Whoa," and then there was the sound of glass smashing, followed by his laughter.

She stopped scraping the plates and closed her eyes, sighing.

"Lou's a good man, you know," Gabe said softly.

"Thank you, Gabe. Believe it or not, that is exactly what I need to hear right now, but I was rather hoping it wouldn't come from one of his work buddies. I'd like for his mother to be able to say it." She looked up at him, eyes glassy. "Or his father. Or it would be nice to hear it from his daughter. But no, at work, Lou is the man." She scraped the plates angrily.

"I'm not a work buddy, believe me. Lou can't stand me."

She looked at him curiously.

"I used to sit outside his building every morning, and yesterday, totally out of the blue, he stopped and gave me a coffee and offered me a job."

"He mentioned something about that last night." Ruth searched her brain. "Lou really did that?"

"You sound surprised."

"No, I'm not. Well, I am. I mean . . . what job did he give you?"

"A job in the mailroom."

"How does that help him out?" She frowned.

Gabe laughed. "You think he did it for his own good?"

"Oh, that's a terrible thing for me to say." She bit her lip to hide her smile. "I didn't mean it that way. I know Lou is a good man, but lately he's just been very . . . busy. Or more *distracted*; there's nothing wrong with being busy, as long as you're not distracted." She waved her hand dismissively. "But he's not all here. It's like he's in two places at once. His body with us, his mind constantly elsewhere." She composed herself. "You obviously brought out the good side in him, Gabe."

"He's a good man," Gabe repeated.

Ruth didn't answer, but it was almost as though Gabe

read her mind when he said, "But you want him to become a better one, don't you?"

She looked at him in surprise.

"Don't worry." He placed his hand over hers, and it was immediately comforting. "He will be."

CHAPTER 14

The Wake-Up Call

L OU AWOKE THE MORNING AFTER to a wood-pecker sitting on his head hammering away with great gregariousness at the top of his skull. The pain worked its way from his frontal lobe through both his temples and down to the base of his head. Somewhere outside, a car horn beeped, ridiculous for this hour, and an engine was running. He closed his eyes again and tried to disappear into the world of sleep, but responsibilities, the woodpecker, and what sounded like the front door slamming wouldn't allow him safe haven in his sweet dreams.

His mouth was so dry, he found himself smacking his lips together and thrashing his tongue around in order to gather the smallest amount of moisture. And then the saliva came, and he found himself in that awful place—between his bed and the toilet bowl—where his body temperature went up, his mind dizzied, and the moisture came to his mouth in waves. He kicked off his bed-clothes, ran for the toilet, and fell to his knees in a heavy, heaving worship of the toilet bowl. It was only when he no longer had any energy, or anything left inside his stomach, that he sat on the heated tiles in physical and mental exhaustion, and noticed that the sky outside was bright. Unlike the darkness of his usual morning rises at this time of the year, the sky was a bright blue. And then panic overcame him, far worse than the dash he'd just encountered.

Lou dragged himself up from the floor and returned to the bedroom with the desire to grab the alarm clock and strangle the nine a.m. that flashed boldly in red. He'd slept in. They'd all missed their wake-up call. Only they hadn't, because Ruth wasn't in bed. Then he noticed the smell of food drifting upstairs, almost mockingly doing the cancan under his nose. He heard the clattering and clinking of cups and saucers. A baby's babbles. Morning sounds. Long, lazy sounds that he shouldn't be hearing. He should be hearing the hum of the fax machine and photocopier; the noise of the elevator as it moved up and down the shaft, its ping, every now and then, as though the people inside had been cooked. He should be hearing Alison's acrylic nails on the keyboard. He should be hearing the squeaking of the mail cart as Gabe made his way down the hallways . . .

Gabe.

He pulled on a robe and rushed downstairs, almost falling over the shoes and briefcase he'd left at the bottom step, before bursting through the door into the kitchen. There they were, the three usual suspects: Ruth, Lucy, and Bud. Gabe wasn't anywhere to be seen, thankfully. Egg was dribbling down Lucy's chin, Ruth was still in her nightgown. Bud was the only one to make a sound as he sang and babbled, his eyebrows moving up and down with such expression it was as though his sentences actually meant something. Lou took this scene in, but at the same time failed to appreciate a single pixel of it.

"What the hell, Ruth?" he said loudly, causing all heads to look up and turn to him.

"Dada?" Bud asked, his voice sweet as an angel's.

"Excuse me?" Ruth looked at him with widened eyes.

"It's nine a.m. Nine o-fucking-clock. Why the hell didn't you wake me?" He came closer to her.

"Lou, why are you talking like this?" Ruth frowned, then turned to her son. "Come on, Bud, a few more spoons, honey."

"Because you're trying to get me fired, is what you're doing. Isn't it? Why the hell didn't you wake me?"

"Lucy, why don't you go and wash your hands," Ruth spoke calmly, her eyes following her daughter out of the room and then turning to Lou. "I was going to wake you, but Gabe said not to. He said to let you rest until about ten o'clock, that a rest would do you good, and I agreed," she said matter-of-factly.

"Gabe?" He looked at her as though she were the most ludicrous thing on the planet. "GABE?" he shouted now. "Gabe the mailboy? The fucking MAILBOY? You listened to him? He's an imbecile!"

"Well, that imbecile"—Ruth fought to stay calm—"drove you home last night instead of leaving you to drive to your death."

Remembering then that Gabe had driven him home, Lou rushed outside to the driveway. He made his way around the perimeter of his car, hopping from foot to foot on the pebbles outside, his concern for his vehicle so great that he could barely feel them pinching his bare skin. He examined his Porsche from all angles, running his fingers along the surface to make sure there weren't any scratches or dents. Finding nothing wrong, he calmed a little, though he still couldn't understand what had made Ruth value Gabe's opinion so highly. What was going on in the world that had everybody eating out of Gabe's palm?

He returned to the kitchen, where Ruth was still sitting at the table feeding Bud.

"Ruthy." He cleared his throat and made an attempt at a Lou-style apology, the kind of apology that never involved the word *sorry*. "It's just that Gabe is after my job, you see. You didn't understand that, I know, but he is. So when he arrived at work this morning bright and early, knowing that I was still asleep—"

"He left five minutes ago." She cut him off right away, not turning around, not even looking at him. "He stayed in one of the spare rooms because I'm not too sure if he's got anywhere else to go. He got up and made us all breakfast, and then I called him a taxi, which I paid for so that he could get to work. So I suggest you get out of this house and take your accusations with you."

"Ruthy, I—"

"You're right, Lou, and I'm wrong. It's clear from this morning's behavior that you're totally in control of things and not in the least bit stressed," she said sarcastically. "I was such a fool to think you needed an extra hour's sleep. Now, Bud," Ruth said as she lifted the baby from his chair and kissed his food-stained face, "let's go give you a bath."

Bud clapped his hands and turned to jelly under her raspberry kisses. Ruth walked toward Lou with Bud in her arms, and for a moment Lou softened at the big smile on his son's face. He prepared to take Bud in his arms but didn't get a chance. Ruth walked right on by, cuddling Bud tightly while he laughed uproariously at her kisses. Lou acknowledged the rejection. For about five seconds. And then he realized that he needed to get to work. And so he dashed.

In record timing, and thankfully due to Sergeant O'Reilly's not being on duty as Lou fired his way to work, Lou arrived at the office at ten fifteen a.m.: the latest he had ever arrived at the office. He still had a few minutes before the weekly in-house meeting ended, and so, spitting on his hand and smoothing down his hair, which hadn't been washed, and running his hands across his face, which hadn't been shaved, he shook off the remaining waves of dizziness of his hangover, took a deep breath, and entered the boardroom.

Inside, there was a collective intake of breath at the sight of him. It wasn't that he looked so bad. It was just that, for Lou, he wasn't perfect. He took a seat opposite Alfred, who beamed with astonishment and absolute delight at his friend's apparent breakdown.

"I'm so sorry I'm late," Lou addressed the table more calmly than he felt. "I was up all night with one of those stomach bugs, but I'm okay now, I think."

Twelve faces nodded in sympathy and understanding.

"Bruce Archer has that very same bug," Alfred smirked, and he winked at Mr. Patterson.

The switch was flicked, and Lou's blood began to heat up, expecting any minute for a loud whistling to drift from his nose as he reached boiling point. He sat quietly through the meeting, though fighting flushes and nausea while the vein in his forehead pulsated at full force.

"And so, tonight is an important night, lads." Mr. Patterson turned to Lou, and Lou zoned in on the conversation.

"Yes, I have the audiovisual conference call with Arthur Lynch," Lou spoke up. "That's at seven thirty, and I'm sure it will all go without a hitch. I've come up with a great number of responses to his concerns, which we all went through last week. I don't think we need to go through them again—"

"Hold on, hold on." Mr. Patterson lifted a finger to stall him, and it was only then that Lou noticed that Alfred's cheeks had lifted into a great big smile.

Lou stared at Alfred to catch his eye, hoping for a hint, a giveaway, but Alfred avoided him.

"No, Lou, you and Alfred have a dinner with Thomas Crooke and his partner. This is the meeting we've been trying to get all year," Mr. Patterson said, looking concerned.

Crumble, crumble, crumble. It was all coming tumbling down. Lou shuffled through his schedule and ran shaky fingers through his hair. He pointed his finger along the freshly printed schedule, his tired eyes finding it hard to focus, his clammy forefinger smudging the words as he moved it along the page. There it was, the audiovisual conference call with Arthur Lynch. No mention of a dinner. No damn mention of a damn dinner.

"Mr. Patterson, I'm well aware of the long-hoped-for meeting with Thomas Crooke." Lou cleared his throat. "But nobody confirmed a dinner with me, and I made it known to Alfred last week that I have a meeting with Arthur Lynch at seven thirty tonight." He looked at Alfred with confusion. "Alfred? Do you know about this dinner meeting?"

"Well, yeah, Lou," Alfred said in a mocking tone with a shrug that went with it. "Of course I do. I cleared my schedule as soon as they confirmed it. It's the biggest chance we've got to make the Manhattan development work. We've all been talking about this for months."

The others around the table squirmed uncomfortably in their seats, though there were some, Lou was certain, who were enjoying this moment profusely, documenting every sigh, look, and word to rehash it with others as soon as they were out of the room.

"Everybody, you can all get back to work," Mr. Patterson said, looking forward. "We need to deal with this rather urgently."

The others emptied the room and left Lou, Alfred, and Mr. Patterson at the table; Lou instantly knew by Alfred's stance and the look on his face, by his stubby fingers pressed together in prayer below his chin, that Alfred had already taken the higher moral ground on this one. Alfred was in his favorite mode, his most comfortable position of attack.

"Alfred, how long have you known about this dinner and why didn't you tell me?" Lou immediately went on the offensive.

"I told you, Lou," Alfred responded calmly.

With Lou a sweaty, unshaven mess and Alfred appearing so cool, Lou knew he wasn't coming out of this looking the best. He removed his shaky fingers from the schedule and clasped his hands together.

"It's a mess, a bloody mess." Mr. Patterson rubbed his chin roughly with his hands. "I needed both of you at that dinner, but I can't have you missing the call with Arthur. The dinner can't be changed; it took us too long to get it in the first place. How about the call with Arthur?"

Lou swallowed. "I'll work on it."

"If not, there's nothing we can do, except for Alfred to begin the dinner, and Lou, as soon as you've finished your meeting, you make your way as quickly as you can to join Alfred."

"Lou has serious negotiations to discuss with Arthur, so he'll be lucky if he makes it to the restaurant for after-dinner mints. But I'll be well able to manage it, Laurence." Alfred spoke from the side of his mouth with his usual smirk. "I'm capable of doing it alone."

"Yes, well, let's hope Lou negotiates fast and that he's successful; otherwise this entire day will have been a waste of time. This is the second time this week there's been a mix-up with meetings, isn't it?" Mr. Patterson asked.

"No, no, this is the first. Alfred scheduled the other meeting *after* I told him I wasn't available." Lou felt drips of perspiration rolling down his back. His shirt clung to him, his tie choked his neck, and his hair felt matted to his head. He hoped neither of them could smell, like black coffee, the stench emanating from his underarms.

Alfred turned to Lou in surprise. It wasn't like Lou to throw something like that at Alfred in front of Mr. Patterson. But the accusation was like blood to a shark, and Alfred was done with circling and was ready to bite. The corner of his lip turned up in a snarl as he said, "I know, Lou, and I apologize for that, but it was a development deal worth one hundred million euros. I couldn't hold back on that just because you needed to take the morning off."

Mr. Patterson looked to Lou.

"I didn't take the morning off." Lou leaned in, his voice breaking as it rose in pitch. He realized he sounded like a teenager standing up to his parents, but he couldn't help it. He wiped the sweat from his lip with the back of his hand. "It was an hour. Just to collect my mother from the hospital. Then I was straight back in. You could have waited. That was the first hour I've taken off in five years working here."

"Wow." Alfred smiled. "Then you really know how to choose your hours. You could have picked a lunch break or something. Anyway, I closed the deal, Lou," Alfred said, taking that first bite into Lou's flesh. "I did it alone. So there's no need to worry."

Lou, trembling with rage, looked from one man to the other. He wanted to punch Alfred. Alfred wanted him to punch him. Lou looked to the water jug filled at the center of the table and thought about flinging it at Alfred's head. Alfred's eyes followed Lou's gaze. He smiled knowingly.

"Do you need a glass of water, Lou?" Alfred asked. "You don't look well."

Mr. Patterson finally spoke up, "Is something the matter, Lou? You do look—"

"No," Lou interrupted Mr. Patterson, cutting him off far more rudely than intended. "I'm fine. All is fine. In fact, I'm feeling better than usual." He tried to perk himself up but felt a bead of sweat drip down his forehead. He quickly brushed it away. "I'm ready to go, ready for *two* important meetings this evening, both of which will be an absolute success."

Mr. Patterson frowned. "Lou." He was silent for a moment. "Are you sure you'll be able to—"

"Absolutely," he interrupted again. "I have never let

you down before, Mr. Patterson, and I don't intend on doing it now." Not when so much was at stake.

Mr. Patterson looked at him with concern, then grumbled something inaudible, gathered his papers, and stood up. Meeting adjourned.

Lou felt like he was in the middle of a nightmare; everything was falling apart, all his good work was being sabotaged. He stormed out of the meeting room, ignoring Alfred's faux-concerned voice calling to have a private word with him. Lou headed straight to Alison's desk, where he threw the details of that evening's dinner on her keyboard, stopping her acrylic nails midtap. She narrowed her eyes and scanned the brief.

"What's this?"

"A dinner tonight. A very important one. At eight p.m. That I *have* to be at." He paced the area in front of her while she read it more carefully.

"But you can't; you have the conference call. It took us weeks to set that up. If you don't talk to them tonight, they'll go with Raven and Byrne, and you don't want that."

"I know, Alison," he snapped. "But I need to be at this." He stabbed a finger on the page. "Make it happen." Then he rushed into his office and slammed the door. He froze before he got to his desk. On it his mail was laid out neatly.

He backtracked and opened his office door again.

Alison snapped to it quickly and looked up at him. "Yes?" she said eagerly.

"The mail."

"Yes?"

"When did it get here?"

"First thing this morning. Gabe delivered it the same time as always."

"He couldn't have," Lou objected. "Did you see him?"

"Yes," she said, looking concerned. "He brought me a coffee, too. Just before nine, I think. Are you okay?"

"I'm fine," he snapped.

"Em, Lou, just one thing before you go . . . Is this a bad time to go over some details for your dad's party?"

She'd barely finished her sentence before he'd gone back into his office and slammed the door behind him once again.

THERE ARE MANY TYPES OF wake-up calls in the world. For Lou Suffern, a wake-up call was a duty for his devoted alarm clock to perform on a daily basis. At six a.m. every day, when he was in bed sleeping and dreaming, thinking of yesterday and planning tomorrow, his alarm would ring dutifully and loudly. It would reach out from the bedside table and prod him right in the subconscious, taking him away from his slumber and dragging him into the world of the awakened. Lou would wake up; eyes closed, then open. Body in bed, then out of bed; naked, then clothed. This, for Lou, was what waking up was about. It was the transition period from sleep to work.

For other people wake-up calls took a different form. For Alison, it was the pregnancy scare at sixteen that had forced her to make some choices; for Mr. Patterson, it was the birth of his first child that had made him see the world in a different light. For Alfred, it was his father's loss of their millions when Alfred was a child, forcing him to attend public school for a year before his father made it all back. It changed him forever. For Ruth, her wake-up call happened on their last summer holiday, when she walked in on her husband with their twenty-six-year-old Polish nanny. For little five-year-old Lucy, it was when she looked out into the audience during her school play to see an empty seat beside her mother.

Today, though, Lou was experiencing a very different kind of wake-up call. Lou Suffern, you see, wasn't aware that a person could be awakened when his eyes were already open. He didn't realize that a person could be awakened when he was already out of his bed, dressed in a smart suit, doing deals and overseeing meetings. He didn't realize a person could be awakened when he considered himself to be calm, composed, and collected, able to deal with life and all it had to throw at him. The alarm bells were ringing now, louder and louder in his ear, and only his subconscious could hear them. He was trying to turn the bells off, to hit the snooze button so that he could nestle back down in the lifestyle he felt cozy with, but it wasn't working. He didn't know that he couldn't tell life when he was ready to learn, that life would instead teach him when it felt he was good and ready. He didn't know that he couldn't press buttons and suddenly know it all; that it was the buttons in him that would be pressed.

Lou Suffern thought he already knew it all.

But he had only scratched the surface.

CHAPTER 15

Bump in the Night

AT SEVEN THAT EVENING, WHEN the rest of his
colleagues had been spat out of the office building
and then sucked in by the spreading Christmas mania
outside, Lou Suffern remained inside at his desk, staring at some files, feeling less like the dapper business-
man and more like Aloysius, the schoolboy in detention
whom he'd fought so hard over the years to leave behind.

Outside was black and cold. Lines of traffic filled every bridge and quay as people made their way home,
counting down the days of this mad rush to Christmas.
Harry in the mailroom was right: it was all moving too
quickly, the buildup feeling more of an occasion than
the moment itself. Lou's head pulsated more than it had
that morning, and his left eye throbbed as the migraine
worsened. He lowered the intensity of the lamp on his
desk, feeling sensitive to the light. He could barely think,
let alone string a sentence together, and so he wrapped
himself up in his cashmere coat and scarf and left his

office to go to the nearest pharmacy for some headache pills. He knew he was hung over, but he was also sure he was coming down with something; the last few days he'd felt extraordinarily unlike himself. Disorganized, unsure—traits that were surely due to illness.

Lights were out in all the offices; the hallways were dark, apart from a few emergency lights that remained on for the security guards doing their rounds. Lou pressed the elevator call button and waited for the sound of the thick wires pulling the elevator up the shaft to start up. Instead, the doors opened instantly, and he caught sight of himself in the elevator mirror: disheveled, tired. He pulled his coat around him tighter, stepped into the car, and before he had the opportunity to press a button, the doors automatically closed and the elevator immediately descended.

He pressed the ground-floor button, but it failed to light up. He pressed it again harder. Still nothing. He thumped it a few times and, with growing concern, watched as the light moved from each number on the panel to the next. Twelve, eleven, ten . . . The elevator picked up speed as it descended. Nine, eight, seven . . . It showed no signs of slowing. The elevator was rattling now as it sped along the wires, and, with growing fear and anxiety, Lou began to press all of the buttons in front of him, alarm included, but it was to no avail. The elevator didn't respond, and it continued to fall through the shaft on a course of its own choosing.

Only floors away from the ground level, Lou moved

away from the doors quickly and hunched down, huddling in the corner of the car. He tucked his head between his knees, crossed his fingers, and braced himself in the crash position.

But seconds later, the elevator slowed and suddenly stopped, shuddering a little from its abrupt halt. When Lou opened his eyes, which until that moment had been scrunched shut, he saw that he'd stopped on the basement floor. Then the elevator omitted a cheery *ping*, and its doors slid open. He shuddered at the sight in front of him as he looked out. The basement was cold and dark, and the concrete ground dusty. Not wanting to get off in the basement, he pressed the ground-floor button again to return quickly to marble surfaces and carpets, to creamy toffee swirls and chromes, but the button still failed to light up; the elevator stayed open. He had no choice but to try to find the stairs so that he could climb up to the ground floor. As soon as he stepped out of the elevator and placed both feet on the basement floor, the doors behind him slid closed and the elevator ascended.

The basement was dimly lit. At the end of the corridor a fluorescent strip of light flashed on and off, which didn't help his headache and made him lose his footing a few times. There was the loud hum of machines all around, and the ceilings revealed a complicated mess of electrics and wiring. The floor was cold and hard beneath his leather shoes and dust motes bounced up to cover his polished tips. As he moved along, searching for the exit, he heard the sound of music drifting out from under the door at the end of a hallway that veered off to the right. "Driving Home for Christmas" by Chris Rea. Along the hallway on the opposite side, he saw a green sign depicting a man running illuminated above a metal door. He looked from the exit, back to the room from which music and light emanated. He glanced at his watch. He still had time to make his way to the pharmacy and— providing the elevators worked—back to his office for the conference call. Curiosity got the better of him, and so he made his way down the hall and drummed his knuckles against the closed door. The music was so loud he could barely hear his own knock, so he slowly opened the door and stuck his head in the room.

The sight stole words straight from his mouth.

Inside was a small stockroom, the walls lined from floor to ceiling with metal shelves, filled with everything from lightbulbs to toilet rolls. There were two aisles, both of them no more than ten feet in length, and it was the second aisle that caught Lou's attention. Through the shelving units, light came from the ground. Walking closer to the aisle, he could see the familiar sleeping bag laid out from the wall. On the sleeping bag was Gabe, reading a book, so engrossed that he didn't look up as Lou approached. On the lower shelves a row of candles was lit, the same scented kind that were dotted around all the office bathrooms, and a shadeless lamp sent out a small amount of orange light in the corner of the room. Gabe was wrapped up in the same dirty blanket that Lou recognized from Gabe's days out on the street. A kettle was on a shelf and a plastic sandwich bag was half empty beside him. Gabe's new suit hung from a shelf, still covered in plastic.

Gabe looked up then, and his book went flying from his hands, just missing one of the candles, as he sat up straight and alert.

"Lou," he said, with a fright.

"Gabe," Lou said, and he didn't feel the satisfaction he thought he should. The sight before him was sad. No wonder the man had been first at the office every morning. This small storeroom piled high with shelves of miscellaneous junk had become Gabe's home.

"Are you going to tell?" Gabe asked, though he didn't sound concerned, just interested.

Lou looked back at him and felt pity. "Does Harry know you're here?"

Gabe shook his head.

Lou thought about it. "I won't say a word."

"Thanks."

"You've been staying here all week?"

Gabe nodded.

"It's cold in here."

"Yeah. Heat goes off when everyone leaves."

"I can get you a few blankets or, em, an electric heater or something, if you want," Lou said, feeling foolish as soon as the words were out.

"Yeah, thanks, that would be good. Sit down." Gabe pointed to a crate that was on the bottom shelf. "Please."

Lou pushed up his coat sleeves as he reached for the crate, not wanting the dust and dirt to get on him, and he slowly sat down.

"Do you want a coffee? It's black, I'm afraid; the latte machine isn't working."

"No, thanks. I just stepped out to get a few headache pills," Lou replied, missing the joke while looking around in distraction. "By the way, I appreciate your driving me home last night."

"You're welcome."

"How did you know where I lived?"

"I guessed," Gabe said sarcastically, pouring himself some coffee from the kettle. At Lou's look, he added, "Your house was the only one on the street with gates. Bad tasting gates, at that. They had a bird on top. A bird?"

"It's an eagle," Lou said defensively, and then finally came out with it. "Why did you want me to be late for work this morning?"

Gabe fixed those blue eyes on him, and despite the fact Lou had a six-figure salary and a multimillion-euro house in one of the most affluent areas in Dublin, and all Gabe had was this, Lou once again felt like the underdog, like he was being judged.

"Figured you needed the rest," Gabe responded.

"Who are you to decide that?"

Gabe simply smiled.

"What's so funny?"

"You don't like me, do you, Lou?"

Well, it was direct. It was to the point, no beating around the bush, and Lou appreciated that. But before Lou had the opportunity to answer, Gabe continued.

"You're worried about my presence in this building," he said simply.

"Worried? No. You can sleep where you like. This doesn't bother me."

"That's not what I mean. Do I threaten you, Lou?"

Lou threw his head back and laughed. It was exaggerated and he knew it, but he didn't care. It had the desired effect. His laugh filled the room and echoed in the small concrete cell against the open ceiling of exposed wires. "Intimidated by you? Well, let's see . . ." He held his hands out to indicate the room Gabe was living in. "Do I really need to say any more?" he said pompously.

"Oh, I get it." Gabe smiled broadly, as though guessing the winning answer to a quiz. "I have fewer *things* than you. I forgot that meant something to you." He laughed lightly and snapped his fingers, leaving Lou feeling stupid.

"Things aren't important to me," Lou defended himself weakly. "I'm involved in lots of charities. I give things away all the time."

"Yes," Gabe nodded solemnly, "even your word."

"What are you talking about?"

"You don't keep that, either." He started rooting in a shoe box on the second shelf. "Your head still at you?"

Lou nodded and rubbed his eyes tiredly.

"Here." Gabe retrieved a small container of pills. "You always wonder how I get from place to place? Take one of these." He tossed them over to Lou.

Lou studied them. There was no label on the container.

"What are they?"

"They're a little bit of magic," Gabe said with a laugh. "When taken, everything becomes clear."

"I don't do drugs." Lou handed them back, placing them on the end of Gabe's sleeping bag.

"They're not drugs."

"Then what's in them?"

"I'm not a pharmacist, just take them. All I know is that they work."

"No, thanks." Lou stood and prepared to leave.

"They'd help you a lot, you know, Lou."

"Who says I need help?" Lou said. "You know what, Gabe? You asked me if I don't like you. Overall, I don't really mind you. I'm a busy man, I'm not much bothered by you. But this, *this* is what I don't like about you, patronizing statements like that. I'm fine, thank you very much. My life is fine. All I have is a headache—and that's it. Okay?"

Gabe simply nodded, and Lou turned around and made his way toward the door.

Gabe started again. "People like you—"

"Like what, Gabe?" Lou turned around and snapped, his voice rising with each sentence. "People like me what? Work hard? Like to provide for their families? Don't sit on their asses on the ground all day waiting for handouts? People like me who help people like you, who go out of their way to give you a job and make your life better . . ."

Had Lou waited to hear the end of Gabe's sentence, he would have learned that Gabe was implying quite the opposite. Gabe was referring to people like Lou who were competitive. Ambitious people, with their eye on the prize instead of the task at hand. People who wanted to be the best for all the wrong reasons and who'd take almost any path to get there. Being the best was only slightly better than being in the middle, which was equal to being the worst. All were merely a state of being. It was how a person *felt* in that state and *why* that was the important thing.

Gabe wanted to explain to Lou that people like him were always looking at what the next person was doing, always looking to achieve more and greater things. Always wanting to be better. And the entire point of Gabe's telling Lou Suffern about people like Lou Suffern was to warn him that people who constantly looked over their shoulders often bumped into things.

Paths are so much clearer when people stop looking at what everyone else is doing and instead concentrate on themselves. Lou couldn't afford to bump into any more things at this point in the story. If he had, it would have surely ruined the ending, to which we've yet to arrive. Yes, Lou still had much to do.

But Lou didn't stick around to hear any of that. He left the storeroom, shaking his head with disbelief at

Gabe's cheekiness as he walked back down the corridor with the dodgy fluorescent lighting. He found his way to the exit and ran up the stairs to the ground floor.

Once he reached the warmth above, Lou was back in his comfort zone. The security guard looked up as Lou emerged from the emergency exit.

"There's something wrong with the elevators," Lou called out to him as he approached the elevator bank, not enough time now for him to get to a pharmacy and back for the conference call. He'd have to go straight up, feeling like this, head hot and mushy, with Gabe's ridiculous words ringing in his ears.

"That's the first I've heard of it." The security guard made his way over to Lou. He leaned over and pressed the call button, which lit up immediately. The elevator doors opened.

He looked at Lou oddly.

"Oh. Never mind. Thanks." Lou got back in the elevator and made his way up to the fourteenth floor. He leaned his head against the mirror and closed his eyes, dreamed of being at home in bed with Ruth cozied up beside him, wrapping her arm and leg around him as she used to do while she slept.

When the elevator pinged on the fourteenth floor and the doors slid apart, Lou opened his eyes and screamed with fright.

Gabe stood directly before him, looking solemn, his nose almost touching the doors. He rattled the container of pills in Lou's face.

"SHIT! GABE!"

"You forgot these."

"I didn't forget them."

"They'll get rid of that headache for you."

Lou snatched the container of pills from Gabe's hand and stuffed them deep into his trouser pocket.

"Enjoy." Gabe smiled with satisfaction.

"I told you, I don't do drugs." Lou kept his voice low, even though he knew they were alone on the floor.

"And I told you they're not drugs. Think of them as an herbal remedy."

"A remedy for what, exactly?"

"For your problems, of which there are many. I believe I listed them for you already."

"Says you, who's sleeping on the floor of a bloody basement stockroom," Lou hissed. "How's about you take a pill and go about fixing your own life? Or is that what got you in this mess in the first place? You know, I'm getting tired of your judging me, Gabe, when I'm up here and you're the one down there."

Gabe's expression looked curious in response, which made Lou feel guilty. "Sorry," Lou sighed.

Gabe simply nodded.

Lou examined the pills as his head pounded, heavier now. "Why should I trust you?"

"Think of it as a gift." Gabe repeated the words Lou had spoken only days before, bringing chills down Lou Suffern's spine.

CHAPTER 16

Granted

ALONE IN HIS OFFICE, LOU took the pills from his pocket and placed them on his desk. He laid his head down and finally closed his eyes.

"Christ, you're a mess," he heard a voice say close to his ear, and he jumped up.

"Alfred," he said, spotting his nemesis. He rubbed his eyes. "What time is it?"

"Seven twenty-five. Don't worry, you haven't missed your meeting. Thanks to me." Alfred smirked, running his nicotine-stained fingers along Lou's desk, his one touch enough to tarnish everything and annoy Lou. The term *grubby little mitts* applied here.

"Hey, what are these?" Alfred picked up the pills and popped open the lid.

"Give them to me." Lou reached out for them, but Alfred pulled away. He emptied a few into his open, clammy palm.

"Alfred, give them to me," Lou said sternly, trying to keep the desperation out of his voice as Alfred moved about the room waving the container in the air, teasing him with the same air as a school bully.

"Naughty, naughty, Lou, what are you up to?" Alfred asked in an accusing singsong that chilled Lou to the core.

Knowing that Alfred was already devising to use these against him, Lou thought fast.

"Looks like you're concocting a story." Alfred smiled. "I know when you're bluffing; I've seen you in every meeting, remember? Don't you trust me with the truth?"

Lou fought to keep his tone easy, almost joking, but he was deadly serious. "Honestly? Lately, no. I wouldn't be surprised if you hatched a plan to use that little container against me."

Alfred laughed. "Now, really. Is that any way to treat an old friend?"

Lou's light tone faded. "I don't know, Alfred, you tell me."

They had a moment's staring match. Then Alfred broke it.

"Something on your mind, Lou?"

"What do you think?"

"Look," Alfred's shoulders dropped, the bravado replaced by Alfred's new humble act. "If this is about the meeting tonight, rest assured that I did not meddle with your appointments in any way. Talk to Melissa. With Tracey leaving and Alison taking over, a lot of stuff got lost in the mix." He shrugged. "Though between you and me, Alison seems a little flaky."

"Don't blame it on Alison." Lou folded his arms.

"Indeed," Alfred smiled and nodded slowly to himself. "I forgot that you two have a thing."

"We have no *thing*. For Christ's sake, Alfred."

"Right, sorry." Alfred zipped his lips closed. "Ruth will never know, I promise."

The very fact that he'd mentioned Ruth unnerved Lou. "What's gotten into you?" Lou asked him, serious now. "Really, what's up with you? Is it stress? Is it the crap you're putting up your nose? What the hell is it? Are you worried about the changes—"

"The changes." Alfred snorted. "You make me sound like a menopausal woman."

Lou stared at him.

"I'm fine, Lou," he said slowly. "I'm the same as I've always been. It's you who's acting a little funny around here. Everyone's talking about it, even Mr. Patterson. Maybe it's these." He shook the pills in Lou's face, just as Gabe had done. "You're acting irrationally, sweating in meetings, forgetting appointments. Not exactly a great replacement for Cliff, are you?"

"They're headache pills."

"I don't see a label."

"The kids scratched it off; now can you please stop mauling them and give them back?" Lou held an open hand out toward Alfred.

"Oh, headache pills. I see." Alfred studied the container again. "Is that what they are? Because I thought I heard the homeless guy saying that they were herbal?"

Lou swallowed. "Were you spying on me, Alfred? Is that what you're up to?"

"No." Alfred laughed easily once again. "I wouldn't do that. I'll have some of these checked out for you, to make sure they're nothing stronger than headache pills." He took a pill, pocketed it, and handed back the container. "It'll be nice to be able to find out a few things for myself since my friends are lying to me."

"I know the feeling," Lou agreed, glad to have the container back in his possession. "Like my finding out about the meeting you and Mr. Patterson had a few mornings ago and the lunch you had last Friday."

Unusual for Alfred, he looked genuinely shocked.

"Oh," Lou said softly, "you thought I didn't know, didn't you? Sorry about that. Well, you'd better get to dinner, or you'll miss your appetizer. All work and no caviar makes Alfred a dull boy." Then he led a suddenly silent Alfred to his door, opened it, and winked at him before closing it quietly in his face.

SEVEN THIRTY P.M. CAME AND went without Arthur Lynch appearing on the fifty-inch plasma TV in front of Lou at the boardroom table. Aware that at any moment he could be seen by whoever would be present at the meeting, Lou attempted to relax in his chair and tried not to sleep. At seven forty, Mr. Lynch's secretary informed him that Mr. Lynch would be a few more minutes.

While waiting, the increasingly sleepy Lou pictured

Alfred in the restaurant, brash as could be, the center of attention, loud and doing his best to entertain—stealing the glory, making or breaking a deal that Lou wouldn't be associated with unless Alfred failed. In missing that— the most important meeting of the year—Lou was losing the biggest chance to prove himself to Mr. Patterson. Cliff's job dangled before him day in and day out, like a carrot on a string. So did Cliff's old office down the hall next to Mr. Patterson's, its blinds open and vacant. It was a larger office with better light. It called to him. It had been six months since the memorable morning Cliff had had his breakdown—after weeks and weeks of unusual behavior. Lou had finally found Cliff crouched under his desk, his body trembling, his computer keyboard held tightly and close to his chest. Occasionally his fingers tapped away at the keys in a sort of panicked Morse code. They were coming to get him, he kept repeating, wide-eyed and terrified.

Who exactly *they* were, Lou had been unable to ascertain. He'd tried gently to coax Cliff out from under the desk, to make him put his shoes and socks back on, but Cliff had lashed out as Lou neared and hit him across the face with the computer mouse, swinging the wire around like a lasso. The force of the small plastic mouse hadn't hurt Lou nearly as much as the sight of this young successful man falling apart. But the office had since lain empty for all these months, and as rumors of Cliff's further demise drifted, Lou's sympathy for him lessened while the competition for his job increased.

Lou's frustration grew as he stared at the black plasma screen still yet to come alive. His head pounded, and he could barely think as his migraine spread from the base of his head to his eyes. Feeling desperate, he retrieved pills from his pocket and stared at them.

He thought of Gabe's knowledge of the meeting between Mr. Patterson and Alfred and how he had correctly judged the shoe situation; he considered how Gabe had provided him with coffee the previous morning, had driven him home and somehow won Ruth over. Convincing himself that Gabe had never let him down, Lou shook the open container, and one small white glossy pill rolled out onto the palm of his sweaty hand. He played with it for a while, rolled it around in his fingers, licked it; when nothing drastic happened, he popped it into his mouth and quickly downed it with a glass of water.

Lou held on to the boardroom table with both hands, gripping it so hard that his sweaty prints were visible on the glass surface. He waited. Nothing happened. He lifted his hands from the table and studied them as though the effects would be seen on his palms. Still nothing out of the ordinary happened, no unusual trip, nothing life-threatening, apart from his head, which continued to pound.

At seven forty-five there was still no sign of Arthur Lynch. Lou tapped his pen against the table impatiently, no longer caring about how he'd appear to the people on the other side of the camera. Already paranoid beyond reason, Lou began to convince himself that there was no meeting at all, that Alfred had somehow orchestrated this so that he could conduct the dinner by himself and negotiate the deal. Lou wasn't going to allow Alfred to sabotage any more of his hard work. He stood quickly, grabbed his overcoat, and charged for the door. He'd pulled it open and had one foot over the threshold when he heard a voice coming from the plasma behind him.

"I'm very sorry for keeping you waiting, Mr. Suffern."

The voice stalled Lou in his march. He closed his eyes and sighed, kissing his dream of Cliff's office with the three-hundred-sixty-degree view of Dublin good-bye. He quickly thought about what to do: run and make it in time for dinner, or turn around and face the music. Before he had time to make the decision, the sound of another voice in the office almost stopped his heart.

"No problem, Mr. Lynch, and please call me Lou. I understand how things can run overtime, so no apologies are needed. Let's get down to business, shall we? We have a lot to discuss."

"Certainly, Lou. And call me Arthur, please. We do have a lot to get through, but before I introduce you to these two gentlemen beside me, would you like to finish your business up there? I see you have company?"

"No, Arthur, it's just me here in the office," Lou heard himself say. "Everyone else has deserted me."

"Oh, I thought I could see a man there by the door."

Spotted, Lou slowly turned around and, quite impossibly, came face-to-face with himself. He was still seated at the boardroom table, in the same place where he had been waiting before making a run for the door. The face that greeted him was also a picture of shock. The ground swirled beneath Lou, and he clutched the door frame to stop himself from falling.

"Lou? Are you there?" Arthur asked, and both heads turned to face the plasma.

"Erm, yes, I'm here," Lou at the table stammered. "I'm sorry, Arthur, that gentleman is a . . . colleague of mine. He's just leaving, I believe he has an important *dinner* meeting to get to." Lou turned around and threw his counterpart at the door a warning look. "Don't you?"

Lou simply nodded and left the room, his knees and legs shaking with his every step. At the elevators, he held on to the wall as he tried to catch his breath and let the dizziness subside. The elevator doors opened and he fell inside, thumping the ground-floor button before hunkering down in the corner of the space, moving farther and farther away from himself on the fourteenth floor.

At eight p.m., as Lou was in the boardroom of the Patterson Development offices negotiating with Arthur Lynch, Lou entered the restaurant just as Alfred and the team of men were being led to their tables. He offered his cashmere coat to the host, adjusted his tie, smoothed down his hair, and made his way to the tables, one hand in his pocket, the other swinging by his side. His body was loose again, nothing rigid, nothing contained. In order to function he needed to feel the swing of his body, the casual motion of a man who personally doesn't care about the decision either way, but who would do his best to convince you otherwise, because his only concern is you.

"Pardon me, gentlemen, for being a little delayed," he said smoothly to the men whose noses were already buried deep in their menus.

They all looked up, and Lou was exceptionally happy to see the expression on Alfred's face: a wave of emotions ranging from surprise to disappointment to resentment to anger. Each look told Lou that this mix-up had indeed been planned by Alfred. Lou made his way around the table greeting the dinner guests, and by the time he reached Alfred, his coworker had regained his smug face.

"Patterson is going to kill you," Alfred spoke quietly from the side of his mouth. "But at least one deal will be done tonight. Welcome, my friend." He shook Lou's hand, his anticipation of Lou's sacking tomorrow lighting up his face.

"It's all been taken care of," Lou simply replied, turning to take his place a few seats away.

"What do you mean?" Alfred asked harshly, for a moment forgetting where he was, his tight grip around Lou's arm preventing him from moving away.

Lou looked around at the table and smiled, then leaned down and discreetly removed each of Alfred's fingers from his arm. "I said, it's all been taken care of," Lou repeated.

"You canceled the conference call? I don't get it." Alfred smiled nervously. "Let me in on it."

"No, no, it's not canceled. Don't worry, Alfred, let's pay our guests some attention now, shall we?" Lou flashed his pearly whites and finally moved to his chair. "Now, gentlemen, what looks good on this menu? I can recommend the foie gras; I've had it here before, and it's a treat." He smiled at the team and immersed himself in the pleasure of deal making.

At nine twenty p.m., after the visual conference call with Arthur Lynch, an exhausted yet exhilarated and triumphant Lou stood outside the window of the Saddle Room restaurant. He was wrapped up in his coat as the December wind picked up, his scarf tight around his neck, yet he didn't feel the cold as he watched himself through the window, suave and sophisticated and holding everyone's attention as he told a story. Everybody's face was interested, all but Alfred, and after five minutes of his animated hand gestures and facial expressions, all the men started laughing. Lou could tell from his body movements that he was telling the story of how he and his colleagues had wandered into what turned out to be a gay bar in London instead of the lap-dancing bar they had expected. Looking at himself telling the story, he decided then and there never to tell it again. He looked like a prat.

He felt a presence beside him, and he didn't need to turn around to know who it was.

"You're following me?" he asked, still watching through the window.

"Nah, just figured you'd come here," Gabe responded,

shivering and stuffing his hands into his pockets. "How are you doing in there? Entertaining the crowd as usual, I see. Ah, it's the one about the three blondes in the elevator. You do like telling that joke, don't you?"

"What's going on, Gabe?"

"Busy man like you? You got what you wished for. Now you can do everything. Mind you, it'll wear off by the morning, so watch out for that."

"Which one of us is the real me?"

"Neither of you, if you ask me."

Lou finally turned to look at him then, and frowned. "Enough of the deep insights, please. They don't work on me."

Gabe sighed. "Both of you are real. You both function as you always do. You'll eventually merge back into one and be as right as rain again."

"And who are you?"

Gabe rolled his eyes. "You've been watching too many holiday movies. I'm Gabe. The same guy you dragged off the streets."

"What's in these?" Lou took the pills out of his pocket. "Are they dangerous?"

"Just a little bit of insight. And that never killed anyone."

"But these things . . . you could make some real money. Who else knows about them?"

"All the right people—the people who made them—and don't you go trying to make a fortune off them, or you'll have a few serious people to answer to."

Lou backed off for the moment. "Gabe, you can't just double me up and then expect me to accept it without question. This could have dire medical consequences for me, not to mention life-changing psychological reactions. And the rest of the world really needs to know about this. This is insane! We really need to talk about this—I need to know much more."

"Sure, we will." Gabe studied him. "And then, when you tell the world, you'll either be locked up in a padded cell or you'll become a freak-show act, and every day you can read about yourself in exactly the same amount of column inches as Dolly the cloned sheep. If I were you, I'd just keep quiet about it all and make the best of a very fortunate situation." He paused. "Wait, you're very pale. Are you okay?"

Lou laughed hysterically. "No, I'm not okay! This is not normal. Why are you behaving like this is normal?!"

Gabe shrugged. "I'm just used to it, I guess."

"Used to it?" Lou asked, bewildered. "Then you tell me, where do I go now?"

"Well, you've taken care of business at the office, and it looks like your other half is taking care of business here." Gabe smiled. "That would leave one special place for you to go."

Lou thought about that, and then a smile slowly crawled onto his face as he finally understood Gabe for the first time that evening. "Okay, let's go."

"I think Ruth would rather you come home alone tonight," Gabe said. "She liked me, but she didn't like me *that* much."

"What the hell are you talking about? I'm not going home. Let's go to the pub. We have to celebrate."

Gabe stared at him.

"What's wrong?"

"Go *home*, Lou."

"Home?" Lou scrunched up his face. "Why would I do that? You've just given me a free ticket to stay out late. *He* can bloody well go home." He turned back to watch himself at the dinner table, launching into yet another story. "Oh, I'm telling the one about the time I was stranded in the Boston airport. There was this woman on the same flight as me . . ." He grinned, turning around to tell Gabe the story, but his friend was gone.

"Suit yourself," Lou mumbled. He watched himself for a little bit longer, still in shock and unsure whether he was really experiencing this night. He definitely deserved a pint, and if the other half of him was heading home after the dinner, that meant he could stay out all night and nobody would notice—nobody, that was, but the person he ended up with. Happy days.

CHAPTER 17

Lou Meets Lou

A TRIUMPHANT LOU ROLLED UP to his home, gratified by the sound of the gravel beneath his wheels and the sight of his electronic gates closing behind him. The dinner meeting had been a success: he had commanded the conversation and had done some of the best convincing, negotiating, and entertaining he'd ever done. They'd laughed at his jokes, all his best ones, and they'd hung on his every word. All the gentlemen had left the table content and in full agreement. He'd shared a final drink with an equally jubilant Alfred before driving home.

The lights in the downstairs rooms were out, but they were all on upstairs, despite this late hour, bright enough to help land a plane.

He stepped inside, into the blackness. Ruth usually left the entrance-hall lamp on, and he felt around the walls for the light switch. There was an ominous smell in the air.

"Hello?" he called. His voice echoed three flights up to the skylight in the roof.

The house was a mess, not the usual tidiness that greeted him when he came home. Toys were scattered around the floor. He tutted.

"Hello?" He made his way upstairs. "Ruth?"

He waited for her shushing to break the silence, but it didn't.

Instead, once he reached the landing, Ruth ran from Lucy's bedroom and dashed by him, hand over her mouth, eyes wide and bulging. She hurried into their bathroom and closed the door. This was followed by the sound of her vomiting.

Down the hall, Lucy started to cry and call for her mother.

Lou stood in the middle of the landing, looking from one room to the other, frozen on the spot.

"Go to her, Lou," Ruth just about managed to say before another encounter with the toilet bowl.

He was hesitant, and Lucy's cries got louder.

"Lou!" Ruth yelled, more urgently this time.

He jumped, startled by her tone, and made his way to Lucy's room. He slowly pushed open the door and peeked inside, feeling like an intruder as he entered a world he had never ventured into before. The smell of vomit was pungent inside. Her bed was empty, but her sheets and pink duvet were unkempt from where she'd been sleeping. He followed her sounds into the bathroom and found her on the tiles, bunny slippers on her feet, throwing up into the toilet. She was weeping quietly as she did so. Spitting and crying, crying and spitting, her sounds echoing into the base of the toilet.

Lou stood there, looking around, briefcase still in his hand, unsure of what to do. He took a handkerchief out of his pocket and covered his nose and mouth, both to block the smell and to prevent the infection from spreading to him.

Ruth returned, much to his relief, and noted him just idly standing by and watching his five-year-old daughter being ill, then barged by him to tend to her.

"It's okay, sweetheart." Ruth fell to her knees and wrapped her arms around her daughter. "Lou, I need you to get me two damp facecloths."

"Damp?"

"Run them under some cold water and wring them out so they're not dripping wet," she explained calmly.

"Of course, yes." He shook his head at himself. He wandered slowly out of the bedroom, then froze once again on the landing. Looked left, looked right. He returned to the bedroom. "Facecloths are in the . . . ?"

"Hall closet," Ruth said.

"Of course." He made his way to the closet and, with his briefcase still in hand and his coat on, fingered the various colors of facecloths inside. Brown, beige, or white. He couldn't decide. Choosing brown, he returned to Lucy and Ruth, ran them under the tap, and handed them to her, hoping what he'd done was correct.

"Not just yet," Ruth explained, rubbing Lucy's back as her daughter took a break.

"Okay, erm, where will I put them?"

"Beside her bed. And can you change her sheets? She had an accident."

Lucy started to weep again, tiredly nuzzling into her mother's chest. Ruth's face was pale, her hair tied back hastily, and her eyes tired, red, and swollen. It seemed it had already been a hectic night.

"The sheets are in the closet, too. And the Dioralyte is in the medicine cabinet in the utility room."

"The what?"

"Dioralyte. Medicine. Lucy likes the black-currant flavor. Oh God," she said, jumping up, hand over her mouth, and running down the hall to their own bathroom again.

Lou was left in the bathroom alone with Lucy, whose eyes were closed as she leaned up against the bathtub. Then she looked at him sleepily. He backed out of the bathroom and started to remove the soiled sheets from her bed. As he was doing so, he heard Bud's cries from the next room. He sighed, finally put down his briefcase, took off his coat and suit jacket, and threw them out of the way, into the Dora the Explorer tent in the corner of Lucy's room. He opened the top button of his shirt, loosened his tie, and rolled up his sleeves.

LOU STARED DEEP INTO HIS Jack Daniel's and ice and ignored the barman, who was leaning over the counter and speaking aggressively into his ear.

"Do you hear me?" the barman growled.

"Yeah, yeah, whatever." Lou's tongue stumbled over his words, already unable to remember what he'd done wrong.

"No, not *whatever*, buddy. Leave her alone, okay? She doesn't want to hear your story; she is not interested in you. Okay?"

"Okay, okay," Lou grumbled then, remembering the rude blonde at the bar who'd kept ignoring him. He'd happily not talk to her—he wasn't getting much conversation out of her anyway—and the journalist he'd just shared a drink with earlier didn't seem much interested in the amazing story that was his life. He kept his eyes down into his whiskey. A phenomenon had occurred tonight, and nobody was interested in hearing about it. Had the world gone mad? Had they all become so used to new inventions and scientific discoveries that the very thought of a man being cloned no longer had shock value? No, the young occupants of this trendy bar would rather sip away at their cocktails, the young women swanning about in the middle of December with their tanned legs, short skirts, and highlighted hair, designer handbags hooked over their arms like candelabras, each one looking as exotic and as at home as a coconut in the North Pole. They didn't care about the greater events of the country. A man had been cloned. There were two Lou Sufferns in the city tonight. Bilocation was a reality. He alone knew the great depths of the universe. He laughed to himself and shook his head at the hilarity of it all.

He felt the barman's stare still searing into him, and so he stopped his solo chortling and concentrated again on his ice. Around the lonesome Lou the noise continued, the sound of people being with other people: after-work flirting, after-work fighting. There were tables of girls huddled together with eyes locked in as they caught up with one another, circles of young men standing with eyes locked outward, their movements shifty.

Lou looked around to catch somebody's eye. He was fussy at first about his chosen confidant, preferring somebody good-looking with whom to share his story for the second time, but then he decided to settle on anybody. Surely somebody would care about the miracle that had occurred to him tonight.

The only eye he succeeded in meeting was that of the barman again.

"Gimme me nuther one," Lou slurred when the barman walked over. "A neat Jack on th' rocks."

"I just gave you another one," the barman responded, a little amused this time, "and you haven't even touched that."

"So?" Lou closed one eye to focus on him.

"So, what good is there in having two at the same time?"

At that, Lou started laughing, a chesty, wheezy laugh with the presence of the bitter December breeze.

"I think I missed the joke." The barman smiled.

"Ah, nobody here cares." Lou got angry again, waving his hand dismissively at the crowd around him. "All

they care about is Sex on the Beach, thirty-year mortgages and Saint-Tropez. I've been listenin' and that's all
they're sayin'.''

The barman laughed. "Just keep your voice down.
What don't they care about?"

Lou turned quiet now and fixed the barman with his
best serious stare. "Cloning."

The barman's face changed, interest lighting up his
eyes. Finally something different for him to hear about,
rather than the usual patron woes. "Cloning? Right. You
have an interest in that, do you?"

"An interest? I have *more* than an *interest*." Lou laughed
patronizingly and then winked at the barman. He took
another sip of his whiskey and prepared to tell the story.
"This may be hard for you to believe, but I"—he took a
deep breath—"have been cloned. This guy gave me pills,
and I took them," he said, then hiccuped. "You probably
don't believe me, but it happened. Saw it with my own
two eyes." He pointed at his eye, misjudged his proximity, and poked himself. Moments later, after the sting
was gone, he continued chatting. "There's two of me,"
he said, holding up three fingers, then one, then finally
two.

"Is that so?" the barman asked, picking up a pint glass
and beginning to pour a Guinness. "Where's the other
one of you? I bet he's as sober as a judge."

Lou laughed, wheezy again. "He's at home with my
wife." He chuckled. "And with my kids. And I'm here,
with her." He directed his thumb to the left of him.

"Who?"

Lou looked to the side and almost toppled off his bar stool in the process. "Oh, she's—where is she?" He turned around to the barman again. "Maybe she's in the toilet. She's gorgeous, we were having a good chat. She's a journalist, she's going to write about this. Anyway, it doesn't matter. I'm here having *all the fun*, and he's"—he laughed again—"he's at home with my wife and kids. And tomorrow, when I wake up, I'm going to take a pill—not drugs; they're herbal, for my headache." He pointed to his head seriously. "And I'm going to stay in bed and he can go to work. Ha! All the things that I get to do, like . . ." He thought hard but failed to come up with anything. "Like, oh, so, so many things. All the places I'm going to go. It's a fucking mir'cle. D'ya know when I last had a day off?"

"When was that?"

Lou thought hard. "Last Christmas. No phone calls, no computer. Last Christmas."

The barman was dubious. "You didn't take a holiday this year?"

"Took a week. With the kids." He wrinkled up his nose. "Fucking sand everywhere. On my laptop, in my phone. And this." He reached into his pocket and took out his BlackBerry and slammed it on the bar counter.

"Careful."

"This thing. Follows me everywhere; sand in it and it still works. The drug of the nation. This thing." He poked it, mistakenly pressing some buttons, which lit up the screen. A picture of Ruth and the kids smiled back at him. Bud with his big silly toothless grin; Lucy's big brown eyes peeping out from under her fringe; Ruth holding them both. Holding them all together. He studied it momentarily with a smile on his face. Then the light went out and the picture faded to black. "In the B'hamas," he continued, "and *beep-beep*, they got me. *Beep-beep, beep-beep*, they get me." He laughed again. "And the red light. I see it in my sleep, in the shower, every time I close my eyes, the red light and the *beep-beep*. I hate the fucking *beep-beep*."

"So take a day off," the barman said.

"Can't. Too much to do."

"Well, now that you're cloned, you can take all the days off that you want," the barman joked.

"Yeah." Lou smiled dreamily. "There's so much I want to do."

"Like what?" The barman leaned in, looking forward to hearing this crazy guy's dream.

"The blonde that was here a minute ago," Lou said, then laughed loudly as the barman shook his head and wandered off to another drunk at the end of the bar.

"IT'S OKAY, SWEETIE, IT'S OKAY, Daddy's here," Lou said, holding Lucy's hair from her face and rubbing her back as she leaned over the toilet and vomited for the twentieth time that night. He sat on the bathroom tiles in a T-shirt and boxer shorts, and leaned against the bathtub as her tiny body convulsed one more time and expelled more vomit.

"Daddy . . ." Her voice was small through her tears.

"It's okay, sweetie, I'm here," he repeated sleepily. "It's almost over." It had to be. How much more could her tiny body get rid of?

Every twenty minutes he'd gone from sleeping in Lucy's bed to assisting her in the bathroom, her body going from freezing to boiling and back again in a matter of minutes. Usually it was Ruth's duty to stay up all night with the children, sick or otherwise, but unfortunately for Lou, and for Ruth, she was having the same experience as Lucy in their own bathroom down the hall. Gastroenteritis, an end-of-the-year gift for those whose systems were ready to wave good-bye to the year.

Lou carried Lucy to her bed again, her small hands clinging around his neck. Already she was asleep, exhausted by what the night had brought her. As he laid her down on the bed, he wrapped her now-cold body in blankets and tucked Beyoncé, her favorite bear, close to her face, as Ruth had shown him. His mobile vibrated again on the pink princess bedside table. At four a.m., it was the fifth time he'd received a phone call from himself. Glancing at the caller display, his own number flashed up on the screen.

"What now?" he whispered into the phone, trying to keep his voice and anger low.

"Lou! It's me, Lou!" came the drunken voice on the other end, followed by a raucous laugh.

"Stop calling me," he said, a little louder now.

In the background was thumping music, loud voices, and a gabble of nonspecific words. He could hear glasses clinking and laughter exploding every few moments from different corners of the room. He could almost smell the alcohol fumes drifting through the phone and penetrating the innocent world of his daughter. Subconsciously, he blocked the receiver with his hand.

"Where are you?"

"Leeson Street. Somewhere," he shouted back. "I met this girl, Lou. Fucking amazing! You'll be proud of me. No, you'll be proud of you!" Raucous laughter again.

"What?!" Lou barked loudly. "No! Don't do anything!" he shouted, and Lucy's eyes fluttered open momentarily like two little butterflies, big brown eyes glancing at him with fright, but then on seeing him— her daddy—she smiled and her eyes closed again with exhaustion. That look of trust, the faith she had put in him with that one simple look, did something to him right then. He knew he was her protector, the one who could take away the fright and put a smile on her face, and it gave him a better feeling than he'd ever felt in his life. Better than the deal at tonight's dinner, better than seeing the look on Alfred's face when he'd arrived at the restaurant. It made him loathe the man at the end of the phone, loathe him so much that he felt like knocking him out. His daughter was at home, throwing her guts up, so much so that her entire body was too exhausted for her to keep her eyes open, and there he was, out getting drunk, chasing skirts, expecting Ruth to do all this without him. He hated the man at the end of the phone.

"But she's hot, if you could just see her," he slurred.

"Don't you even think about it," he said threateningly, his voice low and mean. "I swear to God, if you do anything, I will . . ."

"You'll what? Kill me?" More raucous laughter. "Sounds like you'd be cutting off your nose to spite your face, my friend. Well, where the hell am I supposed to go? Tell me that. I can't go home, I can't go to work."

The door to the bedroom opened then and an equally exhausted Ruth appeared.

"I'll call you back." He hung up quickly.

"Who was on the phone at this hour?" she asked quietly. She was dressed in her robe, her arms hugging her body protectively. Her eyes were bleary and puffed, her hair pulled back in a ponytail; she looked so fragile, as if a raised voice might blow her over and break her. For the second time that night his heart melted, and he moved toward her, arms open.

"It was just a guy I know," he whispered, stroking her hair. "He's out drunk; I wish he'd stop calling. I wish he'd just go away," he added quietly. He tossed his phone aside into a pile of teddy bears on the floor. "How are you?" He pulled away and examined her face closely. Her head was boiling hot, but she shivered in his arms.

"I'm fine." She gave him a wobbly smile.

"No, you're not fine, go back to bed, and I'll get you

a facecloth. I know where they are now," he joked, and she smiled lightly. He kissed her affectionately on the forehead. Her eyes closed, and her body relaxed in his arms.

He almost broke their embrace to jump in the air and holler with celebration, because for the first time in a long time he felt her give up the fight with him. For the past six months, whenever he'd held her she had been rigid and taut, as though she was protesting him somehow, refusing to validate his behavior. He reveled in this moment, feeling her relax against him: a silent but huge victory for their marriage.

Among the pile of teddies his phone vibrated again, bouncing around in Paddington Bear's arms. His screen flashed on again, and he had to look away, not able to stand the thought of himself. Now he could understand how Ruth felt.

"There's your friend again," Ruth said, pulling away slightly, allowing him to reach for his phone.

"No, leave him." He ignored the call, bringing her closer to him again. "Ruth," he said gently, lifting her chin so she could look at him. "I'm sorry."

Ruth looked up at him in shock, then examined him carefully for the catch. There had to be a catch. Lou Suffern had said he was sorry. *Sorry* was not a word in his vocabulary.

From the corner of Lou's eye, the phone kept vibrating, hopping around and falling out of Paddington Bear's paws and onto Winnie the Pooh's head, being passed around from teddy to teddy like a hot potato. Each time the phone stopped, it quickly started again, as if laughing at him, telling him he was weak for uttering those words to Ruth. He fought that side of himself, that drunken, foolish, childish, irrational side of him, and refused to answer the phone, refused to let go of his wife. He swallowed hard.

"I love you, you know."

It was as though it was the first time she'd ever heard it. It was as though they were back at the very first Christmas they'd spent together, sitting in her parents' living room in Galway—the cat curled in a ball on its favorite cushion by the fire; the crazy dog a few years too many in this world outside in the backyard, barking at everything that moved and everything that didn't. Lou had told her then, by the fake white Christmas tree. The gaudy tree would slowly be lit up by tiny green, red, and blue bulbs, and then the lights would slowly fade out before gearing up again. Despite its ugliness, it was relaxing, like a chest heaving slowly up and down. It was the first moment they'd had together all day, the only moments they'd have before he'd have to sleep on the couch and Ruth would disappear to her room. He wasn't planning on saying it; in fact, he was planning on never saying it, but it had popped out. Then the words were out, and his world had immediately changed. Twenty years later in their daughter's bedroom, it felt like the same moment all over again, with that same look of pleasure and surprise on Ruth's face.

"Oh, Lou," she said softly, closing her eyes and savoring the moment. Then suddenly her eyes flicked open, a flash of alarm in them that scared Lou to death about what she was about to say. What did she know? His past behavior came gushing back at him as he panicked. He thought of the other part of him, out there and drunk, possibly destroying this new relationship with his wife, destroying the repairs they had just achieved. He had a vision of the two Lous: one building a brick wall, the other moving behind him with a sledgehammer and knocking down everything as soon as it was built. In reality, that's what Lou had been doing all along. Building his family up with one hand, while the other shattered everything he'd strived so hard to create.

Ruth quickly let go of him and rushed away into Lucy's bathroom, where he heard the toilet seat go up and the contents of her insides empty into the bowl. Hating anyone being with her during moments like this, Ruth, ever the multitasker, managed, in mid-vomit, to lift her foot to kick the bathroom door closed.

Lou sighed and collapsed to the floor on the pile of teddies. He picked up the phone that had begun to vibrate yet again.

"What now?" he said in a dull voice, expecting to hear his own drunken voice on the other end. But he didn't.

CHAPTER 18

The Turkey Boy 3

B ULLSHIT," THE TURKEY BOY SAID as Raphie paused for breath.

Raphie didn't say anything; instead, he chose to wait for something more constructive to come out of the boy's mouth.

"Total bullshit," he said again.

"Okay, that's enough," Raphie said, standing up from the table and gathering the mug, Styrofoam cup, and candy wrappers from the chocolates he'd managed to munch through while he was telling his story. "I'll leave you alone in peace now to wait for your mother."

"No, wait!" Turkey Boy spoke up.

Raphie continued walking to the door.

"You can't just end the story there," the boy said incredulously. "You can't leave me hanging."

"Ah, well, that's what you get for being unappreciative," Raphie said with a shrug, "and for throwing turkeys through windows." He left the interrogation room.

Jessica was in the station's tiny kitchen, having another coffee. Her eyes were red, and the bags under them had darkened.

"Coffee break already?" He pretended not to notice her withering appearance.

"You've been in there for ages." She blew on her coffee and sipped, not moving the mug from her lips as she spoke, eyes looking away in the distance.

"It's a long story. Your face okay?"

She gave a single nod, the closest she'd ever get to commenting on the cuts and scrapes across her skin. She changed the subject. "So how far did you get in the story?"

"Lou Suffern's first pill."

"What did he say?"

"I do believe 'Bullshit' was the expression he used, which was then closely followed by 'Total bullshit.'"

Jessica smiled lightly. "You got further than I thought. You should show him the tapes of that night. They just came in from the audiovisual conference call. They show a guy who looks exactly like Lou walking out of the boardroom, while at the same time another guy, who also looks exactly like Lou, is sitting at the conference table. Still no sight or word from Gabe though."

"It could be Gabe in the conference call video." Raphie thought hard. "He and Lou look very alike."

"That would be much easier to believe but . . ."

"You don't believe it?"

"You don't believe the cloning version?"

"I'm telling it, aren't I?"

Jessica lowered the mug slowly from her lips, and those intense, secretive eyes stared deep into his. "That doesn't answer my question."

Raphie ignored her and instead poured himself another coffee, adding two sugars, which Jessica—sensing his mood—did not protest. Then he filled a Styrofoam cup with water and shuffled off down the corridor again.

"Where are you going?" she called after him.

"To finish the story," he grumbled. "And yes, that still doesn't answer your question."

CHAPTER 19

Man of the Moment

"WAKEY WAKEY," A SINGSONG VOICE penetrated Lou's drunken dreams, where everything was being rerun a hundred times over: mopping Lucy's brow; plugging Bud's pacifier back into his mouth; holding Lucy's hair back as she threw up; hugging Ruth close, her body relaxing against his; then back to Lucy's heated brow again; Bud spitting out his pacifier; Ruth's smile when he'd told her he loved her.

He smelled fresh coffee under his nose. Finally opening his eyes, he jumped back at the sight that greeted him, bumping his already throbbing head against a concrete wall.

Lou took a moment to adjust to his surroundings. Some of the visions that greeted his newly opened eyes in the morning were less comforting than others. Rather than the mug of coffee that at that moment was thrust mere inches from his nose, he was more accustomed to the sound of a toilet flush occasionally as his wake-up call. Often the wait for the mystery toilet flusher to exit the bathroom and show her face was a long and unnerving one, and, on a few occasions, Lou had taken it upon himself to disappear from the bed, and the building, before the mystery woman had the opportunity to show her face.

On this particular morning after Lou Suffern had been doubled up for the very first time, he was faced with a new scenario: a man of similar age was offering him a mug of coffee with a satisfied look on his face. This was certainly a new one for the books. Thankfully, the young man was Gabe, and Lou found, with much relief, that they were both fully dressed. With a throbbing head and the foul stench of something rotting in his mouth, he took in his surroundings.

He was on the ground. That he could tell by his proximity to the concrete and the long distance to the open paneled ceiling with its wires dripping down. The floor was hard despite the sleeping bag beneath him. He had a crick in his neck from the position to which his head had been rather unfortunately lodged. Above him, metal shelves towered to the ceiling: hard, gray, cold, and depressing, they stood like the cranes that littered Dublin's skyline, metal invaders umpiring a developing city. To the left, the new addition of a shadeless lamp was the guilty party behind the unforgiving bright white light that wasn't so much thrown around the room as it was aimed at Lou's head, like a pistol in a steady hand. What was glaringly obvious was that he was in Gabe's room in the basement. Gabe now stood over him. The sight was familiar, a mirror image of only a week ago, when Lou had stopped on the street to offer Gabe a coffee. Only this time the image was as distorted and disturbing as a mirror at a carnival, because when Lou assessed the situation, it was he who was down here, and Gabe who was up there.

"Thanks." He took the mug from Gabe, wrapping his cold hands around the porcelain. He shivered. "It's freezing in here." His first words were a croak, and as he sat up he felt the weight of the world crashing down on his head, another hangover for the second morning running.

"Yeah, someone promised to bring me an electric heater, but I'm still waiting." Gabe grinned. "Don't worry, I hear blue lips are in this season."

"Oh, sorry, I'll get Alison right on that," Lou mumbled, and sipped the black coffee. He had taken his initial wakening moment to figure out where he was. His first sip of caffeine alerted him to another problem.

"What the hell am I doing here?" he asked. He sat up properly, attentive now, and studied himself for clues. He was dressed in yesterday's suit, a crumpled, rumpled mess with some questionable, though mostly self-explanatory, stains on his shirt, tie, and jacket. "What the hell is that smell?"

"I think it's you," Gabe said. "I found you around the back of the building last night throwing up into a trash bin."

"Oh God," Lou whispered, covering his face with his hands. Then he looked up, confused. "But last night I was home. Ruth and Lucy; they were sick. And as soon as they fell asleep, Bud woke up." He rubbed his face tiredly. "Did I just dream that?"

"Nope," Gabe replied chirpily, pouring hot water into his one mug of instant coffee. "You did that, too. You were very busy last night, don't you remember?"

It took a moment for last night's events to register with Lou, but the onslaught of memories of the previous night—the pill, the doubling up—came rushing back to his mind.

"That girl I met." He aborted the sentence, both wanting to know the answer and not wanting to know at the same time. A part of him was sure of his innocence, while the other part of him wanted to take himself outside and beat himself up for possibly jeopardizing his marriage again. His body broke out into a cold sweat, which added a new scent to the mix.

Gabe let him stew for a while as he blew on his coffee and took tiny sips.

"Was I alone when you found me last night?" A loaded question.

"Indeed you were, very alone. Though not lonely. You were quite content to keep yourself company, mumbling about some girl," Gabe teased him. "Seemed as though you'd lost her and couldn't remember where you'd put her. You didn't find her at the bottom of the bin. Though perhaps if we cleared away the layer of vomit you deposited, your cardboard cutout woman may have been revealed."

"What did I say? I mean, don't tell me exactly, just tell me if I said anything about—you know. Shit, if I've done something, Ruth will kill me." Tears sprang into his eyes. "I'm the biggest fucking asshole." He kicked away the blanket on top of him in frustration.

Gabe's smile faded, respecting this side of Lou. "You didn't do anything with her."

"How do you know?"

"I know."

Lou studied him then, warily, curiously, but also with trust. Gabe seemed to be his everything right then: the only person who understood his situation, yet the one who had put him in this situation in the first place. A dangerous relationship.

"Gabe, we really have to talk about these pills. I don't want them anymore." He took them out of his pocket. "I mean, last night was a revelation, it really was, in so many ways." He rubbed his eyes tiredly, remembering the sound of his drunken voice at the end of the phone. "I mean, are there two of me now?"

"No, you're back to one again," Gabe explained. "Fig roll?"

"But Ruth." Lou ignored him. "She'll wake up, and I'll be gone. She'll be worried. Did I just vanish?"

"She'll wake up, and you'll already be off to work, just like always."

Lou absorbed that information and calmed a little. "But it's not right; it doesn't make sense. We really need to discuss where you got these pills from."

"You're right, we do," Gabe said seriously, taking the container from Lou and stuffing them into his pocket. "But not yet. It's not time yet."

"What do you mean, not yet? What are you waiting for?"

"I mean it's almost eight thirty, and you've got a meeting to get to before Alfred sweeps in and steals the limelight. Again."

At that, Lou placed his coffee carelessly on a shelf and jumped to his feet, instantly forgetting his serious concerns about the peculiar pills and failing to question how on earth Gabe knew about his eight thirty meeting.

"You can't go in looking like that." Gabe laughed, looking up and down at Lou's filthy rumpled suit. "And you smell of vomit. And cat urine. Believe me, I know, I've a fine nose for it by now."

"I'll be okay." Lou looked at his watch while taking off his suit jacket at the same time. "I'll grab a quick shower in my office and change into my spare suit."

"You can't. I'm wearing it, remember?"

Lou looked down at Gabe then, and remembered how he'd provided him with his spare clothes on that first day. He'd bet Alison didn't yet know to replace the clothes.

"Shit! Shit, shit, shit!" Lou paced the small room, biting his manicured fingernails, pulling and spitting, pulling and spitting.

"Don't worry, my maid will see to those," Gabe said

with amusement, watching as the chewed bits of nail fell to the cemented floor.

Lou ignored him, pacing some more. "Shops don't open till nine. Where the hell can I get a suit?"

"Never fear, I think I have something here in my walk-in wardrobe," Gabe said, disappearing down the first aisle and reappearing with his new suit draped in plastic. "Like I said, you never know when a new suit will come in handy. And it's your size, fancy that. It's almost like it was made for you." He winked. "May your outer dignity mirror an inner dignity of your soul," he said, handing the suit over.

"Eh, yeah, sure. Thanks," Lou said uncertainly, quickly taking it from Gabe's outstretched hands.

In the empty staff elevator, Lou looked at his reflection in the mirror. He was unrecognizable from the man who'd woken up on the floor half an hour earlier. The suit that Gabe had given him, despite being from an unknown designer, was surprisingly a perfect fit. The blue of the shirt and tie against the navy jacket and trousers made Lou's eyes pop, innocent and cherublike.

Things were looking very good for Lou Suffern so far that day. He was back to his groomed, handsome best, his shoes polished to perfection by Gabe. The swing was back in his step, his left hand casually placed in his pocket, his right arm swinging loosely by his side and available to answer the phone and/or shake a hand at every possible moment. He was the man of the moment.

And after a phone call home, he was also father of the year, according to Lucy.

While he whistled down the halls on the fourteenth floor, Melissa, Mr. Patterson's assistant, chased after him.

"Lou!" she called.

He stopped, swiveled around. "Melissa. Good morning."

"Mr. Patterson wants a brief word with you before the meeting."

Lou froze. "About what?"

"If I was a mind reader, Lou, I would not have gone on that date last night, and I most certainly would not have gone in for that nightcap. Now, quick." She turned on her very high, red-soled heels and ran back down the hall.

Lou composed himself, cleared his throat, and went over to rap on Mr. Patterson's office door.

"Lou." Mr. Patterson looked up from his papers. "I know we have a meeting in a few minutes, but I wanted to have a word before we go in. I just got off the phone with Anthea."

Cliff's wife. "Yes." Lou's heart thudded in his chest.

"Unfortunately, he won't be coming back."

Lou fought the urge to yelp in celebration.

"Oh. I see."

"So we've some decisions to make around here," Mr. Patterson said; then he looked over Lou's shoulder and nodded at Melissa standing in the doorway. "I've got a quick call to make, Lou. I hope you don't mind, but you'll be at the party tomorrow night; we can talk more then."

"Absolutely. I'll be here."

Lou was happy. So happy, in fact, that he started whistling and didn't stop even when he reached his office, where Alison delivered the news that his sister was on the line. He happily picked up the phone and propped himself on the corner of Alison's desk.

"Marcia, good morning," he said cheerily.

"Well, you're in a good mood today. I know you're busy, Lou, so I won't keep you. I just wanted to let you know that we all got Dad's birthday invitations. They were . . . very nice . . . very sophisticated . . . not what I would have chosen but . . . anyway, I've had a few people on the phone to say they haven't received theirs yet."

"Oh, they must have gotten lost in the mail," Lou said, "we'll send theirs again."

"But it's tomorrow, Lou."

"What?" He frowned and squinted his eyes to concentrate on the calendar on Alison's desk.

"Yes, his birthday's tomorrow," she said, sounding slightly panicked. "They won't get the invites if you send them out now. I just wanted to make sure that it would be okay for everyone just to turn up without an invite. It's only a family party, anyway. We could have a guest list or something."

"Tomorrow," Lou's mind was working overtime. He knew he had double-booked tomorrow night, but now the office party wasn't just a party. It was a meeting with Mr. Patterson. "Things have changed, Marcia. Tomorrow is my office party, and I really have to—"

"You missed dinner the other night, Lou. Daddy was hurt enough at that. If you miss his seventieth . . ." She went silent.

"Okay, fine." He rubbed his eyes, feeling his adrenaline shoot up again. "I'll be there."

"Yes, you will. I might just bring a few things to—"

"It's all under control," he said, interrupting her firmly.

"What have you got planned, Lou?" Marcia asked nervously.

"What have I got planned?" Lou faked a laugh. "Oh, well, come on, Marcia, we want it to be a surprise for everyone."

"Do you know what's happening?"

"Do I know what's happening? Are you worried about my organizational skills?"

"I'm worried that you've repeated every single one of my questions just to give yourself more time to think," she said.

"Of course I know what's going on; you think I'd just leave it up to Alison to do alone?" He winked at Alison, who looked horrified. "She's never even met Dad," he said, speaking Marcia's insecurities aloud.

"Exactly, Lou. This Alison seems like a nice girl, but she doesn't really know Dad. I've been calling her to help, but she hasn't been very forthcoming. I just want Dad to have the time of his life."

"He will, Marcia; he will." Lou's stomach turned uneasily. "We'll all have fun, I promise."

HE HANDED THE PHONE BACK to Alison, his smile gone. "It's all under control, isn't it?"

"What?"

"The party," he said firmly. "My dad's party."

"Lou, I've been trying to ask you questions about it all we—"

"Is it all under control? Because if it's not, you'd tell me, wouldn't you?"

"Absolutely." Alison smiled nervously. "The place you picked is very, erm, cool, shall we say, and they have their own events-management team. I told you about this already," she said quickly, "a few times this week. I'd also left some food and music options on your desk, but when you didn't choose any, I had to decide then myse—"

"Okay, Alison, a note for the future: when I ask if it's all under control, I only want a yes or a no," he said firmly. "I don't have time for questions and memos, really; all I need to know is if you can do it or not. If you can't, then that's fine, but I need to know. Okay?"

She nodded quickly.

"Great." He clapped his hands and hopped off the desk. "Now I'd better get to this meeting."

"Here." She handed him his files. "And congratulations on those two deals yesterday; everyone is talking about them."

"They are?"

"Yes," she said, wide-eyed. "Some people are saying you'll get Cliff's job."

That was like music to Lou's ears, but he played it down. "Now, Alison, let's not jump the gun. We're all wishing a speedy recovery for Cliff."

"Of course we are, but . . . anyway"—she smiled—"we can talk more at the party tomorrow?"

"Of course we will." He smiled back, and it was only as she threw him a loaded look that he really understood what she had meant. He hated himself for the flutter of excitement that rushed through him.

"Morning," Gabe suddenly interrupted them, placing a package on the desk.

Lou jumped.

Gabe looked at him, amused.

"Gabe, can I have a word with you, please?" Lou said, once he'd gathered himself.

They walked into his office and closed the door behind them. "Can I have those . . . the container back, please. I was very tired and emotional this morning, and I don't know what got into me. Of *course* I believe in the herbal-remedy thingies."

Gabe didn't respond. He continued laying out envelopes and packages on Lou's desk while Lou looked on with hope on his face.

Lou tried again. "I heard this morning that Cliff's not coming back." He kept his voice down and tried to hide his excitement. "He's totally fried."

"Ah, the poor man who had the breakdown," Gabe said, still flipping through the mail.

"Yes," Lou almost squealed with excitement. "Don't tell anyone I told you."

"That Cliff's not coming back?"

"Yes, that and . . . you know"—he looked around—"other things. Maybe a promotion. A nice big pay raise." He grinned, then got serious. "Problem is, Mr. Patterson wants to talk to me tomorrow at the party, and it just so happens to be my dad's birthday."

"Ah, this is the need for the pills. Well, you can't have them."

At that, Gabe left Lou's office and immediately continued pushing the cart down the hall. Lou quickly followed, yapping at his heels like a Jack Russell after a postman.

"Ah, come on, I'll pay you whatever you want for them. How much?"

"I don't want anything."

"Okay, then you probably want to keep them for yourself, I get it. At least tell me where I can get more?"

"You can't get them anywhere. I threw them away. You were right about them; they're not right. Psychologically. And who knows about the physical side effects? Maybe they were a scientific experiment that found their way out of a lab. Besides, they served their purpose: you learned something very valuable from the experience, and that's that you want to spend more time at home. Shouldn't you just take that and be done with it?"

"What did you do to them?" Lou panicked, ignoring everything that Gabe had just said. "Where did you put them?"

"In the trash."

"Well, get them for me. Go and get them back," Lou said angrily. "Come on, hurry, Gabe." He prodded Gabe in the back.

"They're gone, Lou. I opened the container and emptied the pills into the trash bins outside, and considering what you deposited inside it last night, I'd steer clear."

Lou grabbed him by the arm and led him to the elevators. "Show me."

ONCE OUTSIDE, GABE POINTED THE yellow bin out to Lou, large and filthy. Lou charged over. Looking inside, he could see the container sitting on top, so close he could touch it. Beside it, the pile of pills lay among a greenish-brown ooze of some sort. The smell was dire; he held his nose and tried not to retch. The pills were embedded in whatever that substance was, and his heart sank. He took off his suit jacket and threw it at Gabe to catch. He rolled up his shirtsleeves and prepared to shove his hands in the foul-smelling ooze. He paused before going in.

"If I can't get these pills, where can I get more?" he asked again.

"Nowhere," Gabe responded, standing by the building's back door and watching him, his arms folded. "They don't make them anymore."

"What?" Lou spun around. "Well, who made them? I'll pay them to make more. Shit. Maybe I can wash these." He stepped closer and leaned in. The smell made him retch. "What the hell *is* that?" He gagged again and had to step away from the bin. "Damn it." Lou kicked the bin and then regretted it when the pain hit.

"Oh, look," Gabe said in a bored tone. "It looks like I dropped one on the ground."

"What? Where?" Lou instantly forgot the pain in his toe and raced back to the bin. He examined the ground around it. Between the cracks of the cobbles he saw something white peering up at him. Leaning closer, he noticed it was a pill.

"Aha! Found one!"

"Yeah, I had to throw them away from a distance, the smell was so bad," Gabe explained. "A few fell on the ground."

"A few? How many?"

Lou got down on his hands and knees and started searching.

"I thought you only needed one. Lou, you really should just go back inside. You've had a good day. Why don't you just leave it at that? Learn from it and move on?"

"I *have* learned from it," Lou said, nose close to the cobbles. "I've learned that I'm the hero around here with these things. Aha! There's another one." Satisfied that those two were all he could salvage, he put them in his handkerchief and slipped them into his pocket, then stood up and wiped his knees.

"Two will do for now," he said, wiping his forehead. "I can see two more under the Dumpster, but I'll leave them for the time being."

When Lou turned around, his knees dirty and his hair disheveled, he found he had more company. Alfred was standing beside Gabe, his arms folded, a smug look on his face.

"Drop something, Lou?"

WHEN LOU ENTERED THE BOARDROOM, a little delayed after washing up in the bathroom, all twelve colleagues around the table stood to applaud him, their big, white-toothed smiles beaming from ear to ear, but not quite meeting their tired morning eyes. This was what everybody he knew was faced with. Not enough hours of sleep and the inability to get away from work or work-related devices like laptops, BlackBerrys, and cell phones: distractions that each of their family members wanted to flush down the toilet. Of course they were all happy for him, in a frazzled kind of way. They were all functioning to stay alive, to pay the mortgages, to do the presentations, to meet the quotas, to please the boss, to get in early enough to beat the traffic, to hang around long enough in the evenings until it had gone. Everyone in that room was putting in all the hours under the sun trying to unload their work before Christmas, and as they all did that, the pile of personal problems in their in-boxes only grew higher. That would all be dealt with over Christmas break. Finally, time for festive family issues that had been sidelined all year. 'Twas the season for family folly.

The applause was led by a beaming Mr. Patterson, and everyone joined in but Alfred, who was exceptionally slow to stand. While the others were on their feet, he was slowly pushing his chair back. When the others were clapping, he was adjusting his tie and fastening his gold buttons. He succeeded in clapping just once before the applause died down, a single clap that sounded more like a burst balloon.

Lou worked his way around the table, shaking hands, slapping backs, kissing cheeks. By the time he reached Alfred, his friend had already seated himself, though he offered Lou a limp, clammy hand.

"Ah, the man of the moment," Mr. Patterson said happily, taking Lou's hand warmly and placing his left hand firmly on Lou's upper arm. He stood back and looked at Lou proudly, as a grandfather would his grandson on Communion Day, beaming with pride and admiration.

Feeling like he was floating, Lou sat down and found it hard to keep up with the rest of the morning's discussion. From the corner of his eye, Lou could see Alfred staring at him, the shark beginning to circle again.

"You look tired, Lou, were you out celebrating last night?" a colleague asked.

"I was up all night with my little girl. Vomiting bug. My wife had it, too, so it was a busy night." He smiled, thinking of Lucy tucked in bed, her thick hair hiding half her face.

Alfred laughed, and his wheeze was loud. "You used that excuse just yesterday, Lou."

So he had. A few people laughed.

The aggression was emanating from Alfred in waves. It seeped from his soul, distorting the air around him, and Lou wondered if everybody could see it. Lou felt for him oddly; he could see how lost and fearful Alfred was.

"It's not just me you should be congratulating," Lou announced to the table. "Alfred was in on the New York deal, too. And a fine job he did."

"Absolutely." Alfred brightened up, coming back to the room and fidgeting with his tie. "It was nice of Lou to finally join me at the end, just in time to see me wrap it all up."

Everyone around the table laughed at the joke, but it hit Lou hard.

"Yes, we have already commended Alfred," Mr. Patterson said. "But two deals at once, Lou, how on earth did you manage it? We all know you're a multitasker at the best of times, but what an extraordinary use of time management and, of course, your negotiating skills."

"Yes, extraordinary," Alfred agreed. His tone was playful, but underneath it there was venom. "Almost unbelievable. Perhaps unnatural. What was it, Lou, a magic little pill? Speed?"

There were a few nervous laughs, a cough, and then a silence. Mr. Patterson broke the tension by getting the meeting started, but the damage had already been done. Alfred had left something hanging in the air. A question replaced what had previously been pure admiration; a seed had been planted in each mind. Whether the others believed Alfred or not, each time Lou achieved anything in the future, Alfred's comment would be momentarily, perhaps subconsciously, entertained, and that seed would grow, peep up from dirty soil, and rear its ugly head.

After all his hard work, missing out on important family events, always running out of his home to get to the office, quick pecks on Ruth's cheek for the sake of long handshakes with strangers, he had finally had his moment. Two minutes of handshakes and applause. Followed by a seed of doubt. Had it all been worth it?

CHAPTER 20

'Tis the Season . . .

"Y OU'LL BE THERE, WON'T YOU, Lou?" Ruth asked, trying her best to hide the worry in her voice. She moved around their bedroom in her bare feet, the sound of her skin against the wooden floors like feet splashing in water. Her long brown hair was up in rollers, her body was draped in a towel, and beads of water from her shower glistened on her shoulders.

From their bed, Lou watched his wife of ten years get ready for the evening. They were going into the city center in separate cars at separate times; he had to stop in at his office party before joining the rest of his family at his father's party. Lou hadn't been home long from work; he had showered and dressed in the space of twenty minutes. But instead of pacing downstairs as he normally did, waiting for his wife impatiently, he had chosen to lie on the bed and watch her. He was just learning tonight that staying up here and watching was so much more entertaining than pacing downstairs in anger. Lucy had joined him on their bed only moments ago and was cuddling her loyal blanket that followed her everywhere. Fresh out of the bath, she was dressed in her pajamas and smelled so freshly of strawberries that he almost wanted to eat her.

"Of course I'll be there." He smiled at Ruth.

"It's just that you should have left the house a half hour ago, and that would have put you behind as it is." She rushed by him and disappeared into the walk-in closet. The rest of her sentence disappeared along with her, muffling into the clothes neatly folded within. He lay back on the bed and rested his arms behind his head.

"She's talking fast," Lucy whispered.

"She does that." Lou smiled, reached out, and tucked a loose strand of hair behind his daughter's ear.

Ruth reappeared dressed in her underwear.

"You look beautiful," he said.

"Daddy!" Lucy giggled outrageously. "She's in her panties!"

"Yes, well, she looks beautiful in her panties." He kept his eyes on Ruth while Lucy rolled around the bed, laughing at this idea.

Ruth studied him quickly. Lou could see her swallow, her face curious, not used to the sudden attention, perhaps worrying that he was acting this way out of guilt. A big part of her was afraid to become hopeful, afraid that it was yet another buildup to a later letdown. She disappeared into the bathroom for a few moments, and when she reentered the room she hopped around, still in her underwear.

Lucy and Lou started laughing while watching her.

"What are you doing?" Lou asked.

"I'm drying my lotion." She ran in place, smiling. Lucy hopped up and joined her, giggling and dancing, before deciding her mother was dry and joining her father back on the bed.

"Why are you still here?" Ruth asked gently. "You don't want to be late for Mr. Patterson."

"This is far more fun."

"Lou," she laughed, "while I appreciate the fact that you are not constantly moving for the first time in ten years, you really have to go. I know you say you'll be there tonight, but—"

"I will be there tonight," he replied, starting to feel insulted.

"Okay, but please don't be too late," she continued, racing around the room. "Most people going to your dad's party are over the age of seventy, and they might have fallen asleep or have gone home by the time you get there." She darted back into the wardrobe.

"I'll be there," he replied, more to himself this time. He knew he had to be. And this time, he actually wanted to be.

He heard her rooting around in the drawers. She bumped into something, swore, dropped something else, and when she reappeared in the bedroom she was dressed in a black cocktail dress.

Usually Lou would automatically tell her she was beautiful, hardly even looking at her while saying it.

He felt that it was his duty, that it was what she wanted to hear, that it would get them out of the house faster, but tonight he found himself unable to speak. She was truly beautiful. It was as though all his life he had been told the sky was blue, and for the first time he had actually looked up to see it for himself. Why didn't he look at it every day? He turned to lie on his stomach and lean his head on his hand. Lucy imitated him. They both watched the wonder that was Ruth. Ten years of this display and he'd been pacing downstairs the whole time.

"And remember," she said, zipping up her dress at the back, "you got your father a cruise for his birthday."

"I thought we were getting him a golf membership."

"Lou, he hates golf."

"He does?"

"Granddad hates golf," Lucy confirmed with a knowing nod.

"He's always wanted to go to Saint Lucia," Ruth said. "Remember the story about Douglas and Ann and how they won the trip on the back of a cereal box, blah, blah, blah?"

"No." Lou frowned.

"The cereal box competition." She stopped on her way to the closet to stare at him in surprise.

"Yeah, what about it?"

"He tells this story all the time, Lou. About how Douglas entered the competition and they won a trip to

Saint Lucia . . . Anything?" She looked at him for a glimmer of recognition.

Lou shook his head.

"Wow, how could you not know that story?"

Ruth disappeared inside the closet one last time and reappeared with one shoe on her foot and the other under her arm. Up, down, up, down, she made her way across the room to her dressing table to put on her jewelry.

"Oh," she said as she put on her earrings. "When you see Mary Walsh, don't mention Patrick." Half of her hair was still covered in rollers, the other half loose and curled. Her face was sad. "He left her."

"Okay," Lou nodded, trying to remain as solemn as possible.

When Ruth ducked into the bathroom again, Lou turned to Lucy. "Patrick left Mary Walsh," he said. "Did you know that?"

Lucy shook her head wildly.

"Did you tell him to do that?"

She shook her head, giggling.

"Who knew that would happen?"

Lucy shrugged. "Maybe Mary did."

Lou laughed. "Maybe."

"Oh, and *please* don't ask Laura if she's lost weight," Ruth called out. "You always do that, and she hates it."

"Isn't that a nice thing to say?" He frowned.

Ruth laughed. "Honey, she's been putting on weight consistently for the past ten years. When you say that to her, it's like you're making fun."

"Laura's a fatty," he whispered to Lucy, and she collapsed on the bed laughing.

He took a deep breath as he noticed the time. "Okay, I should go now. See you tomorrow," he said to Lucy, kissing her on the head.

"I like you much better now, Daddy," she said happily.

Lou froze, still half on the bed. "What did you say?"

"I said I like you much better now." She smiled, revealing a missing bottom tooth. "Me, Mummy, and Bud are going ice-skating tomorrow. Will you come?"

Still taken aback by her comment, he simply said, "Yes. Sure."

Ruth came back into the room again, bringing a wave of her perfume with her, her hair in loose waves down past her shoulders. Lou couldn't take his eyes off her.

"Mummy, Mummy!" Lucy jumped up on the bed and started bouncing up and down. "Daddy's coming ice-skating tomorrow."

"Lucy, get down, you're not allowed to jump on the bed. Get down, sweetheart, thank you. Remember I told you that Daddy is a very busy man, he doesn't have time to be—"

"I'm coming," Lou interrupted firmly.

Ruth's mouth fell open. "Oh."

"Is that okay?"

"Yes, sure, I just . . . Yes. Absolutely. Great." She nodded, then headed back into the bathroom. This time the door closed softly behind her.

He gave her a couple of minutes alone but then couldn't afford to wait any longer.

"Ruth"—Lou rapped gently on the bathroom door— "you okay?"

"Yes, I'm fine." She cleared her throat and sounded overly perky. "I'm just . . . blowing my nose."

"Okay, I'll see you later," he said, wanting to go inside and hug her good-bye, but knowing that the door would open if she wanted him to.

"Okay," she said, a little less perky now. "See you at the party."

The door remained closed, and so he left.

THE OFFICES OF PATTERSON DEVELOPMENTS were swarming with Lou Suffern's colleagues in various states of disarray. It was only seven thirty p.m.—and already some were set for the night. Unlike Lou, who'd gone home after work, most people had gone straight to the pub and returned to the party to continue their revelry. There were women he barely recognized, in dresses that revealed bodies he'd never known existed beneath their suits; and there were some whose bodies were made only for their suits. The uniformity of the day had been broken down: there was an air of adolescence, of the desire to show off and prove to one another who they really were. It was a night for rule breaking, for saying what they felt; it was a dangerous environment to be in. Mistletoe hung from almost every doorway—in fact, Lou had already received two kisses as soon as he'd stepped out of the elevator, from the opportunists hanging around there.

Suit jackets were off; novelty musical ties, Santa hats, and reindeer antlers were on. They all worked hard, and it was clear that tonight they were all going to play hard.

"Where's Mr. Patterson?" Lou asked Alison, finding her sitting on the lap of the fifth Santa Claus he'd seen so far. Her eyes were glassy, the focus already gone. She was wearing a tight red dress that showed every curve of her body. He forced himself to look away.

"And what do you want for Christmas, little boy?" the voice beneath the costume bellowed.

"Oh, hi, James," Lou said politely.

"He wants any promotion," somebody in the crowd yelled, which was followed by a few titters.

"Not just a promotion, he wants Cliff's job," somebody with reindeer antlers shouted, and the crowd laughed again.

Smiling to hide his frustration and minor embarrassment, Lou laughed along with them; then when the conversation turned to something else, he quietly slipped away. He retreated to his office, which was quiet and still, with not a glimpse of tinsel or mistletoe in sight. He sat with his head in his hands, awaiting Mr. Patterson's call to his office, listening to "Grandma Got Run Over by a Reindeer" being half sung and half shouted by the crowd outside. He shouldn't be here, he realized. He should be across the river Liffey at his father's party.

He reached into his pocket and retrieved the pill he had wrapped in a handkerchief. He placed it on the table and poured a glass of water. He placed the glass beside the pill and stared at them both. Took a deep breath.

Suddenly the music got louder as the door to his office opened; then it quietened as the door closed. He knew who it was before he even looked up.

Alison walked toward him, a glass of red wine in one hand, a whiskey in the other, her hips swinging in her slinky red dress and looking like the dangly thing at the back of a throat. Her ankles wobbled in her platform heels, and the wine jumped up a few times from the glass to splash her thumb.

"Careful there." Lou's eyes followed her every move, his head staying put, both sure and uncertain at the same time.

"It's okay." She put her glass down on the table and sucked her thumb, licking the spilled wine from her skin while looking at Lou seductively. "I brought you a whiskey." She handed it to him and sidled up beside him at the desk. "Cheers." Picking up her glass again, she clinked his and then, her eyes not once moving from his, drank.

Lou cleared his throat, suddenly feeling crowded, and pushed his chair back. Alison misunderstood and slid her behind along the desk so that she was directly in front of him now. Her chest was in his sight line, and he tore his eyes away, looking instead at the door. His position was dangerous. It looked very bad. But he felt extremely good.

"We never got to finish up what we were doing before." She smiled. "Everybody's talking about clearing their desks before Christmas." Her voice was low and sultry. "Thought I'd come in and give you a hand."

She pushed away a few files from his desk; they slid down onto the floor, scattering everywhere. The pill flew up and got lost among the files on the ground.

"Oops," she said with a smile, sitting on the desk before him, her short red dress rising even farther up her thighs, revealing long, toned legs.

Beads of sweat broke out on Lou's brow. His mind ran through every possibility. Go outside and search for Mr. Patterson or stay inside with Alison. He could take the pill lying somewhere on the ground and do both. No, remember his priorities: be with Alison and go to his dad's party. No, be with Mr. Patterson and go to his dad's party. Both at the same time.

Uncrossing her legs, Alison used her foot to pull his chair in closer to the desk, red lace between her thighs greeting him as he was wheeled slowly closer to her. She scooted forward to the edge of the desk, pushing her dress up even higher. So high there was nowhere else for him to look now. He could take a pill: be with Alison and be with Ruth.

Ruth.

Alison reached out and pulled him closer, her hands

now on his face. He felt the acrylic nails. The *tap-tap* sound against the keyboards that drove him insane every day. There they were, on his face, on his chest, running down his body. Long fingers on the fabric of his suit, the suit that was supposed to mirror his inner dignity.

"I'm married," he sputtered as her hand reached his groin. His voice was panicked, sounding childlike.

Alison threw her head back and laughed. "I know," she purred, and her hands continued roving.

"That wasn't a joke," he said firmly, and she stopped suddenly to look at him. He stared back at her solemnly, and they held each other's gaze. Then the corner of Alison's lips lifted in a smile, despite her attempts to prevent it. Then, when she couldn't keep it in anymore, she exploded. Her long blond hair reached down to his desktop as she threw her head back to laugh once again.

"Oh, Lou," she sighed, finally wiping the corners of her eyes.

"It's not a joke," he said, more firmly and with more dignity and confidence, he hoped. More of a man now than he was five minutes ago.

As she realized he really wasn't teasing, her smile faded instantly.

"Isn't it?" She cocked an eyebrow, looked him dead in the eye. "Because you might have fooled *her*, Lou, but you haven't fooled us."

"Us?"

She waved a hand behind her dismissively. "Us. Everyone. Whatever."

He pushed his chair away from the desk.

"Oh, okay, you want me to be specific? I'll be specific. Gemma in accounts, Rebecca in marketing, Louise in personnel, Tracey—your secretary before me—and I never did get the nanny's name. Shall I continue?" She smiled, then took a sip of wine, watching him. Her eyes watered slightly, her corneas reddened as though the wine was traveling directly to her eyes. "Remember all of them?"

"They were"—Lou swallowed, feeling breathless—"they were a long time ago. I'm different now."

"The nanny was six months ago." She laughed. "Christ, Lou, how much do you think a man like you can change in six months, if at all?"

Lou felt dizzy, sickened all of a sudden. He ran his sweaty hands through his hair, panic setting in. What had he done?

"Just think about it." She perked up. "When you become Number Two around here, you can have whoever you want; but just remember, I got you first." She laughed, putting down the wine and reaching out her foot to pull his chair toward her again. "But if you take me with you, I can tend to all your needs."

She took the whiskey glass from his hand and placed it on the desk. Then she took his hand and pulled him to his feet, and he followed, numb and lifeless like a dummy. She rubbed her hands across his chest, grabbed his lapels, and pulled him closer.

So much went through his mind right then, a strobe-light effect of thoughts; manic and not fully formed, they flashed in and out of his head as he failed to hold on to one and really register it. Each was a warning he couldn't fully grasp. If he could just bring himself back into the moment and stop smelling Alison's perfume, stop feeling her fingertips, which were gentle on his cheeks . . . Gabe spoke his words of wisdom in one ear; Lou Suffern's dark side whispered in the other. But suddenly, he watched with great clarity as what he had been slowly learning over the past few days came flying toward him like a meteor headed toward the Earth. Its impact yielded a result. What he was doing with Alison was wrong. This was all wrong. He wasn't that man anymore. His great life, his achievements, were so only because of his family. Take them away, take Ruth away, and he was and had nothing.

Just as their lips were about to meet, he stopped and moved his lips to her ear. Ever so softly, he whispered, "My marriage is not a joke, Alison."

With that, he pulled back and walked away from the desk.

Alison sat frozen on the desk. The only movement was her mouth, which had fallen open, and her hand, which fidgeted and tried to pull at the bottom of her skirt.

"Yeah," he said as he watched her fix herself, "you should cover that up. You can take a minute to gather your thoughts, but please replace the files on my desk before you leave," he said calmly, moving the files around with his shoe to find the displaced pill. Finding it nestled in the thick carpet, he quickly picked it up and placed it in his pocket. Leaving his hands there to hide how much his body shook, he strode out of his office and into the middle of a karaoke, where Alex from accounts was drunkingly singing Mariah Carey's "All I Want for Christmas." Streamers popped around Lou, and drunken colleagues smothered him with kisses as he left his office.

"I have to go," he said to no one in particular, trying to make his way to the elevator. He pushed right through the crowd, some people grabbing him and trying to dance with him, others blocking his path and spilling their drinks. "I have to go," he said a little more aggressively now. His head was pounding; he was nauseous; he felt as though he had just woken up in the body of a man who had taken over his life and had almost thrown it all away. "I have to go," he said, continuing to make his way to the elevator. Finally he reached it and pressed the call button. He didn't want to meet Mr. Patterson, didn't care about the job; he just wanted to be with his family. He kept his head down and waited.

"Lou!" He heard his name. He kept his head down, ignoring the voice. "Lou! I need a minute with you!" He ignored it again, watching the floors rising on the elevator panel and shaking his leg anxiously, hoping he'd get inside before it was too late.

He felt a hand on his shoulder.

"Lou! I've been calling you!" a friendly voice said.

He turned around. "Ah, Mr. Patterson, hello. Sorry." Lou was aware his voice was edgy, but he needed to get out of there. He'd promised Ruth. He pressed down on the elevator button again. "I'm in a bit of a rush, it's my dad's se—"

"We won't take long, I promise. Just a word." Mr. Patterson pulled gently on his arm.

"Okay." Lou turned around, biting his lip.

"I was rather hoping we could talk in my office, if you don't mind." Mr. Patterson smiled.

He led Lou down to his office, where they sat down opposite each other on aged brown leather couches. Lou felt around in his pocket for his pills. He shouldn't be here. He really shouldn't be here. He reached for the glass of water Mr. Patterson poured for him, trying to control the tremble in his hand.

"Would you like something stronger, Lou?"

"No, thank you, Mr. Patterson." He waited for the opportunity to take the pill, but Mr. Patterson kept his eyes on him at all times.

"Laurence, please." Mr. Patterson shook his head again. "Honestly, Lou, you make me feel like a schoolteacher when you address me so. Well, I'm going to have one, anyway." Mr. Patterson stood up and made his way over to his drinks cabinet. He poured himself a brandy from a crystal decanter. "You sure you won't have one?" he offered again. "Rémy XO." He swirled it midair, tauntingly.

"Okay, I will, thank you." Lou smiled and relaxed a

little, his panic to get across the river to the other party subsiding slightly.

"Good." Mr. Patterson smiled. "So, Lou, let's talk about your future. It's going to be a long one. How much time do you have?"

Lou took his first sip of the expensive brandy, and he was brought back to the room, back to the present. He pulled his cuffs over his watch and took a deep breath, trying to ignore the clock ticking away on the wall, trying to put his father's party out of his head. It would all be worth it. They would all understand. They would all be too busy celebrating to notice he wasn't even there.

"I have all the time you need." Lou smiled nervously.

CHAPTER 21

Surprise!

WHEN LOU ARRIVED AT THE venue for his father's party—late—he was sweating profusely as though he'd broken out in a high fever, despite the December chill outside that squeezed into the joints and whistled around the body. He was breathless and nauseous at the same time. Relieved and exhilarated.

He'd decided to host his father's party in the famous building that Gabe had admired the very first day they'd met. Shaped like a sail, it was lit up in blue, Patterson Development's award-winning building, which was sure to impress his father and relatives from around the country. Directly in front of the building, the Viking longship's tall mast was decorated in Christmas lights.

When he reached the door, Marcia was outside giving it to a large doorman dressed in black. Bundled in coats, hats, and scarves, a crowd of twenty or so were standing around, stamping their feet on the pavement in order to stay warm.

"Hi, Marcia," Lou said happily, trying to break up the

argument. He was bursting to tell her about the promotion, but he had to bite his lip; he had to find Ruth to tell her first.

Marcia turned to face him, her eyes red and blotchy, her mascara smudged. "Lou," she spat, her anger now fully aimed at him.

His stomach did somersaults, which was rare. He never usually cared what his sister thought of him, but tonight he cared more than usual.

"What's wrong?"

She walked him a few paces from the crowd and came firing at him. "I've been trying to call you for an hour."

"I was at my work party, I told you that. What's wrong?"

"*You* are what's wrong," she said shakily, her voice somewhere between anger and deep sadness. She inhaled deeply, then slowly exhaled. "It's Daddy's birthday, and for his sake I won't ruin it any more than it already has been by causing an argument, so all I have to say is, would you please tell this brute to let our family in. Our family"—she raised her voice to a quivering screech—"who has traveled from all over the country to share in"—her voice went weepy again—"in Dad's special day. But instead of being with his family, he's up there in a practically empty room while everybody is out here being turned away. Five people have already gone home."

"What? What?" Lou's heart leapt into his throat. He rushed to the doormen. "Hi, guys, Lou Suffern." He held out his hand, and the doormen shook it with all the life of a dead fish. "I'm organizing the party tonight. What seems to be the problem here?" He looked around at the crowd and instantly recognized all the faces. Most were close family friends whose homes he'd grown up visiting, and all were over the age of sixty. They stood on the freezing cold pavement in December, elderly couples hanging on to one another, trembling with the cold, some leaning on crutches, one man in a wheelchair. In their hands were sparkly bags and cards, bottles of wine and champagne, gifts that had been wrapped neatly and thoughtfully for the big night.

"No invites, no entry," one doorman explained.

One couple flagged down a taxi and slowly made their way to where it had pulled over, while Marcia chased after them, trying to convince them to stay.

Lou laughed angrily. "Gentlemen, do you think that these people are *party crashing*?" He lowered his voice. "Come on, look at them. My father is celebrating his seventieth birthday. These are his friends. There was obviously a mistake with the invitations. I arranged with my secretary Alison for there to be a guest list."

"These people aren't on the list. This building has strict guidelines as to who comes in and who—"

"Fuck the guidelines," Lou said through gritted teeth so that those behind him couldn't hear. "It is my father's birthday, and these are his guests. And as the person who is paying for this party, and as the man who got this building off the ground, I'm telling you to let these people in."

Moments later the members of the group were shuffling inside, warming themselves while waiting in the grand lobby for the elevators to take them up to the top floor.

"You can relax now, Marcia; it's all sorted out." Lou tried to make amends with his sister as they got in the last elevator. She had refused to speak to him or even look at him for the last ten minutes while they'd managed to get everyone inside and up to the penthouse. "Marcia, come on," he laughed lightly. "Don't be like this."

The look she gave him was enough to stop his smile and make him swallow hard.

"I know you think I'm dramatic and controlling and annoying, and whatever else you think about me that I'm sure I don't want to know about, but I'm not being dramatic now. I'm hurt. Not for me, but for Mummy and Daddy." Her eyes filled again, and her voice, which was always so gentle and understanding, became hard. "Of all the selfish things you've done, this is right up there as the most fucking selfish of them all. I have sat back and bitten my tongue while you've taken Mummy and Daddy for granted, while you've screwed around on your wife, while you've jeered at your brother, flirted with his wife, ignored your kids, and taunted me on every possible occasion. I have been—we *all* have been—as patient as pie with you, Lou, but not anymore. You don't deserve any of us."

"Marcia," Lou simply said. He had never been spoken to like that before, and it hurt him deeply.

Marcia laughed bitterly. "What you saw outside isn't even the half of it. Surprise," she said dully as the elevators opened and the sight of the room greeted him.

As he looked out, Lou's heart immediately sank to his stomach, where the acid there began to burn it away. Around the room there were blackjack tables and roulette, and scantily clad cocktail waitresses who paraded around with cocktails on trays. It was an impressive party, and one that Lou remembered attending when the building first opened, but it wasn't a party for his seventy-year-old father. It wasn't for his father, who hated celebrations for himself, who hated forcing friends and family to gather together just for him, whose idea of a good day was being alone out fishing. A modest man, he was embarrassed by the very thought of a party, but the family had talked him into celebrating this milestone birthday, a big occasion where his family and friends from all around the country would join in and celebrate with him. Somewhere along the way he had warmed to the idea, and there he was, in his best suit, standing in the middle of the scene: short skirts and red bow ties, a DJ playing dance music, and a twenty-five-euro minimum at the casino tables. Lying in the center of one table, a near-naked man was covered in little cakes and fruit.

Standing together awkwardly at one side of the room was Lou's family. His mother, with her hair freshly blown dry, was wearing a new lilac trouser suit and a scarf tied neatly around her neck. Her handbag was draped over her shoulder, and she clasped it tightly in both hands as she looked around uncertainly. His father stood with his brother and sister—a nun and a priest—looking more lost in this environment than Lou had ever seen him look. Each family member looked up at him and then away again, freezing him out. The only person who smiled faintly at him was his father, who nodded and saluted him.

Lou looked around for Ruth and found her standing on the far side of the room, making small talk with the rest of the equally uncomfortable-looking partygoers. She caught his eye, and her look was cold. There was an awkward tension in the room, and it was all Lou's fault. He felt embarrassed, beyond ashamed. In that instant he wanted to make it up to them; he wanted to make it up to everybody.

"Excuse me." Lou approached a man in a suit looking over the crowd. "Are you the person in charge?"

"Yes, Jacob Morrison, manager." He held his hand out. "You're Lou Suffern; we met at the opening night a few months ago. I recall it was a late one." He winked at him.

"Yes, I remember," Lou replied, at the same time not remembering him at all. "I'm just wondering if you could help me with making some changes in here."

"Oh." Jacob looked taken aback. "Of course we'll try to accommodate you in any way that we can. What were you thinking of?"

"Chairs." Lou tried not to speak rudely. "This is my father's seventieth. Could we please get him and his guests some chairs?"

"Oh." Jacob made a face. "I'm afraid this is a standing-only event. We didn't charge for—"

"I'll pay you for whatever, of course." Lou flashed his pearly whites through a tight smile.

"Yes, of course." Jacob began to leave when Lou called him back.

"And the music," Lou said, "is there anything more traditional than this?"

"Traditional?" Jacob smiled questioningly.

"Yes, traditional Irish music. For my seventy-year-old father." Lou spoke through gritted teeth. "Instead of this acid jazz funky house music that my seventy-year-old father isn't so much into."

"I'll see what we can do."

The atmosphere between the two men was darkening.

"And what about food? Did Alison arrange food? Apart from the naked man covered in cream that my mother is currently standing beside."

"Yes, of course. We have shepherd's pies, lasagna, that kind of thing."

Lou quietly celebrated.

"You know, we discussed all of our concerns with Alison before," Jacob explained. "We don't usually hold seventieth parties." His fake smile quickly faded. "It's just that we have a standard setup here, particularly for the Christmas period, and this is it." He gestured to the room proudly. "The casino theme is very successful for corporate events, launches, that kind of thing," he explained.

"I see. Well, it would have been nice to know that," Lou said politely.

"You did sign off on it," Jacob assured him.

"Right." Lou swallowed and looked around the room. His fault. Of course.

As Lou approached his family, they stepped away and separated themselves from him as though he were a bad smell. His father, though, greeted his middle child as he always did: with a smile.

"Dad, happy birthday," Lou said quietly, reaching his hand out to his father.

"Thank you." His father took his son's hand warmly. Despite all this, despite what Lou had done, his father still loved him.

"So are you happy to be going to Saint Lucia?" Lou asked.

"Saint Lucia?" His father looked shocked; his mouth dropped open. "Oh my Lord."

"Oh for fuck's sake, Lou." Lou's brother, Quentin, overheard the conversation and went racing over to Marcia, who was over by the DJ area getting a microphone stand ready. She listened to Quentin whisper in her ear and then Lou saw her face fall.

"Let me get you a Guinness," Lou said, turning around to look for the bar, trying to change the subject.

"Oh," his father said, finally snapping out of his shock. "They don't have any."

"What? But that's all you drink."

"They have champagne, and some funny-looking green cocktail," his father said, sipping on his glass. "I'm just drinking water. Your mother's happy, though. She likes champagne, though far from it she was reared." He laughed, trying to make light of the situation.

On hearing herself being mentioned, Lou's mother turned around and threw Lou a withering look.

"Ah, now," his father said softly, "I can't drink tonight anyway. I'm sailing with Quentin tomorrow in Howth," he said proudly. "He's racing in the Brass Monkeys and he's down a man, so yours truly is filling in." He thumbed himself in the chest.

"You are not racing, Fred." Lou's mother rolled her eyes. "You can barely stand upright on a windy day, never mind on a boat. It's December. Those waters are choppy."

"I'm seventy years old. I can do what I like."

"You're seventy years old, you have to *stop* doing what you like, or you won't see seventy-one," she snapped, and the family laughed, including Lou.

"You'll just have to find someone else, dear." She looked at Quentin, who had rejoined them.

"I'll do it for you," Alexandra said to her husband, wrapping her arms around him, and Lou found himself having to look away, feeling mildly jealous.

"You've never raced before." Quentin smiled. "No way."

"What time is the race?" Lou asked.

Nobody answered.

"Of course I can do it," Alexandra said with a smile. "Isn't it easy? I'll bring my bikini, and I'll let the rest of the crew bring the strawberries and champagne."

The family laughed again.

"What time is the race?" Lou asked again.

"Well, if she races in her bikini, then I'll definitely let her take part," Quentin teased.

More laughter.

As though suddenly hearing his brother's question, Quentin responded without looking him in the eye, "Race starts at eleven a.m. Maybe I'll give Stephen a quick call." He took his cell phone out of his pocket.

"I'll do it," Lou said, and everyone looked at him in shock.

"I'll do it," he repeated.

"Maybe you could call Stephen first, love," Alexandra said gently.

"Yes," Quentin responded, turning back to his phone. "Good idea. I'll just go somewhere quiet." He brushed by Lou and left the room.

Lou felt the sting as the family turned away from him again and talked about places he'd never been, about people he'd never met. He stood by idly while they laughed at inside jokes he didn't understand. It was as though they were speaking a secret language, one that Lou was entirely unable to comprehend. Eventually he stopped bothering to ask the questions that were never answered, and eventually he stopped listening, realizing nobody cared if he did or not. He was too detached from the family to make it up in one evening, to check himself into a place where there was currently no vacancy.

CHAPTER 22

The Soul Catches Up

L OU'S FATHER WAS BESIDE HIM, looking around the room like a lost child, no doubt feeling nervous and embarrassed that everyone had come tonight for him.

"Where's Ruth?" his father asked.

"Eh," Lou looked around for the hundredth time, unable to find her, "she's just chatting with some guests."

"Right . . . Nice view from up here." He nodded out the window. "City's come a long way."

"Yeah, I thought you'd like it," Lou said, glad he'd gotten one thing right.

"So which one is your office?" His father looked across the river Liffey at the office buildings, which remained lit up at this hour.

"That one there, directly opposite." Lou pointed. "Thirteen floors up, on the fourteenth floor."

Lou's father glanced at him, obviously thinking the numbering peculiar, and for the first time Lou felt it too, could see how it could be perceived as odd and confusing. This rattled him. He had always been so sure about it.

"It's the one with all the lights on," Lou explained more simply. "Office party."

"Ah, so that's where it is." His father nodded. "That's where it all happens."

"Yes," Lou said proudly. "I just got a promotion tonight, Dad." He smiled. "I haven't told anybody yet. It's your night, of course," he backtracked.

"A promotion?" His father's bushy eyebrows rose.

"Yes."

"More work?"

"Bigger office, better light," he joked. When his dad didn't laugh, he became serious. "Yes, more work. More hours. But I like to work hard."

"I see." His father was silent.

Frustration rose within Lou. A single congratulations was all he wanted.

"You're happy there?" his father asked casually, still looking out the window, the party behind them visible in the reflection. "No point in working that hard if you're not, because at the end of the day, that's what it's all about, isn't it?"

Lou pondered that, both disappointed by the lack of praise and intrigued by his father's thinking at the same time.

"But you always told me to work hard," Lou said suddenly, feeling an anger he had never known was there. "You always taught us not to rest on our laurels for a second, if I recall the phrase exactly." He felt tense.

"I didn't want you all to be lazy, by any means," his dad responded, and he turned to look Lou in the eye. "In *any* aspect of your life, not just in your work. Any tightrope walker can walk in a straight line and hold a cane at the same time. It's the balancing on the rope at those dizzying heights that they have to practice," he said simply.

A staff member carrying a chair in her hand came up and broke the quiet tension. "Excuse me, who is this for?" She looked around at the family. "My boss told me that someone in this party asked for a chair."

"Em, yes, I did," Lou laughed bitterly. "But I asked for *chairs*. Plural. For all the guests."

"Oh, well, we don't have that amount of chairs on the premises," she apologized. "So who would like this chair?"

"Your mother," Lou's father said quickly, turning to the others, not wanting any fuss. "Let your mother sit down."

"No, I'm fine, Fred," Lou's mother objected. "It's your birthday; you have the chair."

Lou closed his eyes and breathed deeply. He had paid twelve thousand euro for his family to fight over the use of a chair.

"Also, the DJ said that the only traditional music he has is the Irish National Anthem. Would you like him to play it?"

"What?" Lou snapped.

"It's what he plays at the end of the night, but he has no other Irish songs with him," she apologized. "Shall I tell him to play it for you all now?"

"No!" Lou snapped. "That's ludicrous. Tell him no."

"Can you please give him this?" Marcia interjected politely, reaching into a cardboard box she had underneath the table. From it, party hats, streamers, and banners overflowed. She handed the woman a collection of CDs. Their father's favorite songs. She looked up at Lou briefly while handing them over. "For when you fucked up," she said, then looked away.

It was a short comment, delivered quietly, but it hit him harder than everything else she'd said to him that evening. He'd thought he was the organized one, the one who knew how to throw a party, the one who knew to call in favors and throw the biggest bash. But while he was busy thinking he was all that, his family was busy with Plan B, in preparation for his failures. All in a cardboard box.

Suddenly the room cheered as Quentin stepped out of the elevator along with Gabe—whom Lou hadn't known was invited—each with a pile of chairs stacked up in their arms.

"There are more on the way!" Quentin announced to the crowd, and suddenly the atmosphere picked up as everyone looked to one another with relief.

"Lou!" Gabe's face lit up when he saw him. "I'm so glad you came." He laid the chairs out for a few elderly people nearby and approached Lou, hand held out, leaving Lou confused as to whose party it was. Gabe leaned in close to Lou's ear. "Did you double up?"

"What? No." Lou shook him off, annoyed.

"Oh," Gabe said with surprise. "The last I saw of you, you and Alison were having a meeting in your office. I didn't realize you left the office party."

"Yes, of course I did. Why do you have to assume the worst, that I had to take one of those pills to show up at my own father's party?" Lou feigned insult.

Gabe merely smiled. "Hey, it's funny how life works, isn't it?" Then he nudged Lou.

"What do you mean?"

"Well, the way one minute you can be up here, and then the next minute all the way down there?" On Lou's puzzled look, Gabe continued, "I just mean that when we met last week, I was down there, looking up and dreaming about being here. And now look at me. It's funny how it all switches around. I'm up in the penthouse; Mr. Patterson gave me a new job—"

"He what?"

"Yeah, he gave me a job." Gabe grinned and winked. "A promotion."

Before Lou had the opportunity to respond, a waitress approached them with a tray.

"Would anybody like some food?" She smiled.

"Oh, no, thank you, I'll wait for the shepherd's pie." Lou's mother smiled at her.

"This *is* the shepherd's pie." The woman pointed

to a mini blob of potato sitting in a minuscule cupcake holder.

There was a moment's silence, and Lou's heart almost ripped through his skin from its hectic beating.

"Is there more food coming later?" Marcia asked.

"Apart from the cake? No"—she shook her head—"this is it for the evening. Trays of hors d'oeuvres." She smiled again as though not picking up on the hostility that was currently swirling around her.

"Oh," Lou's father said, trying to sound upbeat. "Then you can just leave the tray here."

"The whole tray?" She looked dubious.

"Yes, we've a hungry family here," Lou's father said, taking the tray from her hands and placing it on the tall table so that everybody had to stand up from their chairs in order to reach.

"Oh, okay." She watched it being placed down and slowly backed away, trayless.

"You mentioned a cake?" Marcia asked, her voice high-pitched and screechy.

"Yes."

"Let me see it, please," she said, casting a look of terror at Lou. "What color is it? What's on it? Does it have raisins? Daddy hates raisins." They could hear her questioning the waitress as she headed to the kitchen, her cardboard box of damage-limitation items in hand.

"So, who invited you, Gabe?" Lou felt anxious, not wanting to discuss Gabe's promotion any longer.

"Ruth did," Gabe said, reaching for a mini shepherd's pie.

"Oh, she did, did she? I don't think so." Lou laughed.

"Why wouldn't you think so?" Gabe shrugged. "She invited me the night I had dinner and stayed over at your house."

"Why do you say it like that? Don't say it like that," Lou said childishly, squaring his shoulders at him. "You weren't invited to dinner in my house. You dropped me home and ate leftovers."

Gabe looked at him curiously. "Okay."

"Where is Ruth, anyway? I haven't seen her all night."

"Oh, we've been talking all evening on the balcony. I really like her," Gabe responded, mashed potato dribbling down his chin and landing on his borrowed tie. Lou's tie.

At that, Lou's jaw clenched. "You really like her? You really like my *wife*? Well, that's funny, Gabe, because I really like my wife, too. You and I have so fucking much in common, don't we?"

"Lou," Gabe said, smiling nervously, "you might want to keep your voice down just a little."

Lou looked around and smiled at the attention they'd attracted and playfully wrapped his arm around Gabe's shoulder to show all was good. When the eyes looked away, he turned to face Gabe and dropped the smile.

"You really want my life, don't you, Gabe?"

Gabe seemed taken aback, but he didn't have the

opportunity to respond. Just then, the elevator doors opened and out fell Alfred, Alison, and a crowd from the office party. Despite the noise of Lou's father's favorite songs blaring through the speakers, they managed to announce themselves to the room loud and clear, dressed in their Santa suits and party hats, blowing their noisemakers at anyone who so much as looked their way.

Lou darted from his family and ran up to the elevator, blocking Alfred's path. "What are you all doing here?"

"We're here to par-taay, my friend," Alfred announced, swaying and blowing a party horn in his face.

"Alfred, you weren't invited," Lou said loudly.

"Alison invited me." Alfred laughed. "And I think you know better than anyone how hard it is to turn down an invitation from Alison. But I don't mind being sloppy seconds." He laughed again, wavering drunkenly on the spot. Suddenly his sight line moved past Lou's shoulder and his expression changed. "Ruth! How are you?"

With a swallow, Lou turned around and saw Ruth behind them.

"Alfred." Ruth folded her arms and stared at her husband.

"Well, this is awkward," Alfred said. "I think I'm going to go and join the party. I'll leave you two to bludgeon each other in private."

Alfred disappeared, leaving Lou alone with Ruth, and the hurt on her face was like a dagger through his heart. He'd gladly have anger any time.

"Ruth," he said, "I've been looking for you all evening."

"I see the party planner, Alison, joined us, too," she said, her voice shaking as she tried to remain strong.

Lou looked over his shoulder and saw Alison, little dress and long legs, dancing seductively in the middle of the floor.

Ruth looked at him questioningly.

"I didn't," he said, the fight going out of him, not wanting to be that man anymore. "Hand on heart, I didn't. She tried tonight, and I didn't."

Ruth laughed bitterly. "Oh, I bet she did."

"I swear I didn't."

"Anything? Ever?" She studied his face intently, clearly hating herself, embarrassed and angry at having to ask.

He swallowed. He didn't want to lose her, but he didn't want to lie. "A kiss. Once, is all. Nothing else." He spoke faster now, panicking. "But I'm different now, Ruth, I'm—"

She didn't listen to the rest of it. She turned away from him, trying to hide her face and her tears from him. She walked over and opened the door to the balcony.

"Ruth—" He tried to grab her arm and pull her back inside.

"Lou, let go of me. I swear to God, I'm not in the mood to talk to you now," she said angrily.

He followed her out onto the balcony, and they moved away from the window so that they couldn't be seen by anyone inside. Ruth leaned on the edge of the railing and looked out at the city, the cold air blowing around them. Lou moved close behind her, wrapped his arms tightly around her body, and refused to let go, despite her body's going rigid as soon as he touched her.

"Help me fix this," he whispered, close to tears. "Please, Ruth, help me fix this."

She sighed, but her anger was still raw. "What the hell were you thinking? How many times did we all tell you how important this night was?"

"I know, I know," he stuttered, thinking fast. "I was trying to prove to you all that I could—"

"Don't you dare lie to me again." She stopped him short. "Don't you dare lie when you've just asked for my help. You weren't trying to prove *anything*. You were fed up with Marcia ringing you, fed up with all the details, you were too busy—"

"Please, I don't need to hear this right now." He winced.

"This is *exactly* what you need to hear. You were too busy at work to care about your father or about Marcia's plans. You got a stranger who knew *nothing* about your father's seventy years on this Earth to plan the whole thing for you. Her." She pointed inside at Alison, who was now doing the limbo, revealing her red lace underwear to all who were looking. "A little tramp whom you probably screwed while dictating the party guest list," she spat.

"That didn't happen, I swear. I know I messed everything up. I'm sorry." He was so used to saying that word now.

"And what was it all for? For a promotion? A pay raise that you don't even need? More work hours in a day that just aren't humanly possible to achieve? When will you stop? When will it all be enough for you? How high do you want to climb, Lou?" She paused. "Last week you said that a job can fire you, but a family can't. I think you're about to realize that the latter is possible after all."

"Ruth." He closed his eyes, ready to jump off the balcony then and there. "Please don't leave me."

"Not me, Lou," she said. "I'm talking about them."

He turned around and watched his family now dancing in a train around the room, kicking up their legs every few steps.

"I'm racing with Quentin tomorrow. On the boat." He looked at her for praise.

"I thought Gabe was doing that?" Ruth asked in confusion. "Gabe volunteered right here in front of me. Quentin said yes."

Lou's blood boiled. "No, I'm definitely going to do it." He would make sure of it.

"Oh, really? Is that before or after you're coming ice-skating with me and the kids?" she asked before walking off and leaving him alone on the balcony, cursing himself for forgetting his promise to Lucy.

As Ruth opened the door to go back inside, music rushed out, along with a burst of warm air. Then the door closed again, but he felt a presence behind him. She hadn't gone inside. She hadn't left him.

"I'm sorry about everything I've ever done. I want to fix it all," he said with exhaustion. "I'm tired now. I want to fix it. I want everyone to know that I'm sorry. I'd do anything for them to know that and to believe me. Please help me fix it," he repeated.

Had Lou turned around then he would have seen that his wife had indeed left him, that she'd rushed off inside to once again cry her tears of frustration for a man who had convinced her only hours previously that he had changed. It was Gabe who had stepped out onto the balcony when Ruth had rushed off, and it was Gabe who'd just heard Lou's confessions.

Gabe knew that Lou Suffern was exhausted. Lou had spent so many years moving so quickly through the minutes, hours, and days that he'd stopped noticing life. The looks, gestures, and emotions of other people had long stopped being important or visible to him. Passion had driven him at first, and then, while on his way to the somewhere he wanted to be, he'd left it behind. He'd moved too fast, he'd taken no pause for breath; his rhythm was too quick, his heart could barely keep up.

As Lou breathed in the cold December air and lifted his face up to the sky, to feel—and appreciate—the icy droplets of rain that started to fall onto his skin, he knew that his soul was coming to get him.

He could feel it.

CHAPTER 23

The Best Day

AT NINE A.M. ON SATURDAY, the day after his father's seventieth birthday party, Lou Suffern sat out in his backyard and lifted his face and closed his eyes to the morning sun. He'd clambered over the fence that separated their one-acre landscaped garden—where pathways and pebbles, garden beds and giant pots were neatly organized—from the rugged and wild terrain that lay beyond human meddling. Splashes of yellow gorse were everywhere, as though somebody in Dalkey had taken a paintball gun and fired carelessly in the direction of the northside headland. Lou and Ruth's house sat at the very top of the summit, their back garden looking out to the north with vast views of Howth village below, the harbor, and out farther again to Ireland's Eye.

Lou sat on a rock and breathed in the fresh air. His numb nose dribbled, his cheeks were frozen stiff, and his ears ached from the nip in the wind. His fingers had turned a purplish blue, as though they were being strangled at the knuckles—not good weather for vital parts,

but ideal weather for sailing. Unlike the carefully main-
tained gardens of his and his neighbors' houses, the wild
and rugged gorse had been even more lovingly left to
grow as it wanted. It had roamed the mountainside and
stamped its authority firmly around the headland. The
land here was hilly and uneven; it rose and fell without
warning, apologized for nothing, and offered no assis-
tance to trekkers. It was the student in the last row in
class, quiet but suggestive, sitting back to view the traps
it had laid. Despite Howth's wild streak in the mountains and the hustle and bustle of the fishing village, the
town itself always had a sense of calm. It had a patient,
grandparental feel about it: lighthouses that guided in-
habitants of the waters safely to shore; cliffs that stood
like a line of impenetrable Spartans with heaving chests,
fierce against the elements. There was the pier that acted
as a mediator between land and sea and dutifully fer-
ried people out as far as humanly possible; the martello
tower that stood like a lone aging soldier who refused to
leave his zone long after the trouble had ended. Despite
the constant gust that attacked the headland, the town
was steady and stubborn.

Lou wasn't alone this morning as he pondered his
life looking out at all this. Beside him sat himself. They
were dressed differently: one ready for sailing with his
brother, the other for ice-skating with the family. They
stared out to sea, both watching the shimmer of the sun
on the horizon, looking like a giant silver dime that had
been dropped in for luck and now glimmered under the

waves. They'd been sitting there for a while, not saying anything, merely comfortable with their own company.

Lou on the mossy grass looked at Lou on the rock, and smiled. "You know how happy I am right now? I'm beside myself." He chuckled.

Lou, sitting on the rock, fought his smile. "The more I hear myself joke, the more I realize I'm not funny."

"Yeah, me, too." Lou pulled a long strand of wild grass from the ground and rolled it around in his purple fingers. "But I also notice what a handsome bastard I am."

They both laughed.

"You talk over people a lot, though," Lou on the rock said, having witnessed his other self in conversation.

"I noticed that. I really should—"

"And you don't really listen," he added. "And your stories are always too long. People don't seem to be as interested as you think," he said. "You don't ask people about what they're doing. You should start doing that."

"Speak for yourself," Lou on the grass said, unimpressed.

"I am."

They sat in silence again because Lou Suffern had recently learned that a lot could come from silence and from being still. A gull swooped and squawked nearby, eyed them suspiciously, and then flew off.

"He's off to tell his mates about us," Lou on the rock said.

"Let's not take whatever they say to heart; they all look the same to me," the other Lou said.

They both laughed again.

"I can't believe I'm laughing at my own jokes." Lou on the grass rubbed his eyes. "Embarrassing."

"What's going on here, do you think?" Lou asked seriously, perched on his rock.

"If you don't know, I don't know."

"Yes, but if I have theories, well, then, so do you."

They looked at each other, knowing exactly what the other was thinking.

Lou chose his words wisely, letting them roll around his mouth before saying, "I think we should keep those theories to ourselves, don't you? It is what it is. Let's keep it at that."

"I don't want anybody to get hurt," Lou on the grass said.

"Did you just hear what I said?" he said angrily. "I said don't talk about it."

"Lou!" Ruth was calling them from the garden, and it broke the spell between them.

"Coming!" he yelled, peeping his head above the fence. He saw Bud, new to his feet, escaping to freedom through the kitchen door, racing around the grass unevenly, like a chick that had prematurely hatched from an egg, its legs alone breaking free. He shuffled along after a ball, trying to catch it but mistakenly kicking it with his running feet each time he got near. Finally learning, he stopped running before reaching down to the ball, and instead slowly sneaked up behind it, as though it was going to take off again by itself. He lifted a foot. Not used to having to balance on one leg, he fell backward onto the grass, safely landing on his padded behind. Lucy ran outside in her hat and scarf and helped to pull him up.

"She's so like Ruth." He heard a voice near his ear say before realizing the other Lou had joined him.

"I know. See the way she makes that face." They watched Lucy scolding Bud for being careless. They both laughed.

Bud screeched at Lucy's attempt to take him by the hand and lead him back into the house. He pulled away and threw his hand up in the air in a mini-tantrum, then chose to waddle to the house by himself.

"And who does *he* remind you of?" Lou said.

"Okay, we'd better get moving," he said, ignoring himself. "You walk down to the harbor, and I'll drive Ruth and the kids into town. Make sure you're there on time, okay? I practically had to bribe Quentin into saying yes about helping him today."

"Of course I'll be there. Don't you break a leg."

"Don't you drown."

"We'll enjoy the day." Lou reached out and shook hands with himself. Their handshake turned into an embrace, and Lou stood on the mountainside giving himself the biggest and warmest hug he'd received in a very long time.

LOU ARRIVED DOWN AT THE harbor two hours before the race. He hadn't raced for so many years, he wanted to get reaccustomed to the talk, get a feel for being on a boat again. He also needed to build up a relationship with the rest of the team: communication was key, and he didn't want to let anybody down. Most of all, he didn't want to let Quentin down. He found the beautiful *Alexandra*, the forty-foot sailboat Quentin had bought five years ago and had since spent every spare penny and every free moment on. Already on board, Quentin and five others were in a tight group, going over the course and their tactics.

Lou did the math. There were supposed to be only six on the boat; Lou joining them made seven.

"Hi, there," he said, approaching the boat.

"Lou!" Quentin looked up in surprise, and Lou realized why there were already six people. Quentin hadn't trusted him to show up.

"Not late, am I? You did say nine thirty." He tried to hide his disappointment.

"Yeah, sure, of course." Quentin said, "Absolutely, I just, eh . . ." He turned around to the other men waiting and watching. "Let me introduce you to the rest of the team. Guys, this is my brother, Lou."

Surprise flitted across a few faces.

"We didn't know you had a brother," one of them said, stepping forward to offer his hand. "I'm Geoff, welcome. I hope you know what you're doing."

"It's been a while"—Lou looked over at Quentin—"but Quentin and I were sent on enough sailing courses over the years, it'd be hard for us ever to forget. It's like riding a bike, isn't it?"

They all laughed and welcomed him aboard.

"So where do you want me?" Lou asked.

"Are you really okay to do this?" Quentin asked him quietly, away from the others.

"Of course." Lou tried not to be offended. "Same positions as we used to?"

"Foredeck man?" Quentin asked.

"Aye, aye, Captain," Lou said, saluting him.

Quentin laughed and turned back to the rest of the crew. "Okay, boys, I want us all working in harmony. Remember, let's talk to each other; I want information flowing up and down the boat at all times. If you haven't done what you should have done, then shout, we all need to know exactly what's going on. If we win, I'll buy the first round."

They all cheered.

"Right, Lou"—he looked at his brother and winked— "I know you've been looking forward to this for a long time."

Lou knew better than to correct him.

"Finally you get your opportunity to see what *Alexandra*'s made of."

Lou punched his brother playfully on the shoulder.

RUTH PUSHED BUD'S BUGGY THROUGH Fusilier's Arch and they entered St. Stephen's Green, a park right in the center of Dublin city. An ice rink had been set up in the grounds, attracting shoppers and people from all around the country to join in the unique experience. Passing the duck-filled lake and walking over O'Connell Bridge, they soon entered a wonderland. A Christmas market had been set up, lavishly decorated and looking as if it had come straight out of a Christmas movie. Stalls selling hot chocolate with marshmallows, mince pies, and fruitcakes lined the paths and the smell of cinnamon, cloves, and marzipan wafted into the air. Each stall owner was dressed as an elf, and while Christmas tunes blared out of huge speakers, wind machines blew fake snow through the air.

Santa's Igloo was the center of attention, a long line forming outside, while elves dressed in green suits and pointy shoes did their best to entertain the waiting masses. Giant red-and-white-striped candy canes formed an archway into the igloo, while bubbles blew from the chimney top and floated up into the sky. On a patch of grass off to the side a group of children—umpired by an elf—played tug-of-war with an oversized Christmas cracker. Next to all this a Christmas tree twenty feet tall had been erected and decorated with oversized baubles and tinsel. Hanging from the branches were giant balloons, at which a line of children—but more daddies— threw acorns in an attempt to burst the balloons and release the gifts inside. A red-faced elf ran around collecting gifts from the ground, while his accomplice filled more balloons and passed them to another teammate to hang on the branches. There was no whistling while they worked.

Bud's chubby little forefinger pointed in every direction as something new caught his eye. Lucy, usually chatty, had suddenly gone very quiet, taking in the sights. She was dressed in a bright red double-breasted coat that went to her knees, with oversized black buttons and a black fur collar, and cream tights and shiny black shoes. She held on to Bud's buggy with one hand and floated along beside them all, drifting away in a heaven of her own. Every now and then she'd see something and look up to Lou and Ruth with the biggest smile on her face. Nobody said anything. They didn't need to. They all knew.

Farther away from the Christmas market they found the ice rink, which was swarmed by hundreds of people young and old, the line snaking alongside the rink providing an audience for all those who crashed and fell on the ice.

"Why don't you all go and watch the show?" Lou said, pointing to the mini-pantomime that was being performed in the bandstand next to the rink. Dozens of children sat on deck chairs, entranced by the magical world before them. "I'll get in line for us."

It was a generous gesture and a selfish one both at the same time, for Lou Suffern couldn't possibly change overnight. He had made the attempt to spend the day with his family, but already his BlackBerry was burning a hole in his pocket, and he needed time to check it before he quite simply exploded.

"Okay, thanks," Ruth said, pushing Bud over to join Lou in the line. "We shouldn't be too long."

"What are you doing?" Lou asked.

"Going to watch the show."

"Aren't you taking him?"

"No. *He* is asleep. He'll be fine with you."

Then she headed off hand in hand with a skipping Lucy, while Lou looked at Bud with mild panic, full of prayer for him not to wake. He had one eye on his BlackBerry, the other on Bud, and a third eye he'd never known he had on the group of teenagers in front of them, who had suddenly started shouting and jumping around as their hormones got the better of them, each screech from their mouths and jerk of their gawky movements a threat to his sleeping child. He suddenly became aware of the level of "Jingle Bells" being blasted through the rink's speakers, of the feedback that sounded like a five-car pileup, when a voice cut in to announce a separated family member who was waiting by the Elf Center. He was aware of every single sound, every squeal of a child on the ice, every shout as their fathers fell on their asses, everything. On high alert, as though waiting for somebody to attack at any moment, the BlackBerry and its flashing red light went back in his pocket. People ahead of him moved up, and he ever so slowly pushed the buggy up the line.

In front of him, a greasy-haired adolescent who was telling a story to his friends through the use of serious explosion sounds and the occasional epileptic-fit movements caught Lou's eye because of his dangerous proximity. Sure enough, the boy, getting to the climax of the story, leapt back and landed against the buggy.

"Sorry," the boy said, turning around and rubbing his arm, which he'd bumped. "Sorry, mister, is he okay?"

Lou nodded. Swallowed. He wanted to reach out and throttle the child, wanted to find the boy's parents so that he could tell them about teaching their son the art of storytelling without grand gestures and spittle-flying explosions. He peeped in at Bud. The monster had been woken. Bud's eyes, glassy and tired, and not yet ready to come out of hibernation, opened slowly. They looked left, they looked right, and all around, while Lou held his breath. He and Bud looked at each other for a tense second, and then, deciding he didn't like the horrified expression on his father's face, Bud spat out his pacifier and began screaming. Scream. Ing.

"Eh, shhhh," Lou said awkwardly, looking down at his son.

Bud screamed louder, thick tears forming in his tired eyes.

"Em, come on, Bud." Lou smiled at him, giving him his best porcelain-toothed smile that usually worked on everyone else.

Bud cried louder.

Lou looked around in embarrassment, apologizing to anybody whose eye he caught, particularly the smug father who had a young baby in a pouch on his front and two other children holding his hands. He turned his back on the smug man, trying to end the screech of terror by pushing the buggy back and forth quickly, deliberately clipping the heels of the greasy teen who'd put him in this predicament. He tried pushing the pacifier back in Bud's mouth, ten times over. He tried covering Bud's eyes with his hand, hoping that the darkness would make him want to go back to sleep. That didn't work. Bud's body was contorting, bending backward as he tried to break out of his straps like the Incredible Hulk breaking out of his clothes. He continued to wail. Lou fumbled with the baby bag and offered him toys, which were flung violently out of the buggy and onto the ground.

Smug Family Man with the front pouch bent over to assist Lou in his gathering of dispersed toys. Lou grabbed them while failing to make eye contact, grunting his thanks. Finally Lou decided to release the dough monster from the buggy. He struggled with the straps for some time while Bud's screams intensified, and just as someone was close to calling social services, he finally broke his son free. Bud didn't stop crying, though, and continued to yell, with snot bubbling from his nostrils, his face as purple as a blueberry.

Ten minutes of pointing at trees, dogs, children, planes, birds, Christmas trees, presents, elves, things that moved, things that didn't move, anything that Lou could lay his eye on, and Bud was still crying.

At last Ruth came running over with Lucy.

"What's wrong?"

"Woke up as soon as you left, he won't stop crying." Lou was sweating.

Bud took one look at Ruth and reached his arms out

toward her, almost jumping out of Lou's arms. His cries stopped instantly, he clapped his hands, and his face returned to a normal color. He looked at his mother, played with her necklace, and acted as though nothing had happened to him at all. Lou was sure that when nobody else was looking, Bud turned and smiled cheekily at him.

STARTING TO FEEL IN HIS element, Lou felt his stomach churn with anticipation as he watched the coastline move farther into the distance and they made their way to the starting area, north of Ireland's Eye. Bundled-up family members and friends waved their support from the lighthouse at the end of the pier, binoculars in hands.

There was a magic about the sea. People were drawn to it. People wanted to live by it, swim in it, play in it, look at it. It was a living thing that was as unpredictable as a great stage actor: it could be calm and welcoming one moment, opening its arms to embrace its audience, but then it could explode with its stormy tempers, flinging people around, attacking coastlines, breaking down islands. It had its playful side, too, as it tossed children about, tipped over windsurfers, and occasionally gave sailors helping hands—all with a secret chuckle. For Lou there was nothing like the feel of the wind in his hair and the sun in his face as he glided through the water. It had been a long time since he'd last sailed—he and Ruth had had many holidays on friends' yachts over the years, but it was a long time since Lou had been a team player in any aspect of his life. He was looking forward to the challenge, not only to be in competition with thirty other boats, but also to try to beat the sea, the wind, and all the elements.

In the starting area they sailed near the committee boat *Free Enterprise* for identification purposes. The starting line was between a red-and-white pole on the committee boat and a cylindrical orange buoy that was left to port. Lou got into place at the bow of the boat as they circled the area, trying to get into the best position to time it perfectly so that they'd cross the starting line at just the right time. The wind was northeast force four and the tide flooding, which added to the sea's bad humor. They would have to watch all that to keep the boat moving fast through the choppy, lumpy sea. Just like old times, Lou and Quentin had already talked this out, so both knew what was required. Any premature passing of the starting line would mean an elimination, and it was up to Lou to count them down, position them correctly, and communicate with Quentin, the helmsman. They used to have it down to a fine art when they were in their teens; back then they'd won numerous races and could have competed with their eyes closed, merely feeling the direction of the wind. But that had been so long ago, and the communication between them had broken down rather dramatically over the past few years.

Lou blessed himself as the warning signal appeared

at 11:25. They moved the boat around, trying to get into position so that they'd be one of the first to cross the starting line. At 11:26 the preparatory flag went up. At 11:29 the one-minute signal flag went down. Lou waved his arms around wildly, trying to signal to Quentin where to place the boat.

"Right starboard, starboard right, Quentin!" he yelled, waving his right arm. "Thirty seconds!" he yelled.

They came dangerously close to another yacht. Lou's fault.

"Eh, left port! LEFT!" Lou yelled. "Twenty seconds!"

Each boat fought hard to find a good position, but with thirty boats in the race, there could be only a small number that would make it across the starting line in the favored spot close to the committee boat. The rest would have to do their best with stolen wind on the way up the beat.

Eleven thirty heralded the start signal, and at least ten boats crossed the start line before them. Not the best start, but Lou wasn't going to let it get to him. He was rusty, he needed some practice, but he didn't have time for that. This was the real thing.

They raced along with Ireland's Eye on their right and the headland to their left, but there was no time to take in the view now. Lou thought fast and looked around him at all the yachts racing by, with the wind blowing in his hair, his blood pumping through his veins, feeling more alive than he'd ever felt. It was all coming back to him, what it felt like to be on the boat. He was slower, perhaps, but he hadn't lost his instincts. They raced along, the boat crashing over the waves as they headed toward the weather mark, one mile up in the wind from the starting line.

"Tacking!" Quentin shouted, watching and steering as the team prepared. The runners trimmer, Alan, checked that the slack on the old runners had been pulled in. The genoa trimmer, Luke, made sure that the new sheet had the slack pulled in and gave a couple of turns on the winch. Lou didn't move an inch, thinking ahead about what he needed to do and watching the other boats around them to make sure nothing was too close. He instinctively knew they were tacking onto port and would have no right of way over boats on starboard. His old racing tactics came flooding back, and he was quietly pleased with how he had positioned the boat right on the lay line to the weather mark. He could sense Quentin's confidence in him gaining at their now favorable position when the tack was completed, powering toward the mark with a clear passage in. It was Quentin's belief in him that Lou was fighting to win, just as much as first place.

Quentin made sure that there was room to take and started the turn. Geoff, the cockpit man, moved quickly to the old genoa, and as the genoa backwinded, he released it. The boat went through the wind, the mainsheet was eased a couple of feet, and the boom came across. Luke pulled as fast as possible, and when he couldn't pull anymore, he put a couple more turns on the winch and the grinding began. Quentin steered the new course.

"HIGH SIDE!" Lou yelled, and they all raced to hang their legs over the windward side.

Quentin whooped, and Lou laughed into the wind.

After rounding the first mark and heading toward the second with the wind on their side, Lou jumped into action in time to hoist the spinnaker, then gave Quentin the thumbs-up. The rest of the team instantly got busy, tending to their individual duties. Lou was a little too much fingers and thumbs, but he could tell it was coming together.

Watching it rise to the top, Lou happily called, "UP!"

Alan trimmed the spinnaker while Robert grinded. They sailed fast, and Lou punched the air and roared. Behind the wheel, Quentin laughed as the spinny filled with wind like a windsock, and the wind with them, they raced to the next mark. Quentin allowed himself a quick look astern, and it was some sight: there must have been twenty-five boats with spinnakers filling, chasing them down. Not bad. He and Lou caught each other's eyes and smiled.

AFTER THIRTY MINUTES OF QUEUING for the ice rink, Lou and his family finally reached the front.

"You guys have fun," Lou said, clapping his hands together and stamping his feet to keep warm. "I'll just go to the coffee place over there and watch you."

Ruth started laughing. "Lou, I thought you were coming skating with us."

"No." He scrunched up his face. "I've just spent the last half an hour watching men my age making fools of themselves out there. What if someone sees me? I'd rather stay here, thank you. Plus, these are new and dry clean only," he added, pointing to his trousers.

"Right," Ruth said firmly, "then you won't mind taking care of Bud while Lucy and I skate."

"Come on, Lucy." Lou had an instant change of heart at that and grabbed his daughter's hand. "Let's get us some skates." He winked at Ruth, who looked amused, and made off to get their ice skates. He got to the counter ahead of Smug Family Man. Ha. He felt a sense of silent victory.

"What size?" The man behind the desk looked at him.

"Ten, please," Lou responded, and looked down at Lucy and waited for her to speak up. Her big brown eyes stared back up at him.

"Tell the man your size, sweetheart," he said, feeling Smug Family Man breathing down his neck as he waited.

"I don't know, Daddy," she said, almost in a whisper.

"Well, you're four, aren't you?"

"Five." She frowned.

"She's five," he told the man. "So whatever size a five-year-old would take."

"It really depends on the child."

Lou sighed and took out his BlackBerry, refusing to have to line up again. Behind him, Smug Family Man with the baby in the pouch called over his head, "Two size fours, a size three, and an eleven, please."

Lou rolled his eyes and mimicked him as he waited for his call to be answered.

"Hello?"

"What size is Lucy?"

Ruth laughed. "She's a twenty-six."

"Okay, thanks." He hung up.

Once on the ice, he held on to the side of the rink carefully. He took Lucy's hand and guided her along. Ruth stood nearby with Bud, who kicked his legs excitedly while bouncing up and down and pointing at nothing in particular.

"Now, sweetheart"—Lou's voice and ankles wobbled as he stepped on the ice—"it's very dangerous, so you have to be very careful. Hold on to the sides now, okay?"

Lucy held on to the side with one hand and slowly got used to moving along the ice while Lou's ankles still wobbled on his thin blades.

Lucy started to skate faster. "Honey," Lou said, his voice shaky as he looked down at the cold, hard ice, dreading what it would feel like to fall.

The distance between Lucy and Lou widened.

"Keep up with her, Lou," Ruth called from the other side of the barrier, walking alongside him as he moved. He could swear he heard teasing in her voice.

"I bet you're enjoying this." He could barely look up at her, he was concentrating so much.

"Absolutely."

He pushed with his left foot, which skidded out farther than he planned, and he almost broke into a split.
Feeling like Bambi getting to his feet for the first time, he
wobbled and spun, arms waving around in circles as he
tried to keep his balance. But he was making progress.
He looked up now and then to keep his eye on Lucy,
who was clearly visible in her fire-engine-red coat, halfway around the rink ahead of him.

Smug Family Man went flying by him, arms swinging as though he was about to take part in a bobsled
race, the speed of him alone almost toppling Lou. Behind him, Smug Family Man's kids raced along, holding
hands, and were they actually singing? That was it, Lou
decided. Slowly letting go of the barrier at the side, he
tried to balance on wobbly legs. Then, bit by bit, he slid
a foot forward, almost toppling backward, his back arch-
ing as though about to fall into a crab position, but he
somehow managed to rescue himself.

"Hi, Daddy," Lucy said, speeding by him as she completed the first round of the rink.

Lou moved out from the side of the rink, away from
the beginners who were shuffling around inch by inch,
determined, albeit foolishly, to beat Smug Family Man.

Halfway now between the center of the rink and the
barrier, Lou was out on his own. Feeling a little more
confident, he pushed himself farther, trying to swing his
arms for balance as he saw the others doing. He picked
up speed. Dodging children and old people, he quite un-

sophisticatedly darted around the rink, hunched over and swinging his arms, more like an ice-hockey player than a graceful skater. He bumped against children, knocking some over, causing others to topple. He heard one child cry. He broke through a couple holding hands. He was concentrating on not falling over so much that he could barely find the time to apologize. At one point he passed Lucy but, unable to stop, had to keep moving, his speed picking up as he went round and round. The lights that decorated the park trees above them blurred as he raced around, along with the sounds and colors of the other skaters. Feeling like he was on a merry-go-round, Lou smiled and finally relaxed a little bit, as he raced round and round and round. He passed Smug Family Guy; he passed by Lucy for a third time; he passed by Ruth, whom he heard call his name and take a photograph. He couldn't stop, and he wouldn't stop; he didn't know how. He was enjoying the feel of the wind in his hair, the lights of the city around him, the crispness of the air, the sky so filled with stars as the evening began to close in at the early hour. He felt free and alive, happier than he remembered being for a long time. Round and round he went.

ALEXANDRA AND THE CREW HAD taken on the course for the third and final time. Their speed and coordination had come together better over the last hour, and Lou had fixed any previous hiccups that he'd had. They were coming up to rounding the bottom mark, and they needed to once again execute the spinnaker drop.

Lou made sure that the ropes were free to run. Geoff hoisted the genoa, Lou guided it into the luff groove, and Luke made sure that the genoa sheet was cleated off. Robert positioned himself to grab the loose sheet under the mainsail so that it could be used to pull in the spinnaker. As soon as he was in position, everyone prepared for everything to happen at once. Geoff released the halyard and helped to stuff the spinnaker down below. Joey released the guy and made sure it ran out fast so that the spinnaker could fly flaglike outside the boat. When the spinnaker was in the boat, Luke trimmed the genoa for the new course, Joey trimmed the main, Geoff lowered the pole, and Lou stowed the pole.

Spinnaker down for the last time and approaching the finishing line, they radioed the race officer on Channel 37 and waited for recognition. Not first in, but they were all happy. Lou looked at Quentin as they sailed in, and they smiled. Neither of them said anything. They didn't need to. They both knew.

LYING ON HIS BACK WITH people flying by him, Lou held on to his sore rib cage and tried to stop laughing, but he just couldn't. He had done what he had been dreading and achieved the most dramatic and comical fall of the day. He lay in the center of the rink; Lucy was by his side, laughing, trying to lift his arm and pull him up.

They had been holding hands and skating around slowly together when, too cocky, Lou had tripped over his own feet, gone flying, and landed on his back. Nothing was broken, thankfully, other than his pride, but even that he surprisingly didn't care about. He allowed Lucy to believe she was helping him up from the ice as she pulled on his arm. He looked over to Ruth and saw a flash as she took yet another photo. They caught each other's eyes, and he smiled.

They didn't say anything about that day. They didn't need to. They all knew.

It had been the best day of their lives.

CHAPTER 24

The Turkey Boy 4

S O HE SPENT THE DAY with his brother *and* he spent the day with his wife at exactly the same time." The Turkey Boy wrinkled his nose.

"Indeed," Raphie sighed, knowing how incredible it sounded.

"How do you know that? Did Lou tell you? I wouldn't trust that Lou bloke, if I were you; he sounds like a bit of a sap."

"No, I didn't hear it from Lou. I heard it from his wife, and I heard it from his brother."

"Oh." The boy went silent. Then he perked up. "Hey, what are you doing investigating him, anyway? What did he do?"

Raphie was silent.

"Yes!" The boy rubbed his hands together with glee. "I knew you'd get the flash bastard on somethin'. Go on, tell us the rest." He smiled with excitement, pulling his chair closer to the table so that he'd hear Raphie's words as soon as they left his mouth.

CHAPTER 25

It All Started with a Mouse

ON THE MONDAY MORNING FOLLOWING his weekend of sailing and skating, Lou Suffern found himself floating down the hall to the office with the bigger desk and better light. It was Christmas Eve and the office floor was near empty, but the few souls that haunted the halls—dressed in their casuals—offered pats on the back and firm handshakes of congratulations. He had made it. Behind him, Gabe helped carry a box of his files. Being Christmas Eve, it was the last day Lou would have to prepare himself before the Christmas break. Ruth had wanted him to accompany her and the kids into the city for some last-minute shopping, but he knew the best thing to do was to get a head start in his new job.

So down he and Gabe went, to his bigger office with better light. When they opened the door, it was almost as though angels were singing inside, the morning sun lighting a pathway from the door to the desk and shining directly on his new oversized leather chair as though it were an apparition. Having already breathed a sigh of relief, Lou now took another deep breath for the new task ahead of him. No matter what he previously achieved, the feelings of having to reach again were never ending. Life for him felt like an endless ladder that disappeared somewhere in the clouds, constantly wobbling and threatening to topple and bring him down with it. He couldn't look down now or he would freeze. He had to keep his eyes upward. Onward and upward.

Gabe placed the boxes down and whistled as he looked around.

"Some office, Lou."

"Yeah, it is." Lou grinned.

"It's warm," Gabe added, hands in pockets and strolling around.

Lou frowned. "Warm is . . . a word I wouldn't use to describe this"—he spread his hands out in the vast space—"enormous fucking office." He started laughing, feeling slightly delirious. Tired and emotional, proud and a little fearful, he tried to take it all in.

"So what exactly is it that you do now?" Gabe asked.

"I'm the business development director, which means I now have the authority to tell certain little shits exactly what to do."

"Little shits like you?"

Lou's head snapped around to face Gabe, like a radar that had found a signal.

"I mean, just a few days ago you would have been one

of those little shits being told what to . . . never mind,"
Gabe trailed off. "So how did Cliff take it?"

"Take what?"

"That his job was gone?"

"Oh." Lou looked up. He shrugged. "I don't know. I
didn't tell him."

Gabe left a silence.

"I don't think he's well enough yet to talk to anyone,"
Lou added, feeling the need to explain.

"He's perfectly fine," Gabe told him.

"How do you know?"

"I know. You should go and see him. He might have
some good advice for you. You could learn from him.
He's decided to become a landscaper. Something he's
always wanted to do."

Lou laughed at that.

Gabe didn't blink, and stood looking at him as if disappointed.

Lou cleared his throat awkwardly.

"It's Christmas Eve, Lou. What are you doing here?"
Gabe's voice was gentle.

"What do you mean, what am I doing?" Lou held
his hands up questioningly. "What does it look like? I'm
working."

"Except for security, and a few stragglers, you're the
only person left in the building. Haven't you noticed?
Everybody's out there." Gabe pointed out at the busy
city.

"Yeah, well, everybody out there isn't as busy as I

am," Lou said childishly. "Besides, you're here, too, aren't you?"

"I don't count."

"Well, that's a great answer. I don't count then, either."

"You keep on going like this and you won't," Gabe said. "You know, one of the most successful businessmen of all time, a certain Walt Disney—I'm sure you've heard of him, he has a company or two here and there— said, 'A man should never neglect his family for business.'"

There was a long, awkward silence during which Lou clenched and unclenched his jaw, trying to decide whether to ask Gabe to leave or physically throw him out.

"But then"—Gabe laughed—"he also said, 'It all started with a mouse.'"

"Okay, well, I'd better get to work now, Gabe. I hope you have a happy Christmas." Lou tried to control his tone.

"Thank you, Lou. A very happy Christmas to you, too. And congratulations on your warm, enormous fucking office."

Lou couldn't help but laugh at that, and as Gabe closed the door behind him, Lou was alone for the first time in his space. He made his way to the desk, ran his finger along the walnut border to the pigskin surface. All that was on the desk was a large white computer, a keyboard, and a mouse.

He sat down on the leather chair and swung around to face the window, watching the city below him preparing for the celebrations. A part of him felt pulled outside, yet he felt trapped behind the window. In fact, he often felt as though he were trapped inside an oversized snow globe, responsibilities and failures sprinkling down around him. He sat in that chair, at that desk, for over an hour, just thinking. Thinking about Cliff; thinking about the events of the past few weeks and about the best day of all with his family, about the lessons he had learned. He thought about everything. When a mild panic began to grow inside him, he turned in his chair and faced the office. Faced up to it all.

He stared at the keyboard. Stared at it hard. Then he followed the thin white wire that was connected to the mouse. He thought about Cliff, about finding him underneath this very desk, clutching this very keyboard, swinging that very mouse at him with wide, haunted eyes.

To honor Cliff—something that Lou realized he hadn't managed to do in the entire time that the man had been out of work—he kicked off his shoes, unhooked the keyboard from the computer monitor, and pushed back the leather chair. He got onto his hands and knees and crawled underneath the desk, clutching the keyboard close to him. From there he looked out the floor-to-ceiling windows and watched the city go racing by. He sat there for another hour, just pondering, watching people live while he was still and alone.

The clock on the wall ticked loudly in the silence. Gone was the usual hustle and bustle of the office floor. No phones ringing, no photocopiers going, no hum of the computers, no voices, no footsteps passing by. He'd never before heard the seconds on the clock, but now that he'd registered them, the ticking seemed to get louder and louder. Lou looked down at the keyboard in his hands, and then he looked at the mouse. What on Earth was he doing here, again, when everything he loved in the world was out there? It was then that he had a jolt, he felt it smack him in the head for the second time that year; for the first time, Cliff's message finally reached him. Whatever Cliff had been so afraid was coming to get him, Lou sure as hell didn't want it chasing him, either.

He clambered out from under the desk, shoved his feet into his polished black leather shoes, and walked out of the office to join the living.

CHAPTER 26

Christmas Eve

GRAFTON STREET, THE BUSY PEDESTRIAN street in Dublin city, was awash with people doing their last-minute shopping. Hands were fighting to grab the last remaining items on shelves, budgets and all thought gone out the window as rash decisions were made according to availability and time, and not necessarily with the recipient in mind. Presents first; for whom, later.

For once not keeping up with the pace around him, Lou held Ruth's hand and slowly wandered the streets of Dublin, allowing others to rush by them. Lou had all the time in the world. Ruth had been more than taken aback earlier when he'd arranged to meet up with them out in the city but, as usual, hadn't asked any questions. She'd welcomed his new change with silent delight but with equal amounts of cynicism. Lou Suffern still had much to prove to her.

They walked down Henry Street, where hawkers cleared the last of their stock in their market stalls: toys and wrapping paper, tinsel and baubles, remote-control cars that ran up and down the street, everything on show for the last few hours of manic Christmas shopping. On the ever-changing Moore Street, displays included a lively ethnic mix of Asian and African stores. They attended early Christmas Eve mass and ate lunch together in the Westin Hotel in College Green, the historic nineteenth-century building, that had been transformed from a bank to a five-star hotel. They ate in the Banking Hall, where Bud spent the entire time with his head tilted to the ceiling, looking in awe at the intricately hand-carved ornate ceiling and the four chandeliers that glistened with eight thousand pieces of Egyptian crystal, and shouting over and over again just to hear the echo of his voice in the high ceiling.

Lou Suffern saw the world differently that day. Instead of viewing it from thirteen floors up, behind tinted reinforced glass in an oversized leather chair, he had chosen to join in. Gabe had been right about the mouse; he'd been right about Cliff teaching him something all along—in fact, it had started six months ago, as soon as the plastic mouse had hit him across the face, causing Lou's fears and his conscience to slowly resurface after long being buried. In fact, when Lou thought about it, Gabe had been right about a lot of things. The voice that had been grating so much in his ear over the past week had actually been speaking the words he hadn't wanted to hear. He owed Gabe a lot, he realized. As the evening was closing in, the children having to return home before Santa took to the skies, Lou kissed Ruth and the kids good-bye, saw them safely into the car, and then headed back to the office. He had one more thing to do.

Lou waited in the building lobby for the elevators, and when the doors opened, Lou about to step in, Mr. Patterson stepped out.

"Lou," he said in surprise, "I can't believe you're working today. You really are a piece of work." He eyed the box in Lou's hand.

"Oh no, I'm not working. Not on a holiday," Lou smiled, trying to make a point, subtly attempting to set the ground rules for his new position. "I just have to . . ." He didn't want to get Gabe into trouble by revealing his whereabouts. "I just left something behind in the office."

"Good, good. Well, Lou," Mr. Patterson said tiredly. "I'm afraid I have to tell you something. I deliberated over whether to or not to, but I think it's best that I do." He paused. "I didn't come in this evening to work, either," he admitted. "Alfred called me in. Said it was urgent. After what happened to Cliff we're all on tenterhooks, I'm afraid, and so I came in quickly."

"I'm all ears," Lou said, worried. The elevator doors closed again. Escape route gone.

"He wanted to have a few words about . . . well, about you."

"Yes," Lou said slowly.

"He brought me these." Mr. Patterson reached into his pocket and retrieved the container of pills that Gabe had given Lou. There was only one pill inside. Alfred, the rat, had obviously scuttled to the trash bin to collect the one piece of evidence to destroy him.

Lou looked at the container in shock and tried to decide whether to deny the pills or not. Sweat broke out on his upper lip as he thought quickly for a story. They were his father's. No. His mother's. For her hip. No. He had back pain. Then he realized Mr. Patterson was talking.

"He said something about finding them under the trash." Mr. Patterson frowned. "And that he knew them to be yours . . ." He studied Lou, searching for recognition.

Lou's heart beat loudly in his ears.

"I know that you and Alfred are friends," Mr. Patterson said, his face suddenly showing his sixty-five years. "But his concern for you seemed a little misguided. It seemed to me that the purpose of this was to get you into trouble."

"Eh," Lou swallowed, eyeing up the brown container, "that's not, em, they're not, em . . ." He stuttered while trying to formulate a sentence.

"I'm not one to pry into people's personal lives, Lou—what my colleagues do in their own time is their own business, so long as it's not going to affect the company in any way. So I didn't take too kindly to Alfred giving me these," he said. When Lou didn't answer, Mr. Patterson added, "But maybe that's what you wanted him to do?"

"What?" Lou wiped his brow. "Why would I want Alfred to bring these to you?"

Mr. Patterson stared at him, his lips twitching ever so slightly. "I don't know, Lou, you're a clever man."

"What?" Lou responded, totally confused. "I don't understand."

"Correct me if I'm wrong, but *I* assumed," Mr. Patterson said, his twitching lips eventually growing into a smile, "that you deliberately tried to mislead Alfred with these pills. That you somehow made him believe they were more than they are. Am I right?"

Lou's mouth fell open, and he looked at his boss in surprise.

"I knew it." Mr. Patterson chuckled and shook his head. "You are good. But not that good. I recognized the blue mark on the pill."

"What do you mean? What blue mark?"

"You didn't manage to scratch the entire symbol off this last one," he explained, opening the container and emptying it into his palm. "See the blue mark? If you look close enough you can also see the trace of the *D* where it used to be. I should know. Working here, I swear by these fellas."

Lou swallowed. "That was the only one with the blue mark?" Lazy till the end, Alfred couldn't even reach into the trash to save his own skin, he'd had to scrape an initial off a simple headache tablet.

"No, there were two pills. Both with blue marks. I took one, I hope you don't mind. Trash or no trash, my head was pounding so much I had to have one. This bloody Christmas season is enough to drive me to an early grave."

"You took one?" Lou gasped.

"I'll replace it." He waved his hand dismissively. "You can get them at any pharmacy. Newsagents even, they're just over-the-counter pills."

"What happened when you took it?"

"Well, it got rid of my headache, didn't it?" He frowned. "Though to tell you the truth, if I don't get home in the next hour, I'll have to take another one before I know it." He looked at his watch.

Lou was gobsmacked into silence.

"Anyway, I just wanted to let you know that I didn't like what Alfred was trying to do, and that I don't think you're a . . . well, whatever Alfred was trying to make me believe. There's no place in the company for people like him. I had to let him go. Christmas Eve, Christ, this job makes a monster of us sometimes," he said, tiredly now.

Lou was silent, his mind screaming questions at him. Either Alfred had replaced the pills with fake ones, or Lou, too, had taken headache pills on the two occasions he had doubled up. Lou took out the handkerchief from his pocket, unwrapped it, and examined the one remaining pill. His heart froze in his chest. The faint initial of the headache tablet could be seen on its surface. Why hadn't he noticed it before?

"Ah, I see you have another one there," Mr. Patterson

chuckled. "Caught red-handed, Lou. Well, here you go, you can have the last one. Add it to your collection." He handed him the container.

Lou looked at him and opened and closed his mouth like a goldfish, no words coming out, as he shifted the box into one hand and took the remaining pill in the other.

"I'd better go now." Mr. Patterson slowly backed away. "I have a train set to put together and batteries to insert into a Little Miss Something-or-Other with a mouth as dirty as a toilet bowl, which I'll no doubt be forced to listen to all week. Have a lovely Christmas, Lou." He held his hand out.

Lou gulped, his mind still in a whirl about the headache tablets. Was he allergic to them? Had the doubling up been some sort of side effect? Had he dreamed it? No. No, it had happened, his family had witnessed his presence on both occasions. So if it wasn't the pills . . .

"Lou," Mr. Patterson said, his hand still in midair.

"Bye," Lou said croakily, and then cleared his throat. "I mean, Happy Christmas." He shoved the pills deep into his pocket before he reached out and shook his boss's hand.

As soon as Mr. Patterson had turned his back, Lou ran to the stairwell and charged down to the basement. It was colder than usual, and the fluorescent tube at the end of the hall had finally been fixed, no longer flashing like an eighties strobe light. Christmas music drifted out from under the door Lou was heading toward, "Driving

Home for Christmas" by Chris Rea echoing down the long, cold, sterile hallway.

Lou didn't knock before entering. He pushed the door with his foot, still carrying the box in his arm. The room was significantly emptier than it had been. Gabe was down the second aisle, rolling up the sleeping bag and blanket.

"Hi, Lou," he said without turning around.

"Who are you?" Lou asked, his voice shaking as he put the box down on a shelf.

Gabe stood up and stepped out of the aisle. "Okay," he said slowly, looking Lou up and down. "That's an interesting way to start a conversation." His eyes went to the box on the shelf, and he smiled. "A gift for me?" he said softly. "You really shouldn't have." He stepped forward to receive it, and Lou took a step backward while eyeing him.

"Hmm," Gabe said, frowning, then turning to the gift-wrapped box on the shelf. "Can I open it now?"

Lou didn't answer. Sweat glistened on his face, and his eyes moved sharply to follow Gabe's every movement.

Taking his time, Gabe carefully opened the perfectly wrapped gift. Approaching it from the ends, he slowly removed the tape, taking care not to rip the paper.

"I love giving people gifts," he explained, still keeping the same easy tone. "But it's not often that people give them to me. But you're different, Lou. I've always thought that." He unwrapped the box and finally revealed the gift inside, a small electric heater for his store-room. "Well, this is certainly very thoughtful. Thank you. It will definitely warm up my next space, but not here, unfortunately, as I'm moving on."

Lou had moved up against the wall now, as far away from Gabe as he could get before he spoke with a trem-ble. "The pills you gave me were headache tablets."

Gabe kept studying the heater. "Mr. Patterson told you that, I suspect."

Lou was taken aback, having expected Gabe to deny it. "Yes," he responded. "Alfred took them from the trash and gave them to him."

"The little rat." Gabe shook his head, smiling. "Pre-dictable old Alfred. I thought he might do that. Well, we can give him points for persistence. He *really* didn't want you to have that job, though, did he?"

When Lou didn't answer, Gabe continued, "I bet run-ning to Patterson didn't do him any favors, did it?"

"Mr. Patterson fired him," Lou said quietly, still try-ing to figure the situation out.

Gabe smiled, not seeming at all surprised. Just satisfied—and very much satisfied with himself.

"Tell me about the pills," Lou found his voice shaking.

"Yeah, they were a packet of headache pills I bought at a newsagent. Took me ages to scrape the little letters off; you know, there aren't many pills without branding on them these days."

"WHO ARE YOU?" Lou shouted, his voice drenched in fear.

Gabe jumped, then looked a little bothered. "You're frightened of me now? Because you found out it wasn't a bunch of pills that cloned you? What is it with science these days? Everyone is so quick to believe in it, in all these new scientific discoveries, new pills for this, new pills for that. Get thinner, grow hair, yada, yada, yada, but when it requires a little faith in something, you all go crazy." He shook his head. "If miracles had chemical equations, then everybody would believe. It's disappointing. I had to pretend they were pills, Lou, because you wouldn't have trusted me otherwise. And I was right, wasn't I?"

"What do you mean, *trust you*? Who the hell are you, and what is this all about?"

"Now," Gabe said, looking at Lou sadly, "I thought that was pretty clear by now."

"Clear? As far as I'm concerned, things couldn't be more messed up."

"The pills. They were just a science con. A con of science. A conscience." He smiled.

Lou rubbed his face, confused and afraid.

"It was all to give you your opportunity, Lou. Everybody deserves an opportunity. Even you, despite what you think."

"Opportunity FOR WHAT?" he yelled.

The following words that Gabe spoke sent shivers down Lou's spine.

"Come on, Lou, you know this one."

They were Ruth's words. They belonged to Ruth.

Lou's body was trembling now, and Gabe continued.

"An opportunity to spend some time with your family, to really get to know them, before . . . well, just to spend time with them."

"To get to know them before what?" Lou asked, quiet now.

Gabe didn't respond and looked away, knowing he'd said too much.

"BEFORE WHAT?" Lou yelled again, coming close to Gabe's face.

Gabe's crystal-blue eyes bore into Lou's.

"Is something going to happen to them?" Lou's voice shook as he began to panic. "I knew it. I was afraid of this. What's going to happen to them?" He ground his teeth together. "If you did something to them, then I will—"

"Nothing has happened to your family, Lou," Gabe responded.

"I don't believe you," he said, reaching into his pocket and retrieving his BlackBerry. He looked at the screen: no missed calls. Dialing the number of his home quickly, he backed out of the stockroom, giving Gabe one last, vicious look, and ran, ran, ran.

"Remember to buckle up, Lou!" Gabe shouted after him, his voice ringing in Lou's ears as Lou ran to the underground parking lot.

With the BlackBerry on autodial to Lou's home, and still ringing, Lou drove out of the lot at a fierce speed. Thick, heavy rain plummeted against his windshield.

Putting the wipers on the fastest speed, he put his foot down on the accelerator and sped by the empty quays. The beeping of the seat-belt warning got louder and louder, but he couldn't hear it for all the worrying he was doing. The wheels of the Porsche slipped a little on the wet roads as he raced down the back roads of the quays, then up the Clontarf coast road to Howth. Across the sea, the two red-and-white-striped chimneys of the electricity-generating station stood seven hundred feet tall, like two fingers raised at him. Rain bucketed down, leaving visibility low, but he knew these streets well, had driven up and down them all his life. All he cared about now was driving over the small thread of land that separated him from his family and getting to them as quickly as possible. It was six thirty and pitch-black since the day had closed in. Most people were at mass or in the pubs, getting ready to wrap final presents and leave a glass of milk and a plate of cookies out for Santa, a few carrots for his chauffeur. Lou's family was at home, having an evening meal—one that he'd promised he'd join—but they weren't answering the phone. He looked down at his BlackBerry to make sure it was still dialing, taking his eye off the road. He swerved a little as he moved over the middle line. A car coming at him beeped loudly, and he quickly moved back into his lane again. He flew up past the Marine Hotel at Sutton Cross, which was busy with Christmas parties. Seeing a clear road ahead of him, he put his foot down. He raced by Sutton Church and by the school along the coast, passed through streets of friendly houses with Christmas trees and candles in the front windows, Santas dangling from roofs. Across the bay, the dozens of cranes lining Dublin's skyline were laced in Christmas lights.

Lou eventually said good-bye to the bay and entered the steep road that began to ascend to his home on the summit. Rain continued to bucket down, falling in sheets, blurring his vision. Condensation was appearing on the windshield, and he leaned forward to wipe it with his cashmere coat sleeve. He pressed the buttons on the dashboard, hoping to clear the glass. The *ping, ping, ping* of the seat-belt warning rang again in his ears, and the condensation rapidly filled the windshield as the car got hotter. Still he sped on, his phone ringing, his desire to be with his family overtaking any other emotion he should have felt then. It had taken him twelve minutes to get to his street on the empty roads.

Finally, his phone beeped to signal a call coming through. He looked down and saw Ruth's face—her caller ID picture. Her smile; her eyes, brown, soft, and welcoming. Glad she was at least safe enough to call him, he looked down with relief and reached for the BlackBerry.

The Porsche 911 Carrera 4S has a unique four-wheel-drive system that grips the road far better than any rear-wheel-drive sports car. It allots 5 to 40 percent of the power to the front wheels, depending on how much resistance the rear wheels have. So if you accelerate out of a corner hard enough to spin the rear wheels, power is channeled to the front, pulling the car in the right direction. All-wheel drive basically means that the Carrera 4S could negotiate the icy road with far more control than most other sports cars.

Unfortunately, Lou did not have that model. He had it on order. It would be arriving in January, only a week away.

And so when Lou looked down at his BlackBerry, so overwhelmed with relief and emotion to see his wife's face, he had taken his eye off the road and had dived into the next corner much too fast. He reflexively lifted his foot from the accelerator, which threw the car's weight forward and lightened the rear wheels; then he got back on the accelerator and turned hard to make the corner. The rear end broke traction, and he spun across to the other side of the road, which was the deep decline down the cliff's edge.

The moments that followed were ones of sheer horror and confusion. The shock numbed the pain. The car turned over once, twice, and then a third time. Each time, Lou let out a yell as his head, body, legs, and arms thrashed about wildly like a doll inside a washing machine. The emergency air bag thumped him in the face, bloodying his nose, knocking him out momentarily so that the next few moments passed in a still but bloody mess.

Some amount of time later, Lou opened his eyes and tried to survey the situation. He couldn't. He was surrounded by blackness and found himself unable to move. A thick, oily substance covered one of his eyes, preventing him from seeing, and with the one hand he could move, he found that every part of his body he touched was covered in the same substance. He moved his tongue around his mouth, tasted rusty iron, and realized it was blood. He tried to move his legs but couldn't. He tried to move his arms and could just about move one. He was silent while he tried to keep calm, to figure out what to do. Then, when for the first time in his life he couldn't formulate one single thought, when the shock wore off and the realization set in, the pain hit him at full force. He couldn't get the images of Ruth out of his mind. Of Lucy, of Bud, of his parents. They weren't far above him, somewhere on the summit; he had almost made it. In the darkness, in a crushed car, in the middle of the gorse and the hebe, somewhere on a mountainside in Howth, Lou Suffern began to whimper.

RAPHIE AND JESSICA WERE DOING their usual rounds and bickering over Raphie's country-music tape, with which he liked to torment Jessica, as they passed the scene where Lou's car had gone off the road.

"Hold on, Raphie," she interrupted Raphie's singing about his achy-breaky heart.

He sang even louder.

"RAPHIE!" she shouted, punching the music off.

He looked at her in surprise.

"Okay, okay, put your Freezing Monkeys on, or whatever you call them."

"Raphie, stop the car," Jessica said in a tone that made him immediately pull over. She leapt out of the car and jogged the few paces back to the scene that had caught her eye, where the trees were broken and twisted. She took her flashlight out and shone it down the mountainside.

"Oh God, Raphie, we need to call emergency services," she shouted to him. "Ambulance and the fire department!"

He stopped his brief jog toward her and made his way back to the car, where he radioed it in.

"I'm going down!" she yelled, immediately making her way through the broken trees and down the steep incline.

"You will not, Jessica!" she heard Raphie yell back, but she didn't listen. "Get back here, it's too dangerous!"

She could hear him, but quickly zoned out from his shouts and could soon hear only her own breath, fast and furious, her heart beating in her ears.

Jessica, new to the squad, should never have seen a sight like this mangled car, upside down and totally unrecognizable, in her life. But she had. For Jessica, it was all too familiar; it was a sight that haunted her dreams and most of her waking moments. Coming face-to-face with her nightmare, and the replaying of a bad memory, dizziness overcame her, and she had to hunker down and put her head between her knees. Jessica had secrets, and one of them had come back to haunt her tonight. She hoped to God nobody was in that car; the car was crushed, unrecognizable, with no license plate, and in the darkness she couldn't even tell whether it was blue or black.

She climbed around the car, the icy rain pelting down on her, soaking her in an instant. The surface was wet and mucky beneath her, causing her to lose her footing numerous times, but as her heart beat wildly in her chest and as she found herself back in that distant memory, reliving it, she couldn't feel the pain in her ankle as she went over on it; she couldn't feel the scrapes of branches and twigs on her face, the hidden rocks among the gorse that bruised her legs.

Around the far side of the car, she saw a person. Or a body, at least, and her heart sank. She shone the light near him. He was bloodied. Covered in it. She discovered that the door had been smashed shut and she couldn't pull it open, but the windowpane of the driver's side had shattered, so at least she had access to his upper half. She tried to keep calm as she shone the flashlight inside the car.

"Tony," she breathed as she saw the figure. "Tony." Tears welled in her eyes. "Tony." She clawed at the man, ran her hands across his face, urged him to wake. "Tony, it's me," she said. "I'm here."

The man groaned, but his eyes remained closed.

"I'm going to get you out of here," she whispered in his ear, kissing him on the forehead. "I'm going to get you home."

His eyes slowly opened, and she felt a jolt. Blue eyes. Not brown. Tony had brown eyes.

He looked at her. She looked at him. Suddenly she was taken out of her nightmare.

"Sir," she said, her voice shakier than she wanted. She took a deep breath and started again. "Sir, can you hear me? My name is Jessica; can you hear me? Help is on the way, okay? We're going to help you."

He groaned and closed his eyes.

"They're on their way now," Raphie called from above her, starting to make his way down.

"Raphie, it's dangerous down here; it's too slippery. Stay up there so they can see you."

"Is anyone alive?" he asked, ignoring her request and continuing to move slowly down, one foot at a time.

"Yes," she called back. Then to Lou, "Sir, give me your hand." She shone the flashlight to look at his hand, and her stomach flipped at the sight. She took a moment to adjust her breathing and brought the light up again. "Sir, take my hand. Here I am, can you feel it?" She gripped him tight.

He groaned.

"Stay with me now. We're going to get you out of here."

He groaned some more.

"What? I can't . . . em . . . Don't worry, sir, an ambulance is on its way."

"Who is it?" Raphie called. "Do you know?"

"No," she called back simply, not wanting to take her attention away from this man, not wanting to lose him.

"My wife," she heard him whisper, so quietly it could have been mistaken for an exhale. She moved her ear to his lips, so close she could feel them on her earlobe, the stickiness of the blood.

"You have a wife?" she asked gently. "You'll see her. I promise, you'll see her. What's your name?"

"Lou," he said. Then he started to cry softly, but even that was such an effort that he had to stop.

"Please hang in there, Lou." She fought back the tears and then put her ear to his lips again as he breathed some more words.

"A pill? Lou, I don't have any—"

He let go of her hand suddenly and started pulling at his coat, thumping his chest with a lifeless hand. He grunted with the effort; he whimpered from the pain. Reaching into his breast pocket, which was soaked with blood, Jessica took out a container. It had one white pill left inside.

"Is this your medication, Lou?" she asked, unsure. "Do I—?" She looked up at Raphie, who was trying to figure out how to make it down through the tricky terrain. "I don't know if I'm supposed to give you—"

Lou took her hand and squeezed it with such sudden strength that she immediately opened the container with a shaking hand and shook the single pill onto her palm. With trembling fingers she lifted his mouth open, placed the pill on his tongue, and closed his mouth. She quickly looked around to see if Raphie had seen her. He was still only halfway down the slope.

When she looked back at Lou, he was staring at her, wide-eyed. He gave her such a look of love, of absolute gratitude for that one simple thing, that it filled her heart with hope. Then he gasped for air and his body shuddered, before he closed his eyes and left the world.

CHAPTER 27

For Old Times' Sake

A T EXACTLY THE SAME TIME as Lou Suffern left one world and entered another, he stood in the front garden of his Howth home, drenched to the very core. He was trembling from the experience he'd just had. He didn't have much time, but there was nowhere in the world he'd rather have been right at that moment.

He stepped through the front door, his shoes squeaking on the tiles. The fire in the living room was crackling, the floor below the tree was filled with presents, all wrapped with pretty ribbons. Lucy and Bud were so far the only children in the family, and so family tradition dictated that Lou's parents, Quentin and Alexandra, and the newly separated Marcia would be staying overnight in his house. Tonight he couldn't imagine not being with all of them; he couldn't think of anything that would fill his heart with any more joy. He entered the dining room, hoping they would see him, hoping that Gabe's last miraculous gift wouldn't fail him now.

"Lou." Ruth looked up from the dinner table and saw him first. She leapt out of her chair and ran to him. "Lou, honey, are you okay? Did something happen?"

His mother rushed to get a towel for him.

"I'm fine." He sniffed, cupping her face with his hands and not taking his eyes off her. "I'm fine now. I was calling," he whispered. "You didn't answer."

"Bud hid the phone again," she said, studying him with concern. "Are you drunk?" she asked in a whisper.

"No." He laughed. "I'm in love," he whispered back, then raised his voice so that the whole room could hear. "I'm in love with my beautiful wife." He kissed her fully on the lips, then breathed in her hair, kissed her neck, kissed her everywhere on her face, not caring who was there to see. "I'm sorry," he whispered to her, barely able to get words out of his mouth, his tears gathering in his throat.

"Sorry about what? What happened?"

"I'm sorry for the things that I've done to you. For being the way I was. I love you. I never meant to hurt you."

Ruth's eyes filled. "Oh, I know that, sweetheart, you already told me. I know."

"I just realized that when I'm not with you, I'm *ruthless*." He smiled, and his mother—who'd returned with a towel and was now tearful at the scene—laughed and clapped her hands, before grabbing her husband's hand at the table.

"To all of you." He pulled away from Ruth but

wouldn't let go of her hand. "I'm so sorry to all of you."

"We know that, Lou." Quentin smiled wobbily, emotion thick in his voice. "It's all water under the bridge now. Okay? Stop worrying, and sit down for dinner; it's all okay."

Lou looked to his parents, who smiled and nodded. His father had tears in his eyes and nodded emphatically that it was all okay. His sister, Marcia, was blinking fiercely to stop her own tears.

They dried him, they kissed him, they loved him, they fed him, though he wouldn't eat much. He told them in turn that he loved them, over and over again, until they were laughing and telling him to stop. He went upstairs to get a change of clothes before, according to his mother, he caught pneumonia. While upstairs, he heard Bud crying and immediately left his bedroom and hurried to his son's room.

The room was almost dark, lit with only a nightlight. He could see Bud wide awake and standing up against the railings of his cot, like a woken prisoner. Lou switched the light on and went inside. Bud viewed him angrily at first.

"Hey there, little man," Lou said gently. "What are you doing awake?"

Bud just gave a quiet little moan.

"Oh, come here." Lou leaned over the railings and lifted him up, holding him close in his arms and shushing him. For the first time in a long time, Bud didn't scream the house down when his father came near him. Instead, he smiled and pointed a finger in Lou's eye, in his nose, then in his mouth, where he tried to grab his teeth.

Lou started laughing. "Hey, you can't have them. You'll have your own soon, though." He kissed Bud on the cheek. "When you're a big boy, all sorts of things will happen." He looked at his son, feeling sad that he would miss all of those things. "Mind Mummy for me, won't you?" he whispered, his voice shaking.

Bud laughed, suddenly hyper, and blew bubbles with his lips.

Lou's tears quickly disappeared at the sound of Bud's laughter. He lifted him up, put Bud's belly on his head, and started jiggling him about. Bud laughed so hard, Lou couldn't help but join in.

From the corner of his eye, Lou saw Lucy at the door watching them.

"Now, Bud," he spoke loudly, "how about you and I go into Lucy's room and jump on her bed to wake her up—what do you think?"

"No, Daddy!" Lucy yelled, exploding into the room. "I'm awake!"

"Oh, you're awake, too! Are you both little elves that help Santa?"

"No." Lucy laughed. Bud laughed, too.

"Well then, you'd better hurry to bed, or else Santa won't come to the house if he sees you awake."

"What if he sees you?" she asked.

"Then he'll leave extra presents." He smiled.

She wrinkled up her nose. "Bud smells of poo. I'm getting Mummy."

"No, I can do it." He looked at Bud, who looked back at him curiously.

Lucy stared at him as though he were insane.

"Don't look at me like that," he joked. "How hard can this be? Now, come on, buddy, help me out here." He smiled at Bud nervously. Bud's open palm smacked his father across the face playfully. Lucy howled with laughter.

Lou lay Bud down on the ground so that he wouldn't wriggle off.

"Mummy puts him up there," Lucy said, pointing to the changing table.

"Well, Daddy doesn't," he said, while trying to figure out how to undo Bud's pajamas.

"The buttons are at the bottom." Lucy said, sitting down beside him.

"Oh. Thanks." He opened the buttons and rolled the pajamas up Bud's body, in an attempt to evacuate all clothes from the area. He untaped a new diaper and slowly opened it. Turned it around in his hands, trying to figure out which way it went.

"Oh, pooh!" Lucy dove backward, her fingers pinching her nose. "Piglet goes on the front," she said through her blocked nose.

Lou moved quickly to try to get the situation under control, while Lucy rolled around fanning the air with exaggerated drama. Impatient with his father's progress,

Bud began kicking his legs, forcing Lou away from him. With Bud now on his knees, his rear end in Lou's face, Lou crawled around behind him, approaching his bottom with a baby wipe. His light swipes were not helping the situation. He needed to get in there. Holding his breath, he went for it. With Bud momentarily under control and playing with a ball that had caught his eye, Lucy handed the various apparatuses to Lou.

"You're supposed to put that cream on next."

"Thanks. You'll always take care of Bud, won't you, Lucy?"

She nodded solemnly.

"And you'll take care of Mummy?"

"Yessss."

"And Bud and Mummy will take care of you," he said, finally grabbing Bud's pudgy legs and pulling him back, while Bud screeched like a pig.

"And we'll all take care of Daddy!" she hurrahed, standing up and dancing around.

"Don't worry about Daddy," he said quietly, trying again to figure out which way to put the diaper on. Finally he got the gist, quickly closed the buttons on Bud's pajamas, and put him back in the crib.

"Mummy puts the lights out so that he gets sleepy," Lucy whispered.

"Oh, okay, let's do that," Lou whispered, turning off the lights so that the Winnie the Pooh night-light was again visible.

Lou hunkered down in the darkness, pulling Lucy

close to him. He sat on the carpet hugging his little girl, watching the bear of very little brain chase a honeypot on the ceiling. As Bud made a few gurgles and spurts, lulling himself to sleep, Lou knew it was his moment to tell her.

"You know that no matter where Daddy is, no matter what's happening in your life, no matter if you're sad or happy or lonely or lost, remember that I'm always there for you. Even if you don't see me, know that I'm in here"—he touched her head—"and I'm in here"—he touched her heart. "And I'm always watching you, and I'm always proud of you and of *everything* you do, and when you sometimes question how I ever felt about you, remember right now, remember me saying that I love you, my sweetheart. Daddy loves you, okay?"

"Okay, Daddy," she said sadly. "But what about when I'm naughty? Will you love me when I'm naughty?"

"When you're naughty," he said, thinking about it, "remember that Daddy is somewhere always hoping that you'll be the best that you can be."

"But where will you be?"

"If I'm not here, I'll be elsewhere."

"Where is that?"

"It's a secret," he whispered, trying to hold back his tears.

"A secret elsewhere," she whispered back, her warm sweet breath on his face.

"Yeah." He hugged her tight and tried not to let a sound pass his lips as his tears fell, hot and thick.

Downstairs in the dining room, there wasn't a dry eye in the house as they listened to the conversation in Bud's nursery over the baby intercom. For the Sufferns they were tears of joy because a son, a brother, and a husband had finally come back to them.

That night, Lou Suffern made love to his wife, and afterward he held her close to him, rubbing his hands down her silky hair until he drifted away, and even then his fingertips continued to trace the contours of her face: the little turn-up of her nose, her high cheekbones, the tip of her chin, along her jawline, then all the way along her hairline, as though he were a blind man seeing her for the first time.

"I'll love you forever," he whispered to her, and she smiled, halfway to her dream world.

IT WAS IN THE MIDDLE of the night that the dream world was shattered when Ruth was awakened by the gate buzzer. Half asleep, she stood in her nightgown and welcomed both Raphie and Jessica into her home. Quentin and Lou's father accompanied her, keen to protect the house against such late-night dangers. But they couldn't protect her from this.

"Morning," Raphie said somberly as they all gathered in the living room. "I'm sorry to disturb you at such a late hour."

Ruth looked at the young police officer standing beside him, at her dark black eyes that seemed cold and

THE GIFT / 293

sad, at the grass and dried muck that was splattered on her boots and that clung to the bottom of her navy-blue trousers. At the small scrapes across her face and the cut that she was trying to hide behind her hair.

"What is it?" Ruth whispered, her voice catching in her throat. "Tell me, please."

"Mrs. Suffern, I think you should sit down," Raphie said gently.

"We should get Lou," she whispered, looking to Quentin. "He wasn't in bed when I woke up; he must be in his study."

"Ruth," the young garda said, so softly that Ruth's heart sank even further, and as her body went limp, she allowed Quentin to reach for her and pull her down to the couch beside him and Lou's father. They grabbed one another's hands, squeezed one another so tightly that they were linked like a chain, and they listened as Raphie and Jessica told them how life for them had changed beyond all comprehension, as they learned that a son, a brother, and a husband had left them as suddenly as he'd arrived.

WHILE SANTA LAID GIFTS IN homes all across the country that night, while lights in windows began to go out for the evening, while wreaths upon doors became fingers upon lips and blinds went down as the eyelids of a sleeping home drooped, hours before a turkey went through a window at another home in another district,

Ruth Suffern had yet to learn that despite losing her husband she had gained his child, and together the family realized—on the most magical night of the year—the true gift that Lou had given them in the early hours of Christmas morning.

CHAPTER 28

The Turkey Boy 5

RAPHIE WATCHED THE TURKEY BOY'S reaction as he heard the last of the story. He was silent for a moment.

"How do you know all of this?"

"We've been piecing it all together today. Talking to the family and to his colleagues."

"Did you talk to Gabe?"

"Briefly, earlier. We've been waiting for him to come back to the station, but we can't seem to find him."

"And you called to Lou's house this morning?"

"We did."

"And Lou wasn't there."

"Nowhere to be seen. Sheets still warm from where he'd lain."

"Are you making this up?"

"Not a word of it."

"Do you expect me to believe this?"

"No, I don't."

"Then what was the point?"

"People tell stories, and it's up to those who listen whether to believe them or not."

"Shouldn't the storyteller believe it?"

"The storyteller should tell it." He winked.

"Do you believe it?"

Raphie looked around the room to make sure nobody had sneaked in without his noticing. He shrugged awkwardly, moving his head at the same time. "One man's lesson is another man's tale, but often, a man's tale can be another's lesson."

"What's that supposed to mean?"

Raphie avoided the question by taking a slug of coffee.

"You said there was a lesson—what was the lesson?"

"If I have to tell you that, boy . . ." Raphie rolled his eyes.

"Ah, come on."

"Appreciating your loved ones," Raphie said, a little embarrassed at first. "Acknowledging all the special people in your life. Concentrating on what's important." He cleared his throat and looked away, not comfortable with preaching.

The Turkey Boy rolled his eyes and faked a yawn.

Raphie tossed his embarrassment to the side, giving himself one more opportunity to get through to the teen before he gave up altogether. He should have been at home, already on his second helping of Christmas dinner, instead of being here with this frustrating boy.

He leaned forward. "Gabe gave Lou a gift, son, a very

special gift. I'm not going to bother asking you what that was, I'm going to tell you, and you'd better listen up, because right after this I'm leaving you, and you'll be alone to think about what you did. If you don't pay attention, then you'll go back out to the world an angry young man who'll feel angry for the rest of his life."

"Okay," the boy said defensively, sitting up in his seat as though being told off by the headmaster.

"Gabe gave Lou the gift of *time*, son."

The Turkey Boy wrinkled up his nose.

"Oh, you're fourteen years old and you think you've all the time in the world, but you don't. None of us have. We're spending it with all the might and indifference of January sales shoppers. A week from now they'll be crowding the streets, swarming the shops with open wallets, just throwing all their cash away." Raphie seemed to crawl into the shell on his back for a moment, his eyes tucked under his gray, bushy eyebrows.

The boy smirked at Raphie, amused by the man's sudden emotion. "But you can earn more money, so who cares?"

Raphie snapped out of his trance and looked up as though seeing the Turkey Boy in the room for the first time. "So that makes time more precious, doesn't it? More precious than money, more precious than anything. You can never earn more time. Once an hour goes by, a week, a month, a year, you'll never get them back. Lou Suffern was running out of time, and Gabe gave him more, to help tie things up, to finish things properly. That's the gift." Raphie's heart beat wildly in his chest. He looked down at his coffee and pushed it away, feeling his heart cramp again. "So we should fix things before . . ."

He ran out of breath and waited for the cramping to fade.

"Do you think it's too late to, you know"—the Turkey Boy twisted the string of his hoodie around his finger, speaking self-consciously—"fix things with my, you know . . ."

"With your dad?"

The boy shrugged and looked away, not wanting to admit it.

"It's never too late—" Raphie stopped abruptly, nodded to himself as though registering a thought, nodded again with an air of agreement and finality, and then pushed back his chair, the legs screeching against the floor, and stood.

"Hold on, where are you going?"

"To fix things, boy. To fix some things. And I suggest you do the same when your mother comes."

The young teenager's blue eyes blinked back at him, innocence still there, though lost somewhere in the mist of his confusion and anger.

Raphie left the room and made his way down the hall, loosening his tie. He heard his voice being called but continued walking anyway. He pushed his way out of the staff quarters, into the public entrance room that was empty on this Christmas Day.

"Raphie," Jessica called, chasing after him.

"Yes," he said, turning around.

"Are you okay? You look like you've seen a ghost. Is it your heart? Are you okay?"

"I'm fine," he nodded. "Everything's fine. What's up?"

Jessica narrowed her eyes and studied him, knowing he was lying. "Is that boy giving you trouble?"

"No, he's fine, purring like a pussy cat now. Everything's fine."

"Then where are you going?"

"Eh?" He looked toward the door, trying to think of another lie, another untruth to tell somebody for the tenth year running. But he sighed—a long sigh that had been held in for many years—and he gave up, the truth finally sounding odd yet comfortable as it fell from his tongue.

"I want to go home," he said, suddenly appearing very old. "I want today to be over so that I can go home to my wife. And my daughter."

"You have a daughter?" she asked with surprise.

"Yes," he said, a simple word filled with emotion. "I do. She lives up there on Howth Summit. That's why I'm there in the car every evening. I just like to keep an eye on her. Even if she doesn't know it."

They stared at each other for a while, knowing that something strange had overcome them that morning, something strange that had changed them forever.

"I had a husband," she said suddenly. "Car crash. I was there. Holding his hand. Just like this morning." She swallowed and lowered her voice. "I always said I'd have done anything to give him at least a few more hours." There, she'd said it. "I gave Lou a pill, Raphie," she said firmly, looking him straight in the eye now. "I know I shouldn't have, but I gave him a pill. I don't know if all that stuff about the pills is true or not—but if I helped Lou have a few more hours with his family, I'm glad, and I'd do it again, if anyone asks."

Raphie simply nodded, acknowledging her two confessions. He'd put it in their statement, but he didn't need to tell her that; she knew.

They just looked at each other, staring but not seeing. Their minds were elsewhere, thinking about the times gone by, the lost time that could never return.

"Where's my son?" A woman's urgent voice broke their silence. As she had opened the door, a burst of cold air filled the station. Snowflakes were trapped in the woman's hair and clothes and fell from her boots as she stamped them on the ground. "He's only a boy." She swallowed. "A fourteen-year-old boy." Her voice shook. "I sent him out to get gravy granules. And the turkey's missing now." She spoke as though delirious.

"I'll take care of this." Jessica nodded at Raphie. "You go home now."

And so he did.

ONE THING OF GREAT IMPORTANCE can affect a small number of people. Equally so, a thing of little importance can affect a multitude. Either way, a happening—big or small—can affect an entire string of people. Occurrences can join us all together. You see, we're all made up of the same stuff. When something happens, it triggers something inside us that connects us to a situation, connects us to other people, lighting us up and linking us like little lights on a Christmas tree, twisted and turned but still connected on a wire. Some go out, others flicker, others burn strong and bright, yet we're all on the same line.

I said at the beginning of this story that this was about people who find out who they are. About people who are unraveled and whose cores are revealed to all who count. And that all that count are revealed to them. You thought I was talking about Lou Suffern and the Turkey Boy, about Raphie, Jessica, and Ruth, didn't you? Wrong. I was talking about each of us.

A lesson finds the common denominator and links us all together, like a chain. At the end of that chain dangles a clock, and on the face of the clock registers the passing of time. We see it and we hear it, the hushed *tick-tock*, but often we don't feel it. Each second makes its mark on every single person's life—comes and then goes, quietly disappearing without fanfare, evaporating into air like steam from a piping hot Christmas pudding. Enough time leaves us warm; when our time is gone, it leaves us cold. Time is more precious than gold, more precious than diamonds, more precious than oil or any valuable treasures. It is time of which we do not have enough; it is time that causes the war within our hearts, and so we must spend it wisely. Time cannot be packaged and ribboned and left under trees for Christmas morning.

Time can't be given. But it can be shared.

Acknowledgments

ALL MY LOVE TO MY family for your friendship, encouragement, and love; Mim, Dad, Georgina, Nicky, Rocco, and Jay. David, thank you. Thanks, Ahoy McCoy, for sharing your boating knowledge. Thank you to the HarperCollins team for your support and belief. Thank you, Jonathan Burnham, Michael Morrison, Kathy Schneider, Katherine Beitner, and Maya Ziv. Special thanks to my wonderful editor, Sally Kim. Thank you, Marianne Gunn O'Connor, for being You. Thank you, Pat Lynch and Vicki Satlow. Thank you to all who read my books, I'm eternally grateful for your support and for allowing me to fulfill my absolute passion.

A⁺

**AUTHOR
INSIGHTS,
EXTRAS, &
MORE...**

FROM

CECELIA
AHERN

AND

WM

WILLIAM MORROW

A Christmas Story from Cecelia
EVERY YEAR

EVERY YEAR I WATCH THEM. Every year I see the changes, how the days and seasons spent apart have somehow softened their tongues. Each year the evidence is faint but palpable all the same. If you look closely at the curve of the smiles once tight, the relaxed shoulders once hunched and the flow of words once clipped, you can see that their edges have blurred like the annual ice sculpture on the lawn sitting in the morning sun. Look more closely and somewhere within its frosty exterior you can see, can hear, the drip, drip, drip of its hard shell slipping away. Transparent cold drops warmed just enough to allow release. Time has been this family's sun. Year after year, I have watched the coldness slipping away from them until I see them now, cocooned together by the warmth of Christmas Day.

Every year I'm taken from the dark dusty confines of

an attic by the same pair of hands, but every year those hands have felt different. Over the years they carried not only me, but the weight of more responsibility. I feel it in his grip now, feel it in the heaviness of his steps down the stairs. I've gone from being carelessly mauled and dropped by his once dirty, childish hands to being carefully cradled in the ones wrapped around me now. I was given to him by his father, a special July deal in the front window of a rundown hardware store in the 1920s, where the paint blistered and peeled from its exterior until it was pared right down to nothing.

Like my carrier I am old, and he shares me with his own family now. We are slow going down the stairs this year, his breathing loud and his hands frail. I don't feel secure in his leatherlike skin as I did in previous years, and I'm fearful of his accidentally releasing me from his clutches as he once did in the giddiness of his childhood. I note the full circle that life has taken for him; he is getting older, yet also younger, as though time were moving in two directions. Every year his body declines but his spirit doesn't. He lives for this time of year, for his family gathering around him, he and his wife the flame to their moths' gathering.

I'm placed on the table before the crackling fire. I see the stockings line the mantelpiece, every year a sock added for a new little one. I see the multicolored presents piled high under the tree, shimmering paper with big delightful bows all heckling to be untied and ripped open. He and she had spent all week wrapping these, I know from hearing their muffled voices below my place in the attic. The month-long lead-up to Christmas has been spent shopping together. Careful, thoughtful, shared decisions made while strolling in shops and boutiques under the decorative lights, the two of them bundled up in hats, scarves, and gloves as the world raced around them. They took it all in, cheered as the lights were turned on, hoisted awestruck grandchildren onto Santa's lap and delighted as more trees appeared in windows in the great big build-up to today.

Those are the irreplaceable weeks where everyone feels the hands of time tick by louder as the day approaches, beating faster in the big rush until hearts are left banging in chests in anticipation and expectation. I wait with the old man for the crowd to arrive. I look around the room with him, see the pride in his eyes, sense the excitement rush through his veins. Another year, another day of all being together. My God, they don't happen often enough, I know he is thinking.

The doorbell rings and time's ticking hands are drowned out by the tinkling Christmas tunes in the living room; the flames of candles by the window dance excitedly on their wicks as the cars pull up outside; the lights on the tree sparkle and wink, encouraging him to make his way to the door. Build-up over, it's time. His troops begin to arrive, one by one.

Big hugs for Mum and Dad, woolly sweaters embracing polo-necks to oohs and aahs of delight as the aromas of cinnamon, pine, and roasting turkey tickle their senses. Children race around in excitement, their little hearts overfilled with the joy of the morning's magic. They poke at the presents, eye the gift tags, stare up at the chimney while shaking their heads, wondering and conferring with each other how on earth Santa did it. And then the annual stories are told: of hearing him on the roof, seeing the reindeer fly off and even meeting the great man himself. Wide eyes from the little ones who have slept through the night, rolled eyes for the elders who hide their smiles. What a great man, they all agree, while munching on mince pies. What a great man.

And then the conversation, stilted at first, of those who once shared bedrooms and secrets, who once fought over toys and friends and who huddled together under bed sheets with flashlights, begins. The room is now a hotpot of past, present, and future family. All eyes are on the kids, the ones who bathe in the excitement of the day and who, in turn, reflect the magic back to their parents.

He announces he's going to put me on top of the tree and the little ones gather around to watch. The old man takes me into his frail hands. The routine applause sounds the same to them every year, but not to me. Like with the ice sculpture, you must pay close attention. The tones have varied as the time has gone by. In the early years it was excitement, the joy of the little ones' first experiences. Then, as time floated away as gently and subtly as a feather in the wind, the cheers turned to jeers and excitement to boredom as hormones flailed around in their changing bodies, kicking and screaming. This year they are adults: mothers and fathers, uncles and aunts who have learned to understand all that was misunderstood in their teenage years. They now applaud loudly and joyously, with their own excited little ones hopping around by their sides, craning their necks to look at me in awe.

My, how everyone's grown. I have sensed already that I won't be carried to my place next year by the same pair of hands. I sensed it by his shaking and by how his eyes filled up when the others weren't looking. But instead of going directly toward the tree, he turns and I find I'm being handed to Tom, whose twelve-year-old mouth gapes open as I'm passed from old hands to new. The eldest grandson looks back to his mother and father, who nod encouragingly and smile with pride.

Tom brings me slowly toward the tree. It looks bigger now than it used to, as I lie in the protective hands of a smaller boy. As we get closer, it looms and the tinsel glitters and the branches smell of glorious pine. I see our reflection in a red bauble. I see the excitement and anxiety in Tom's face as he takes each careful step, not wanting to ruin the moment. With his back turned to the hushed family he goes up the ladder. Then I'm ceremoniously perched in my presiding place.

They think it's going to be the same every year, but I know it's not. They used to think, in their teenage raging hormonal days, that they would rather be anywhere but here in this home, on this day, but now they know differently. I see them now, looking to their parents, as their little ones look to them.

The same every year, they think, but look closely, for it's not.

That is the bittersweet magic of Christmas. It's magical and wonderful and every year rich with the air of too much said and too much unsaid. These are the days when edges are blurred, tongues are burned and softened, and eyes are filled with the drip, drip, drip of never wanting to leave, never wanting to say good-bye to these golden moments, longing to bring back the precious days and all the people in them.

Every day of every year they long for the time when they will feel like this: together, cocooned by the warmth of Christmas Day.

Questions for Discussion: The Gift

1. In the opening pages of the book it is revealed that this story is about "people, secrets, and time." How do these themes play out in the experiences of various characters throughout the book? How do the various plots intersect?

2. Raphie tells The Turkey Boy that Gabe gave Lou the gift of *time* (p. 297). Are there other "gifts" that Gabe gives Lou?

3. Has the rise of social media such as Facebook and Twitter given us more flexibility with time—being able to be in two places at once, like Gabe—or has technology made us busier and actually limited our accessibility?

4. Lou is a complex character: hard and ambitious but with moments of vulnerability, such as his reaction when hearing Ruth cry (p. 75). What are your impressions of Lou? Do they change over the course of the novel? Use scenes from the story to support your viewpoint.

5. Lou always wishes he could be in two places at once, a wish Gabe fulfills when he gives Lou the pills. Why does Lou want this ability? What happens when he takes the pills? Was this "wish come true" what he thought it would be? What are the drawbacks to being in two places at once? If it were physically possible, would you do so?

6. When Lou steps back from his life, he gains some important insights into who he is, how he behaves, and what his impact is on those around him. Have you ever had the opportunity to step "outside" of your life to see if you like what's going on? What was the experience like?

7. Gabe has "special" qualities—moving as quick as light, predicting things before they happen, reading people's feelings. Do you think he's human or something more supernatural, such as an angel? Would you like to have a special ability—if so, what would it be?

8. What insights did reading *The Gift* hold for you and your own work-life balance? Like The Turkey Boy, what did you take away about timing?

9. If you could have a special gift, what would you want?

Cecelia Ahern

Before embarking on her writing career, **CECELIA AHERN** completed a degree in journalism and media communications. At twenty-one, she wrote her first novel, *P.S. I Love You*, which became an international bestseller and was adapted into a major motion picture, starring Hilary Swank. Her successive novels—*Love, Rosie; If You Could See Me Now; There's No Place Like Here; Thanks for the Memories;* and *The Book of Tomorrow*—were also international bestsellers. Her books are published in forty-six countries and have collectively sold more than twelve million copies. The daughter of Ireland's former prime minister, Ahern lives in Dublin, Ireland.

In 2010, Ahern became the youngest recipient of a Nielsen Book Platinum Award, for achieving more than a million sales in the U.K. for *P.S. I Love You*. For more information, go to www.cecelia-ahern.com.

BOOKS BY
CECELIA AHERN

THE GIFT
A Novel

ISBN 978-0-06-178209-1 (paperback)

"This modern-day Scrooge tale is a delightful read with plenty of fun twists and turns."

—*USA Today*

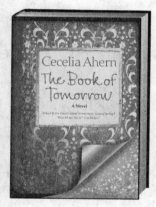

THE BOOK OF TOMORROW
A Novel

ISBN 978-0-06-170630-1 (hardcover)

"[Ahern] takes a more gothic turn in her latest, recasting herself as a lost Brontë sister for the Facebook set. . . . Lovers of stories involving crumbling castles, nefarious family secrets . . . will be ecstatic."

—*Entertainment Weekly*

THANKS FOR THE MEMORIES
A Novel

ISBN 978-0-06-170624-0 (paperback)

"Love and déjà vu feature in this wacky fairy tale about a woman 'transfused' with a stranger's memories. The romance is just what you'd expect from the popular author of *P.S. I Love You*."

—*Good Housekeeping*

Visit www.Cecelia-Ahern.com for more information on Cecelia's books, and find Cecelia on Facebook.

Available wherever books are sold, or call 1-800-331-3761 to order.